Occasion of Murder

A Bekbourg County Novel

by Sherrie Rutherford

Venice, Florida

Bekbourg County Novels

Occasion of Murder

Mindset of Murder

Valley of Murder

Pathos of Murder

Bookends of Murder

Occasion of Murder

A Bekbourg County Novel

By Sherrie Rutherford

Prologue

The lamp post stood alone as the night's mist sought to vanquish its light. Cold perspiration seeped into the murderer's clothing, and cotton seemingly filled the shadowy figure's mouth. As sweaty fingers hugged tight by gloves squeezed around the knife's handle, the killer slowly inhaled to listen. In the distance, music played. All at once, muffled voices could be heard approaching. The killer stood frozen as the couple talked, and the woman giggled at the man's words. As the lovers sauntered away and threat of detection faded, the killer's body unfurled with a quiet exhale. From behind the tall hedges, the killer's eyes swept the area's entrance yet again. The vow was made—*SHE MUST DIE!* Waiting, listening, watching—the killer's vigilance was steadfast. Suddenly—a cough, a click on a paver. *Someone's coming.*

Sherrie Rutherford

Chapter 1

Vera Keller coughed as she stubbed out the cigarette in the car's over-flowing ashtray. Cold ashes and butts fell to the flooring as Vera considered lighting another one. Airwave static distorted the radio's nightly broadcast, which blared in competition with the chugging heater. *Damn thing doesn't warm shit!* Vera fumed as she strained to see ahead. The filmy residue left by the repeated "whomp, whomp, whomp" of the wipers was another aggravation in a long list. It had been many years since she had been back to the town where she grew up. Except for the headlights' dull glare on the dark, damp asphalt, darkness encased her. Somewhere off in the fields was the water tower with "Welcome to Bekbourg," painted on the side. *Wonder if it's still that ugly green?* she pondered as she motored on. She assumed the "roach motel" was still up ahead. It had been flashing that neon sign along the highway leading into Bekbourg longer than she had been alive. She was down to the last of her cash, so until she could make other arrangements, she would have to stay in the dive.

Vera did not fancy returning to Bekbourg, but she had worn out her welcome in the artist community where she had lived near Cleveland.

2

Once again, she found herself being evicted, but this time, acquaintances were unwilling to offer a sofa for even a few nights. Of course, because she did not want to be hounded for money she owed, she was limited in those from whom she could seek favors. Galleries and shops refused to carry her work, and she did not have funds to participate in art fairs.

The drive had given her time to fine-tune plans she had hatched during her final days in Cleveland. *"Ain't nothing holding me back once I take the town,"* she belted to a tune playing in her head. *"Financial problems won't get me down 'cause I'm turning them 'round."* She cackled at her wit.

She mentally patted herself on the back for coming up with a lucrative way to drum up cash. A new art gallery was opening—a place where her paintings could be sold. Not only would that give her a source of income, but she craved the notoriety of being a famous artist around town. She decided on the drive down that the gallery might offer a "twofer"—a place for her artwork and possibly a source of income contributed on the side by the gallery owner herself—*I know your secret, ole girl.* Then, there was her sister. *Hah! Can't wait to see your sour face when you see me knocking on the door!*

She stuck another cigarette in her mouth and pushed the lighter. She squinted as she pressed the lighter to the cigarette's end, bringing about a bright orange glow. But the "cherry on top" had been learning that Brian Lynch was now a state representative. She smirked. *If I'd known that earlier, I wouldn't be broke now. Well, it's never too late.* Off in the distance, she saw the dive's neon sign blinking "Vacancy." Tomorrow, she would start by surprising "Big Sis."

Chapter 2

A gravel driveway pointed to the white two-story house on the rise. Neglect had yielded a forlorn appearance as vines meandered through untamed bushes, and faded siding had succumbed to splotches of loosened paint. Now lackluster in greenery and brown stems, potted ferns hanging along the once regal porch suggested an effort was still being made to cling to appearances by owners, Teri and Gerald Olson. Gerald's injuries sustained over a year-and-a-half ago during a treacherous hiking trip in the Red River Gorge had drained their financial resources and capped their physical abilities to maintain the house. Trying to keep financially afloat when his disability ran out, Teri had taken a job working at the hospital, but her meager earnings were only buying time. She had tried to convince the hospital to hire her full time, but the budget was not there. Looking for other jobs had not been productive.

Gerald had been the assistant fire chief, and the county had held off filling the position in hopes he could return to duty. He still had trouble getting around, though, and pain plagued him most days. Because of his injuries, he was limited in the tasks he could perform. He rejected the prospect he could not become gainfully employed again and adamantly refused to go on full disability. When a county worker was on vacation or temporary leave, he would work, but that was sporadic. He had tried to find jobs around town, but his injury eliminated him from consideration on jobs he would have otherwise qualified for, and other companies were reluctant to hire him because of his injury. The week before, he had been informed the county was going to have to fill the position after the first of the year if the doctor did not clear him. Even he did not hold out much hope the doctor would sign off on him returning to the fire department.

There was one bright spot however. A position for requisitioning equipment and vehicles for county road and construction projects was opening next year due to a retirement. Unfortunately, he could hardly wait until then to start working again. He and Teri were within a couple of months of having to sell their home—a house that had once belonged to Teri's grandparents and where Teri and her sister, Vera, had grown up.

Chapter 3

As she pulled up the driveway to her childhood home, Vera Keller was too self-absorbed to notice the house's decline during the fourteen years she had been away. Visions of the past rolled through her head as she looked at the house which had never felt like a home to her—not because her mother did not try. She did. It was because Vera was incapable of finding contentment, and her heart was therefore never vested there. To many people, her childhood would have seemed idyllic—living in an envious home and having a father who worked hard to support his family, a mother who doted on her daughters and managed their home, and an older sister who could have been a close friend.

But something churned within Vera that could not be turned off—a restlessness that caused her to fault most things and propelled her to inflict chaos and distress. Vera did not understand why she had damaged Teri's toys or hidden her favorite things or spilled chocolate milk on her sister's homework. She did not necessarily revel in seeing her sister upset. She often overheard their mother coaxing Teri to "overlook" Vera's "jests" as she would respond, "She loves you, Honey, and she's just trying to get your attention."

Her feelings toward her older sister were complex. As a child, she admired her big sister, but as Teri started to ignore her, Vera pulled stunts to get her attention. She craved her acceptance and harbored resentment when it proved elusive. As Teri moved into her teenage years, she pulled further away from Vera, which elicited Vera's deep resentment. Their relationship's downward spiral finally crash-landed about the time their mother had died.

Vera's proclivity to pester children spilled over to school. When a parent from school called and complained to her mother that Vera was picking on her child, her mother explained to Vera that she mustn't act that way toward others. Vera eventually set her sights on another victim to bully. During an annual checkup when her mother told the doctor about the calls from the school about bullying, the doctor suggested she find something of interest to Vera. A summer art camp proved to be the ticket. Painting provided a respite to Vera's self-destructive restlessness, but when someone struck her the wrong way, she simply resorted again to her bullying ways.

After slamming the brakes and killing the engine, Vera took time to finish her cigarette before swinging open the squeaky car door and standing. *Might as well get the show on the road,* she thought. She slung the purse strap over her shoulder and looked down as she tugged her tight short dress. *I need new clothes. God, these shoes look bad,* were her last thoughts before she charged forward.

As she approached the door, she considered just walking in. "Why knock? I grew up here," but that would really cause fireworks, especially if that jerk-o husband was here. He hated her. He was so ready to sign all those papers to keep her "out of their hair." *Well, too bad, asshole, I'm back, and I'm not leaving—not unless you and Sister Dear make it worth my while.*

Vera heard her sister's heels clicking on the hardwood floor as she hastened to answer the door. Teri's gracious smile evaporated when she saw Vera. Color drained from her face. "What are you doing here?" Teri asked through firm lips she hoped would not betray the trembling she felt.

Something Teri had dreaded for years had finally happened, she thought as she scrutinized her younger sister through the screen door. Teri had been excited when her parents brought home a baby sister from the hospital. She was eight at the time and coddled her baby sister and spent hours amusing Vera with playful antics and toys. As Vera moved into the toddler years, though, things began to change. Always a fussy baby, she grew prone to tantrums. Teri began to shy away from Vera as very little satisfied her younger sister, and blissful moments were fleeting. Around their large two-story home, Teri found hiding spaces to avoid her cantankerous sister.

As time passed, Teri had grown more embarrassed by Vera's actions in public and tried to distance herself from Vera, hoping not to be associated with her. She grew less inclined to bring friends home because of Vera's harassments and ploys. As Vera grew older, a more menacing side emerged—tattle-telling falsehoods to their mother hoping to get Teri in trouble. Viola loved her daughters and made extra efforts to appease Vera to keep the peace and brushed aside her younger daughter's complaints and "inventions." Their father worked long hours and seemed immune to the family life.

As school years rolled by, Vera became quite adept at manipulating the more vulnerable kids and camouflaging her blighted spirit. An acting award would have been fitting for the "sweetness" she perfected around teachers and other adults. For a long time, Teri held out hope Vera would change. But after numerous misplaced attempts at trusting Vera's pleas and spiels, Teri was determined to never fall prey again.

Vera's voice shook Teri back to reality.

"Surprise," Vera scoffed. "Your prodigal sister has returned." When Teri remained motionless, Vera continued, "I got in town last night and thought I'd stop by and see my favorite sister."

Teri did not smile at Vera's attempted joke or bother to banter in good humor that she was Vera's only sibling. Seeing Teri's stoic expression, Vera pressed, "I thought it's a good time to catch up. Aren't you going to invite me in?" Vera noticed little had changed about her older sister except for some lines around her eyes and forehead.

Teri's heart sank with alarm, but before she could respond, Gerald limped up behind her and looked over her shoulder. His face turned purple. The bellow started deep in the pit of his stomach, "What in the hell is she doing here?"

Teri whirled around, "Go sit down, Gerald. I'll handle this. We'll talk out here on the porch."

She gently pushed his arm, but his body refused to budge as he glared at the unwelcomed visitor. Teri nudged again with more determination. "It's okay, Gerald. I'll handle this. Please," she urged. His eyes narrowed, but he turned and hobbled away. Teri pulled the front door closed and indicated for Vera to sit in one of the wicker chairs, which like everything else, were showing their age.

Teri's initial vexation at seeing her younger sister had blinded her to Vera's appearance. Now, sitting across from her, Teri observed the woman who looked years older than her thirty-three-years—a contradiction to a woman who was clinging to youthfulness in the way she dressed. Vera had never liked that school kids called her "skinny," and even though she had put on a few pounds, she still had an emaciated quality.

Her tight, short dress was faded from numerous washing cycles, and the gaudy necklace drew attention to a neck so thin that the skeletal support was pronounced. Teri wondered how the shabby woven sweater kept such a frail woman warm, but Vera did not appear cold.

Vera's heavy foundation failed to obscure the creases in her forehead and the beginnings of crevices on both sides of her mouth. Hairline furrows from years of smoking lined her upper lip. Although the sisters shared the same reddish-blond hair color, Vera's hair was thinner and frizzy. If Teri did not know her sister better, she would have felt sorry for the woman sitting across from her. The lines in her face told of Vera's joyless existence.

Although Teri could picture Vera when she last saw her fourteen years ago, Teri's most vivid memories were what lay beneath her outward appearance. An ugliness comprised her soul—an insidious spitefulness that was as prevalent as life-blood itself. Pain and suffering were well known to Vera's victims.

Vera pulled out a pack of cigarettes and a lighter. Teri knew Vera would ignore her request not to smoke and sat waiting for Vera to get on with whatever she had come to say. Vera smirked, "I remember you hated it when I smoked. Looks like that hasn't changed." Vera propped her elbow on the chair arm as exhaled smoke floated into the air. As she took another draw, she eyed her sister as if studying a specimen. For her part, Teri's face was pinched with wariness, wondering what had brought Vera back.

Vera took another puff and flicked ashes on the floor. Teri's tolerance faded, "I'll find you an ashtray." When she came back, she slapped the ashtray on the side table. "Vera, just tell me why you're here."

Vera squinted as she inhaled hard and stuck out her lower lip to blow smoke upward. She ground the cigarette into the ashtray, purposefully keeping Teri waiting. For a while, she feigned interest in the front yard. "Well, I guess I might as well tell you. I'm out of money."

Teri's eyes flew wide open, "What?" Her voice hitched. "What do you mean, you're out of money?"

Vera shook out another cigarette and lit it and shrugged. "It's gone. I spent it. My paintings aren't bringing in enough for me to live on, so I'm moving back here."

Teri narrowed her eyes. "That was not the deal, Vera, and you know it. Gerald and I paid the fair market value for this house to mom's estate when she died. I gave you all of my inheritance. You got *everything*. You promised to leave and never come back here."

"Well, things changed, Sister Dear. It didn't work out the way I thought it would."

Teri straightened in the chair. "What about a job? You could work and paint on the side."

"I tried a couple of things, but . . ."

Teri doubted she had ever found a job, and even if she had, she'd likely gotten fired.

"I know Mom taught you better. Shouldn't you be offering your guest something to drink?"

Teri frowned, "I've got some iced tea, or I could make a pot of coffee. Which would you prefer?"

"Oh, I was thinking something stronger. You know. To celebrate us seeing each other for the first time in—what has it been? Fourteen years?"

Teri scowled. "We don't keep alcohol here, Vera. It's got to be tea or coffee."

Vera tilted her head and studied Teri, wondering if that was true. She decided not to push it and shrugged again. "Okay, let me think about it." She snubbed out her cigarette. "I need a place to stay. You don't mind me moving back in for a while? I'm sure my room's not being used. I know there are plenty of rooms."

"That doesn't work, Vera. You can't move in with us, even for just a few nights."

"Oh, come on, Teri. You owe me."

This is disastrous. No way can I let this happen. "I don't owe you, Vera. I'm sorry, but you need to leave and go back to Cleveland. You must be staying somewhere. Where's that?"

"That dive up the highway coming into town."

Teri figured her sister was still incapable of feeling empathy, but she had to find a way to dissuade her. "Look, Gerald had a serious accident going on two years ago. He was nearly killed. His disability ran out, and I had to go to work, but it's not enough. We're barely making it as it is. We're trying to hold onto the house, but I don't know how long that's going to last."

Vera straightened her fingers to look at her chipped nail polish. *This is getting me nowhere,* thought Teri, so she changed tactics. "If your paintings aren't selling where you live, why do you think you'd have more luck here?"

"Well, I read where a new gallery is opening here. What better place to sell my paintings than my home town?" She twitched her lips, "I heard the gallery belongs to Dillie. She finally came back?" Teri continued to stare, so Vera shrugged her shoulder, "I need a place to stay, Teri, and some money until I get some paintings sold."

"You need to leave, Vera. No one can help you here."

Vera took a long drag on the cigarette.

Miles, their son, was due back from a friend's house soon, and Teri did not want her sister here when he returned home. Despite the shaky ground she had experienced when dealing with her sister, Teri had to put her foot down that moving in with them or relying on them for financial support was not an option. "Vera, you *promised* we'd never hear from you again," she gritted through her teeth. "We *cannot* help you. For one time in your life, you're going to have to take care of yourself. I'm through." Teri stood.

Vera's smile was phony as she took her time in gathering her purse and stuffing in the cigarette pack and lighter. She looked at Teri, "Where's the boy? What'd you name him?"

Teri stiffened, "He's not here. I need to check on Gerald."

Teri went to stand by the door. Vera looked at her as she slung her bag over her shoulder. "Don't forget, Teri. I know your big secret. Don't try and bluff me."

Teri's knees weakened as she watched her sister amble toward her car. Vera never looked back as she clicked the engine to life and backed into the grass to turn the car around. *Oh, my Lord! I can't let her destroy our lives. And she will.* Teri's hand shook as she went to open the door.

Vera was not surprised her sister was underwhelmed to see her, but too bad, she thought as she drove to the cheap motel. She had it all figured out, and *like it or not, Big Sis, I will be moving in. I've still got the door key. Bet you and that jerk-o husband of yours never thought to change the lock. I'll find the right time, and once I'm in, there's no way you can get me to leave.*

Teri did not want to face Gerald until she composed herself. She dreaded telling him, but it would eventually come out—her sister would push the issue. She had to convince him not to overreact. *What a mess!*

She heard Gerald approaching the kitchen as she took dishes from the dishwasher. "What'd she want, Teri?" he asked as he stood in the doorway. "I know it's not good. Just tell me."

"Here, Gerald. Sit down. I'll fix you some coffee. Let me finish putting the dishes away, and then we'll talk." This gave her a couple more minutes to arrange her thoughts.

Once they were seated at the table, she told him about Vera needing money, which elicited the outburst she expected. "Damn that woman! I told that damn attorney we needed to put the money in a trust!"

"But if you remember, we didn't have any way to force her to go along with that. Remember, she was afraid we were trying to trick her—keep her from getting the money. Our hands were tied."

"Did you tell her we don't have it?"

"Yes."

"Yeah," he snorted. "She don't give a shit! All she's ever thought about is Number One. When's she leaving town? The sooner—the better."

Teri sipped her coffee as Gerald's frown deepened. "Teri, there's something you're not telling me. Spit it out."

"I'm not sure she is. She said she's going to try to set up her painting business here."

Gerald's eyes burned. "She lied through her teeth, and we fell for it. She told us she'd never be back here or ask for money again. You gave her your entire share of the inheritance. She's going to make our lives a living hell—AGAIN!" Gerald swore under his breath as Teri stared into the cup.

She did not pick it up and let Gerald see her hand trembling. Gerald had been easy going until the accident. At first, she thought it was the pain causing the irritable moods and hoped with time, she would get her old Gerald back. She was beginning to lose hope her unflappable husband would ever return, and this turn of events was not helping. "At least Miles wasn't here. No way do I want him anywhere near that psycho."

Teri could not bring herself to tell him that her sister had asked about their son or her veiled threat about the secret. He would explode. "Yeah, thank goodness."

"I don't want her back up here, Teri. God only knows what she might say or do."

"We'll figure something out. It's too bad Owen Donaldson is dead. I could talk to him about this," said Teri.

"Yeah. He was a good attorney. Anyway, I don't know how we can pay a lawyer."

"Well, if she comes back, I may have to see one," Teri said into her cup as she took another sip of coffee.

"She better not show her face around here again. You made that clear to her?"

"She knows she's not welcome."

"Teri, I'm not kidding," his voice rose. "She better stay away from us. I remember what that bitch put us through, and we're not going through that shit again."

Just then, Miles walked into the kitchen with their dog, a boxer named "Champ," and looked at his parents. "Mom, Dad, what's going on? I heard Dad's voice when I walked in. Who's he talking about?"

Teri jumped up, "It's nothing. Here, I made some brownies. Let me get you some with a glass of milk."

"Listen to your mother, Son," Gerald said as he pushed back from the table. "I got to go fix that faucet in the bathroom. The part finally came in."

Miles looked around at his parents, uncertain about the situation. "Hey, Dad, I'll help you. Mom, I'll eat the brownies after Dad and I have finished."

Teri watched as Gerald limped away with Miles and Champ trailing in his wake. Gerald was a good husband and father. He was a hard worker and good provider. She had never had to work outside the home until his accident. The terror she had experienced when she sat in the hospital not knowing if he was going to make it was still fresh in her memory. The last year-and-a-half had been hard on him. She had to help move him the first few months. Then, his worries about getting a job added to his frustration and despair. He despised being so helpless. Now, Vera showing up could be disastrous. He did not deserve this turmoil and stress. Teri wiped away her angry tears. *I can't let my family be destroyed by her. I'll find a way to stop her.*

19

Chapter 4

Kim Connor, the sheriff department's administrative assistant, was laughing when Sean Neumann, Bekbourg's sheriff, walked into the station. Arlo Lopez, a deputy who had been leaning against the counter, stood. A mischievous glint in Arlo's eyes made Sean leery. "What's up?" *Or, do I want to know?* Sean silently asked himself.

"Chief, have you noticed an unusual vehicle cruising the streets around here?" Arlo could barely contain a grin. Kim was unable to suppress a gleeful smile.

"No. Why?" Sean's serious expression remained unchanged.

"You know who Ms. Beaumont is?"

He nodded. Knowing Dillie was somehow involved was enough to prepare Sean for what might be coming.

"She's driving this souped-up golf cart that looks like a 50's T-Bird. It's a honey, Chief—baby blue with gold accessories."

"She's driving it on the streets?" asked Sean.

"Yep. She has tags and everything."

Kim chuckled, "I can't believe Noel Fischner hasn't already called you complaining."

Arlo nodded. "Oh, I bet it's just a matter of time. He looks for everything he can to zing the sheriff. Although, since it's his brother doing all the work on Dillie's gallery, maybe he'll hold his fire on complaining about Dillie."

A laugh escaped Kim, "I wouldn't count on that. Noel and Cole don't get along. Yep, I bet the sheriff hears from Noel sooner rather than later."

As he turned to head to the shelter of his office, Sean whispered under his breath, "Let's hope he's got better things to do."

Their eyes were sparkling as laugher erupted at Sean's retreat.

Chapter 5

Located in southeastern Ohio, the small rural town of Bekbourg, Ohio, was founded by a Revolutionary War hero as part of a land grant in the Northwest Territory. Early on, massive hardwood forests were cleared, and farming emerged as the predominant way of life. Because of its proximity to the network of pioneer trails intersecting north-south and east-west, Bekbourg grew to be a prosperous trading post. The region flourished as paper mills opened in nearby Chillicothe, and Ohio University was chartered in the city of Athens. Coal and iron-ore mining, brick-making and wheat and corn mills marked the emergence of lucrative area industries. Bekbourg expanded from a trading post into a town with the emergence of farming, dairy products and paper products, and the businesses that catered to these enterprises.

The 1840's brought a major boost to Bekbourg's economy with the construction of the West Virginia Bekbourg and Cincinnati Railroad Company from Wheeling, West Virginia, to Cincinnati, Ohio. The railroad built a switching yard and depot in Bekbourg, and major market expansions for the regional industries were inevitable with access to markets east and west.

During the Depression, the local business owners, through ingenuity and shrewdness, kept their companies viable, and World War II brought a boom as the need for dairy products and paper goods skyrocketed. Bekbourg had a history of growth and economic prosperity until the global economy changed in the 1970's.

Similar to much of the region, Bekbourg's economy began to falter. Cities across the Midwest spiraled downward as manufacturing closed. Bekbourg's milk and paper companies managed to hold on, but barely. Recognizing they were on the cusp of just becoming another rust-belt casualty, Bekbourg's leaders embarked to rebrand Bekbourg as a tourist destination because of its proximity to a national forest, state park, rivers and lakes. Their quest had caused an uptick in visitors and revenues. Business doors, once shuttered, were now open, and new enterprises were moving into the area.

Delphia Beaumont, nicknamed Dillie at birth, was born in Bekbourg and had lived there until she graduated from Schriever High School. Over thirty years later, her brother's memorial had drawn her back to Bekbourg. During her brief visit, she "fell in love" with the town of her childhood and decided that, having recently been divorced from her fifth husband, it was the ideal time to "return home." Vowing to her new friends not to dally, she departed for her California estate to get her affairs in order.

Unbeknownst to the town's people, Dillie had purchased the old factory where cigar boxes had been manufactured from the 1890's until the Schumacher Company closed its doors in the late 1950's. Built in the Richardsonian Romanesque architectural style, the Schumacher factory had been a crown jewel for the city. Hailing from the New England area originally, Konrad Schumacher had wanted to share with his newly-adopted town the majesty of the courthouses, churches, libraries and train stations which had utilized the Richardsonian Romanesque influences.

He had spared no expense as the factory was constructed with a stone exterior set with compelling semicircular-designed arches above the windows and entryways, gabled roofs and a large central tower. The large, round stained-glass window high above the entrance commanded recognition from both outside and inside the grand structure. In the 1960's, the owner, a grandson of Konrad Schumacher, had donated the factory to an order of nuns who had planned to relocate the local elementary school they operated into the larger building and expand their school through the high school grades. Since the nuns had failed to raise the necessary funds, however, the building had remained boarded since its closure in the 1950's.

When Cole Fischner, president of Fischner Construction Company, brought in subcontractors from as far away as Columbus to undertake the renovations planned by Dillie, curiosity began to swirl as to the new owner and the plans. County records listed the purchaser as Livingstone Trust, a private trust. Fischner, and the local architect, Otis Mueller, remained silent as to the nature of the renovations and even the new owner. Excitement blossomed around town as word started to circulate that Dillie was the new owner and planned to open an arts and craft gallery and studio.

With the grand opening days away, Cole Fischner and Otis guided Dillie throughout the structure, explaining the enhancements. "Mrs. Beaumont, Otis and I are happy with the way this has turned out. Since the original factory had the large open space where the employees worked, we built on that openness and constructed the movable walls to accommodate individual work spaces for the artists but with wide open spaces for customers to view their displays and see the artists at work."

Otis, the architect, pointed toward the back. "We kept in place the area where the employee cafeteria was for break rooms, and added off the back a large food preparation area, with state-of-the-art appliances. We'll show you when we get there, but we think you will see that it will service caterers and others for the parties and entertainment you plan for here."

Dillie's smile conveyed her approval. "Gentlemen, I absolutely *love* the transformation of this magnificent structure—absolutely superb. You have simply thought of everything."

"Given that the finest materials and workmanship were used when this factory was built, we had a nice starting point to accomplish what you wanted. Work on the exterior was mostly repair and restoration. The factory's cavernous interior is solid, and since you wanted to leave the large open spaces for artists to work and sell their art, most of the improvements were spent on lighting and on building out apartments above the back part for special guests and artists. Otis saw to it that we used the best in our upgrades and remodels."

"Of course, Darling," said Dillie with approval. Growing up, Dillie had loved passing by the grand building and admiring its beauty and the large stained glass window. She was pleasantly surprised to see the building was vacant when she returned for her brother, Owen Donaldson's, funeral. Upon her return to California, she asked her attorney to look into its availability. Now, seeing the renovations, her dream of returning to her hometown and owning a business that benefitted the city was a reality.

Cole continued, "At first we debated whether to put your office up front, but we decided that by putting it there, you will have the flexibility to adjust the panels to ensure privacy or open them to see what's going on."

"Marvelous idea—and I do love what you have done. Of course, my assistant will adore the large open area there with the tables and equipment to work with the artists and suppliers. Everything is simply splendid. Everyone will fall in love with the exquisite gallery and studio. I do hope you both plan to be at the grand opening so I can show you off for the geniuses you are."

"Yes, ma'am, we both will be there," Cole assured her.

"Wonderful. Now, I would like to see the apartment at the back of the property."

Otis spoke up, "I think you are really going to be pleased with how that turned out. Cole and I took special efforts to transform that old coachman's quarters into a luxury apartment."

"Oh, I'm sure I will love it."

Konrad Schumacher had also built a mansion in the same Richardsonian Romanesque style in town on Oak Street. Except for a time when an order of nuns had lived there, the mansion had stood vacant after his death. Dillie was going to live in the mansion. "Not that there is any hurry, but when do you think I can move into my new home?" Dillie asked.

"Not much longer," Cole said. "We didn't have the open spaces to work with in the house, so it took longer to replace all the piping and wiring and install a heating and cooling system. Otis saw to it that we maintained the beauty of the house but updated everything."

Otis explained, "We have worked closely with your designer. Some of the furnishings are being warehoused, but furniture coming from overseas won't be delivered for several weeks."

"Not to worry, Darling. Bri and Max are spoiling me in their fabulous Bed and Breakfast."

Chapter 6

About fifteen-years ago, Brianna (Bri) Sanderson and her husband, Max Brandt, had taken a gamble when they left their jobs in Cincinnati to restore an abandoned boarding house in Bekbourg's downtown. Both in their 40s, they had a hippy and adventurous flare. Bri's face had a wholesome glow. With her hair typically worn in a long braid or hanging in waves down her back and jeans with long floral smocks or longer dresses, she reminded many of an "earth mother." Max, much more slender than his wife, had a beard and wore his hair in a ponytail.

After opening the B&B, they bought an adjoining building and turned it into a coffee and dining bistro. Max and Bri settled into life in the small town and had become notable for their volunteer pursuits. At the suggestion of friends, Bri had run for mayor of Bekbourg on a reform ticket and won. Max liked to tease her by saying she could top any mayor across the country in baking scones and pastries. Max was proud of Bri's accomplishments as mayor. She had settled into the job, and several initiatives were moving forward to support the town's goal of remaking itself into a tourist destination.

Even though autumn was in the air, hanging baskets of green fern and pots of colorful pansies welcomed visitors to the B&B, which stood out from most of the downtown buildings with its baby blue siding and white shutters. White rocking chairs and wicker tables lined the porch extending the full length of the front. The refurbished large walnut and leaded glass front door drew immediate attention by passersby. Inside, the rich woods on floors, trims and banisters melted into the warm yellows, beiges, blues and greens used on walls, upholstery and accessories.

Cozy warmth filled the parlor from the fire Max had built before starting dinner. Reclining in the plush seating, Dillie and Bri enjoyed pre-dinner drinks.

"Dillie," laughed Bri, "everyone around here was wondering who had purchased the factory and what the plans were. They had no idea who Livingstone Trust was."

"Well, Darling, my first husband, God rest his dear soul, wanted to make sure I was taken care of, so he set up the trust. His people handle things like that for me." Dillie sipped her martini. "Luscious! I must tell Max his martinis are to die for." Dillie's gold bracelets jingled as she moved her arm. "And you dear Bri, you are now the mayor. Congratulations, Darling. So much has transpired since I have been away."

"There has been a lot going on. I guess you heard about Mike Adams' death."

"I was simply devastated when I read the news. Our dear friend, Cheryl, was so gracious to send me publications from her delightful newspaper. I, of course, sent Geri my condolences at the time, but I plan to visit her soon."

Bri tried not to be distracted as the brilliance from Dillie's large jeweled rings danced in concert with the chandelier's glistening prisms. The curls from her long platinum hair were in constant motion as she orchestrated her arm and hand movements with words that mesmerized with a foreign accent. Beauty, aided by makeup, and vibrancy concealed her age.

"Darling, I truly do not wish to raise a heartbreaking topic before dining on the feast Max is preparing, but there is something I have been wondering about."

"What is that, Dillie?"

"The brave woman, Irma Ritter, who was held hostage to entice that handsome sheriff into that awful trap, was quoted in the newspaper as saying that a gentleman named John Pawley saved them all. I was in school with John. Do you know him?"

"Oh, you went to school with him?"

"Yes, but I have not seen him since our senior year. But, Darling, let's not dwell on how long that has been!"

Bri laughed. "To answer your question, I have never met him, and what I do know of him, could fit in a thimble. I don't know if anyone knows much about him. Since you went to school with him, you know he grew up here. He served in the Vietnam War. At some point after the war, he moved back to Bekbourg. He lives on a farm in Mader Valley that belonged to his parents. He's an eccentric mountain man. I understand he lives off the grid and is a loner." Bri shrugged, "That's the extent of my knowledge. Does that sound like the boy you knew?"

"That is not an easy question." Dillie stood to refresh her martini. "Is it true what Ms. Ritter said about him being a hero?"

"Yes. I know some people who attend church with Irma. There was some friction between her and John before the incident. Well, I think that discord was only on Irma's part, because from what I heard, John Pawley ignored Irma."

"Oh, do tell, Darling. This is getting more interesting," smiled Dillie as she returned to her seat.

Bri chuckled. "Well, you see, Irma lives just past John's place, and every time she drives to town, she passes his home. He is a health fanatic, and part of his regiment is to patrol his property, wearing his gun and boots—but that's all."

Dillie's eyes sparked. "You mean he walks around in his birthday suit?"

"Yes. But after John saved the day, Irma decided she could overlook his eccentricity and started cooking food for him, and they struck up a kind of friendship—as best as one can with John.

"Over the winter, she noticed he had not picked up the food she had left him on his porch, so she knocked on the door. She heard his dog whining from inside. The door was unlocked, so she went in and found him gravely ill. She called the ambulance. He nearly died from pneumonia. If it had not been for Irma, I'm afraid John would not have made it."

Dillie had been listening intently. "Thank goodness for that dear woman."

"Yes."

"So, is John back at his home?" asked Dillie as she enjoyed another sip.

"As far as I know. He rarely comes into town. He's an enigma—even to the few who have met him."

Both women's attention was drawn to the slender young man, Frederic St. Fleur, Dillie's personal assistant, as he greeted the women with a bow. Dapper in attire from his plaid silk sports coat and thin scarf to tapered black slacks and leather shoes, he strolled to the bar to pour a drink. After asking if he could refresh their libations, he announced to Dillie, "The artists will be moving their art into the gallery. The display shelving was installed today. I have seen to the final arrangements for the musicians, florist and catering.

Your grand opening will be sensational, Doll, if I say so myself."

"Marvelous." Dillie turned toward Bri, "I simply do not know what I would do without Frederic. He attends to everything."

Bri nodded toward the small leather-bound note pad which she had begun to think of as an appendage to his left hand. "It would take more than that to keep me organized with so many details. I don't know how you do it, Frederic."

"I am delighted with the cooperation from the Cincinnati establishments. Your references for the caterer, equipment rental and valet were superb. I am compiling a database for future references."

"I'm glad you're satisfied with them. I hope it worked out with them agreeing to use locals as much as possible. I want to help the local economy, and to the extent they can hire them for the event, it helps our families here."

"Of course," agreed Frederic. "Also, it brings more interest to Dillie's smashing gallery. A brilliant idea on your part, Bri."

Dillie's thin eyebrow arched, "Frederic, dear. You have been so busy with the grand opening. The corner apartment on the second floor of the gallery is ready to move in." The upper story toward the back of the factory had been converted into apartments for visiting artists.

Bri turned her attention to Frederic as he set the decanter on the tray. "I made arrangements today for my personal belongings to be shipped. I will be moving in there, but only until I find my own place. Perhaps Bri or Max might know someone who can help me with that task."

"Of course we can. You are welcome to stay here as long as you like, and we want you and Dillie to drop by any time after you move into your own places."

Dillie and Frederic raised their glasses in toast as Bri followed their lead. "Cheers."

Max walked to the door, "Whatever we are celebrating, count me in, but let's not delay too long because dinner is ready." The trio was eager to see what fine cuisine awaited them as they headed toward the private dining area off the kitchen.

Chapter 7

Cheryl Seton had spent the first fourteen years of her life in Bekbourg and was then whisked away by her mother to escape a murder scandal involving her beloved grandfather. She had returned to Bekbourg a few years ago as an investigative reporter to cover a murder case making national headlines. Upon her return, Cheryl was pleased to find that the rust bowl had not completely claimed Bekbourg. The heart of the downtown had hundred-year-old buildings that had been refurbished. She never tired of walking along Main Street and studying how the buildings reaching four and five stories toward the sky each offered their own architectural quality.

An unexpected benefit of having recently become the owner of the *Bekbourg Tribune* was delving into the old newspaper files and uncovering stories of interest around the area. Some were cold cases of crimes, and others were stories about events or human interest. Bekbourg had a rich history related to being a railroad town, and many of the old newspaper articles were about railroad happenings.

One day as Cheryl was looking though an archived box, a headline had captured her attention.

As she read, she felt her breath catching. *How many people around Bekbourg would remember this?* she wondered. Her investigative reporter instincts kicked in. She needed more information and reached out to C.P. Traylor, a resident and retired railroad executive, who was in the process of taking operational control of the WVB&C Railroad Company.

Born in the early 1940's, C.P. had grown up in Bekbourg, Ohio, and took a job after high school graduation as a yard clerk with the local railroad to finance his college education. He transferred to Cincinnati where he could continue his railroad job while attending the business college at the University of Cincinnati. He was drafted and assigned to the U. S. Army Railroad Corp at Fort Eustis in Virginia.

After his military service, he completed his degree and quickly moved up the ladder with the railroad company. He was eventually promoted into the executive ranks and successfully oversaw mergers and the transformation of his company from a turn-of-the-century-run corporation to one that relied on technology and streamlined operations. After retiring from the railroad, C. P. took a high-level job with the Department of Transportation working on national transportation initiatives. Growing disillusioned with the federal bureaucracy, however, he had returned to Bekbourg with his sights on acquiring the local railroad.

He had worked with Bri and the City Council to get their support for him to take control of the WVB&C Railroad Company, which had been slated for closure by the OMVX Railroad Corporation. It was a no-brainer for the locals to support C.P.'s plans to keep the train running, and now, his aim to operate his own railroad was days away. His staff had already been combing through all the records and files.

Where some people of C.P.'s stature might make others feel intimidated or uncomfortable, C.P. had a way of engaging with people from different walks of life. For sure, he was a hard-nosed businessman who had long ago mastered negotiation tactics with hardened adversaries, but he could also turn on the charm and affability with those around him. C.P. had been embraced by the citizenry of Bekbourg, and he had championed initiatives to enhance the town's image and had contributed to many philanthropic causes. His goals had grown to include opening a railroad museum in the old depot and turning a twenty-five-mile defunct spur line from downtown Bekbourg to a state park in the Lake Peatmont area into a scenic railroad for tourists.

Losing no time in reaching out to C.P. for any information he might have on the story she had sensed, Cheryl called to ask for an interview, which he immediately granted. C.P. had set up an office in the back corner of the old depot in what had once been the station master's office. On visiting, Cheryl noticed right off that in-coming and out-going trains could be observed through his window. C.P.'s large L-shaped desk looked to have a story behind it as well. He explained that he had combined two desks, both of which had been station master desks. The desk sitting directly in front of his executive chair had been the very first one he had used when he had started working as a yard clerk.

Behind his desk was a large oak unit with slots and cubes. "I take it that is part of railroad history, too?" asked Cheryl.

C.P. grinned. "Yes. It's a mail sorter where the mail was held. The men found it in the station house, and it made sense to put it to good use."

"I like it." She glanced around his office. Hanging on the wall were early photos of the WVB&C rail yard and awards and recognitions earned by C.P. over the years. A functioning railroad clock was mounted on the wall. "Looks like the office of a railroad president."

He laughed. "Yes, I guess it does. Now, what can I do for you?"

"I came across a compelling story. An unfortunate incident back in 1957 shut down the railroad for a good length of time. It wasn't clear from the article just what the impact was to the railroad, so I wanted to see what kind of information you might have."

"Are you talking about when the bridge washed out?"

"Yes, that's it. Do you remember much about it?"

"I was a teenager at the time, but I remember it vividly. It really shut down normal railroad operations. It took nearly six months to reopen the main line. My own father had to go to Cincinnati to work until rail operations through here could resume. He was one of the freight agents."

Cheryl asked him what a freight agent did, and C.P. explained that he scheduled the pickup and delivery of freight cars and scheduled the rail cars to their destination. A freight agent was also responsible for the bills of lading and oversaw the freight house—a temporary holding place for freight. "That's how I ended up hiring on with the railroad as a clerk—my dad got me that job."

"What happened to the businesses around here?" asked Cheryl.

C.P. shook his head. "They had to scramble to stay open, especially the milk plant. As you can imagine, the cows couldn't wait, and the farmers didn't want to dump their milk. Your husband's father can probably help you find out about that, but I remember Dad talking about it. He also said that the paper company had a devil of a time getting materials to make their products."

"What did the businesses do?"

"With the bridge gone, there was no through-rail service, so trains had to be rerouted. Locally, they'd send trains called the 'locals' and pick up cars and take them either to Cincinnati on the west side of the bridge, or to Wheeling on the east side, and from there, they would be rerouted to their destination. It slowed things down, but it kept businesses open. The worst impact was we had no passenger trains. In those days, a lot of people depended on them for travel. Quite a few people didn't have cars, and the roads around here weren't that good." C.P. paused before continuing, "What I remember the most was how many people were laid off on the railroad and how many had to drive into Cincinnati to work."

Cheryl stopped writing and looked up. "I never thought about all the ramifications. It must have been a difficult time."

"It was. I saw the impact an interruption could have on the local economy. Strangely, that memory is one of the reasons I wanted to keep the railroad opened though Bekbourg. Even though things today are a lot different, the railroad's still a vital part of the livelihood around here. This project took such a long time because they had to build a complete replacement from the ground up. They had to remove all the old stuff and put in the new." C.P. smiled, "I can give you a high level view of what happened, but I guess you'd like to know the details."

Cheryl nodded, "I was hoping I could follow up on this by looking through the railroad's records."

"You're in luck. I've recently hired an archivist part-time to organize all the old records for a museum I'm planning to open here about the history of the Bekbourg rail line." He gave Cheryl the contact information and told her he'd tell the archivist she would be in contact. He also suggested others around town who might be able to provide perspectives on what had happened and what life had been like when the bridge was out. "I never knew much at all about what happened that night, Cheryl. You've got my curiosity up on that. I bet if anyone around town can fill you in on the night itself, it would be Jules. He seems to be the resident historian around here."

Cheryl smiled, "He's my go-to on railroad history. I'm going to do as much research as I can; then I'll go to the expert."

C.P. shook his head, "Good game plan."

The more she learned the more interested Cheryl became in the story. Some of the old-timers probably remembered parts of what had happened and what life was like when the train service through town was disrupted, but the series she had planned for the *Tribune* would be an eye-opener for newer residents and the younger generation. She planned to talk to Kye and see what she might remember—since her husband had worked for the railroad at the time. She also had contacts at local businesses which could assist with the impacts they had experienced during that time. Of course, the bridge washing out held the most interest.

Chapter 8

Nell Porter was unpacking pottery pieces she had brought from her home studio and placing them on display shelves when Dillie swooped up wearing her long, silk fuchsia ruana over black slacks and silk camisole. A gold leather belt along with gold jewelry accessories and a multi-carat yellow diamond ring complemented the outfit. "Nell, darling, we have people here who will carry those heavy boxes for you. You must not carry such heavy things!"

"Thank you, Dillie, but I'm used to carrying them. I may not look like it, but I've got a strong back."

"Well, if you insist, but please do not fail to ask for assistance. Oh, this is absolutely glorious artwork!" she exclaimed as she admired the unique shapes and techniques utilized by Nell. "Darling, customers will simply clamor to purchase your stunning creations. Make sure you put any of these marvelous pieces you do not have room for here in the storage area. We absolutely cannot allow your supply to run short during our grand opening. Customers would revolt."

Sherrie Rutherford

Dillie could make a rock smile. Even me, thought Nell as her lips slightly curled up. Nell's pottery was carried by galleries in notable places, such as Gatlinburg, Tennessee; Traverse City, Michigan; and Nashville, Indiana. But she had been commissioned by customers from as far away as California. Nell had grown up in Bekbourg and had been throwing clay on kick-wheels since junior-high. Life had dealt her hard blows, and her life's interests after her daughter's death had shrunk to her clay artworks.

Early in her career, she had mastered using more traditional clays—earthenware, stoneware, and porcelain—and had started mixing and experimenting with other clays and raw materials. Her creativity showed an unchecked boldness in shape, design, motifs and patterns. Her talent in firing clay pieces at different stages and applying over-glazes and textural designs between the steps resulted in unique ceramics. Art enthusiasts commissioned her to create ceramics ranging from vintage to contemporary designs, and her pieces never failed to impress with her ability to work with a spectrum of hues from intense mineral colors to full shades of grays and browns.

When Dillie decided to open the gallery in Bekbourg, Nell was one of the first artists she had reached out to. Nell was happy to have such a magnificent locale to display and sell her ceramics, but she was hesitant to participate—since Dillie wanted the artists available to meet the public, particularly for special events such as the grand opening. The least favorite part of her career was any need to interact with people. Nell simply wanted to live a solitary life and create her art. Even though Dillie offered to staff a sales clerk for her booth and a space in the back of the former cigar box factory to spin her pottery as well as install a kiln, Nell wanted the solitude of her large open studio at the back of her small, two-bedroom home, surrounded by quiet and calm. Out of necessity years ago, she had retained an assistant who would pick up her pottery for shipping and who handled the paperwork and administrative aspects of Nell's business. In the end, Dillie had given her enough assurances that Nell agreed to sign up for a booth.

"Thank you, Dillie. I hope my pieces can live up to your expectations."

"Have no fears, Darling. They already soar. You are a star."

"Excuse me. Are you Ms. Beaumont?"

Both women turned to see the woman. Dillie stepped forward. "Yes, but please call me Dillie. What can I do for you?"

Vera glanced at the scrawny woman wearing jeans and a long-sleeve t-shirt peppered with glaze and turned her attention to Dillie. "My name is Vera Keller, and I'm a painter. I heard you are looking for artists for your gallery."

Nell's eyes widened.

If Dillie whiffed the poignant cigarette smoke from Vera's presence, she never let on. Vera continued as she raised her hand holding a portfolio folder. "I brought some examples of my paintings."

"Of course I would love to see your work. This is Nell Porter—Bekbourg's virtuoso of these beautiful ceramics displayed here for our grand opening."

Nell remained speechless as she continued to stare at Vera. Vera looked at the shelves. "These are nice. I like the color of glazes on those two pieces," she was pointing to a tall vase and a large square tray. "My palette has similar hues."

Nell spun around and yanked back the flaps on a box. Dillie sensed Nell's discomfort and moved with haste to direct Vera toward the front. Her bracelets jingled as she motioned ahead. "Let's move to the area near the entrance where we will have room to talk and look at your lovely paintings. Where are you from?"

Nell turned and stared at Vera with hardened eyes as the women walked toward the front.

Vera replied to Dillie, "I grew up here, but I moved away a long time ago to live around artists like myself and where there were more opportunities to sell my paintings. I lived in an artist colony near Lake Erie. I read about the opening of your art gallery. That was all I needed to pack up my belongings and head back here." A smoker's cough interrupted Vera. "This is a perfect place to sell my work."

Just then, a man with dark hair combed to the side and a smooth face hurried up. Vera wondered if he was a model for some fashion magazine. "Dillie, Doll, I was on the phone with the rental company and the caterer out of Cincinnati." He looked at Vera, who was eyeing him as if he was cotton candy. "I heard the chime but could not get to the door. I take it this is the guest who came in?"

"Yes, Darling, this is Vera Keller, who was just about to show me her enchanting paintings. Vera, this is my assistant, Frederic St. Fleur. Frederic, be a dear and join us."

Frederic and Vera shook hands and moved to a bright area with a large table and easels. Soon after Vera arranged the paintings, Dillie started to excuse herself for another engagement, but Vera hastily spoke, "Oh, I thought we could discuss the terms. I was hoping my paintings would be part of the grand opening this weekend."

Frederic interrupted, "Unfortunately, Ms. Keller, at this late date, we do not have space, but please continue to tell me about your paintings. I would enjoy hearing about your technique and the expression behind each work."

Vera turned only to find Dillie had vanished. "Okay, but I was hoping to talk to Dillie."

Frederic directed her to a painting on the easel. "Please tell me about this one."

Later that afternoon, Frederic materialized in the doorway to Dillie's office with two chilled glasses of sparkling water. "Here, Doll," he said as he set the glass on her desk and glided to the cushioned chair off to the side. As he crossed his legs, he tilted his head, "I must say our opinions of Ms. Keller's paintings are aligned."

Dillie finished sipping, "What did you tell her?"

"Of course I told her how much we appreciated her interest in the gallery but, for now, we had booked a number of painters. I assured her we would keep her in mind for future events and openings."

"I hope she understood?"

Frederic waved his hand as he was apt to do. "Frankly, you should not give it another thought. She is not someone I would recommend. Her paintings are not of the quality of our other artists, but, beyond that, there is something off-putting about her. Not a good mix for our other artists. I was diplomatic, of course."

"You always are. Nell had seemed a bit shaken by her, but neither woman seemed to know the other. If darling Nell feels uncomfortable around her, it is best we not bring her onboard. I appreciate you taking care of it. It is distasteful to me to have to be the bearer of bad news."

He smiled, "Of course it is, Doll. That is what I am here for."

Frederic had been Dillie's personal assistant for five years. He was the son of friends of her latest husband. Although he had been raised in Paris, Frederic had moved to California to get his undergraduate degree from Stanford. After receiving his graduate degree, he had worked for an art museum in San Francisco and dined with Dillie and her husband when they occasionally visited the Bay Area. As it happened one night over dinner, Dillie was telling Frederic how her assistant had resigned to move to Singapore with her husband, and he asked if she would be interested in him taking the position. The arrangement was finalized during dinner, and he had been her devoted right-hand person since—handling the perpetual frenzy that revolved around Dillie. They had worked closely together—it was like he could read her mind and anticipate her next moves.

Her biggest concern when she had decided to relocate to Bekbourg was that he would not be willing to stay on as her assistant. She remembered him sitting much like he was now, sipping wine, when she broke the news about moving to Bekbourg. He looked at her over the edge of the glass as he took an extra-long sip and lowered his glass, "Well, Doll, I know where Ohio is, and after I locate this 'quaint little town of Bekbourg' on the map, I will know where my new home is going to be." It came as no surprise he could make quotation marks with his fingers without spilling a droplet of wine.

Chapter 9

Vera threw open the door to her motel room juggling an ice bucket and a paper bag from the package store. After plopping things on the scarred laminate top, she flung her purse on the bed and mixed the cheap vodka with the warm soft drink left opened from earlier in the plastic cup left by housekeeping. She dropped into the marred vinyl chair. "Shit!" She licked the sloshed liquid from her fingers and hand. She ran her free hand through her disheveled hair as she sipped her sustenance and dwelled on her sorrows. *That jerk acted like he was interested in my paintings, but I know he was giving me the bum's rush. Shit! And now I barely got my car door open when that clod from the office made a bee-line demanding I pay for two nights or else I'm out.* Vera stewed as she gulped from the cup.

It was useless to try and pay with a canceled credit card—she had experience—so she had to give him cash, which was perilously close to running out. Except for her paintings and supplies, old car and personal items, she had nothing of value. She had not considered that her sister would be so low on funds, but even so, they had *some* money they could spare. Once she staked out her old bedroom, no way would they call the cops. Her big sister would not want the embarrassment of bringing in the police for a family matter. Nope, once she was in there, she would have a roof over her head.

But, she had a plan B and a plan C. Too bad she did not get to talk to Dillie—she'd have cash in her pockets right now. All that fancy dress and expensive jewelry told her Dillie Beaumont was loaded. She would find time to commandeer Dillie at the grand opening. Hopefully, that French watchdog would not be hanging around.

I can't rest on my laurels, she thought as she reached for the tattered phone directory and wrote down the information. She pulled a couple of pieces of baloney from the small ice box and devised a plan for tomorrow.

Chapter 10

Anita served the breakfast orders to the railroaders and told the men she would return with more coffee. Mule Head looked around, "Wonder where Jules is this morning? Usually he's here by now."

Dusty drained the last of his coffee and held his cup for Anita to refill. "I don't know. He may be turning in his papers for retirement."

Mule Head tugged a bite of bacon and laid the remaining piece on his plate. "You know, I was down at the depot the other day just nosing around, seeing what was going on. I saw Cheryl, the newspaper owner, leave C.P.'s office."

"Have you seen that office?" Dusty shook his head. "It's something else. He's decorated it with all kinds of things from the depot and freight house."

Chaw spoke up, "Yeah, I've seen it. He took the old crew station master desk and put a new top on. He even took the old mail sorter and put it on the back wall to hold his mail and other things."

Mule Head shook his head, "Well I didn't see any of that, but I saw Cheryl Seton come out of his office and leave. It looked like she had been talking to him about something."

"Well, you know what that means," said Chaw as he buttered his toast.

Dusty and Mule Head nodded, "Yeah, it means it's all about to come down," said Dusty.

Jules walked up to their table and sat down. "Where have you been, old man?" asked Dusty.

Jules had a big grin on his face.

Chaw looked at Dusty and Mule Head, "I know that grin. He turned in his retirement papers."

Jules kept grinning as he wiped his silverware with the paper napkin.

Mule Head scratched his head, "No, I think it's something else. Maybe he got lucky last night with the old lady."

Dusty could not take the suspense. "What are you grinning about, Jules? Do you know something? Is C.P. ready to take over completely?"

Jules finished setting his knife and fork in place and gave Anita his usual order. "Well, boys, do I have a story for you! I just came from meeting with C.P., and all the rumors about the scenic railroad are true."

"What rumors?" Mule Head belted.

"The rumors about the 'Mader Valley Scenic Railroad.'"

"I never heard about that," grumbled Mule Head.

"Well, you'll be hearing about it soon."

"Spit it out," said Chaw. "Quit trying to play games with us."

"Well, since I'm one of the few remaining employees on the railroad who worked on steam engines, C.P. wants me to head up his new steam excursion train for the Mader Valley Scenic Railroad. He's in negotiations to purchase two vintage rebuilt steam engines along with twenty old passenger cars for the scenic railroad. He's also planning to buy an old EMD GP7 diesel that used to work here on our railroad to switch out the cars. In an emergency if a steam engine goes down, it can fill in. It's the old 5706—one of the first diesels we bought back in the 50's."

Mule Head shook his head, "He's pulling our leg."

"No, I'm not pulling your leg. As soon as the final papers are signed on the WVB&C, he's going to start refurbishing the old track and bringing in this old steam equipment. And I'm going to be the chief engineer on this train."

They all looked at him with their mouths open. "You got to be kidding us," said Mule Head.

"There's something else."

While he sipped his coffee, Jules waited to see which man would take the bait. Mule Head could not resist, "What's that?"

"I'm supposed to go to Indiana where they are refurbishing the steam engines and learn about them and renew my old steam engine skills. Once you learn this, you never forget. But I need a refresher course to learn about these steam engines in particular. I'll then be able to train people here how to operate and maintain the engines."

"Well, congratulations, you old codger," hooted Dusty. "The steam engine days are coming back to Bekbourg."

"Eventually, this railroad will go all the way to Cleary, which is about ten miles north—where the old lumber and mining company used to be. They're expecting to have a lot of passengers getting on there and coming down to the state park, and they're even hoping a lot will ride all the way to here. We're starting off just going to the state park, but when he finishes over to Cleary, we'll have people going north and south. That's why we need two trains."

They looked stunned as they watched Jules cut his bacon with the fork and knife. "That is unbelievable," said Mule Head.

Jules nodded as he took a small bite of egg. "Yeah, it's following the old railroad that used to haul iron ore, so its base is in pretty good shape. He just needs to do some work to get it up to speed so we can run our excursion trains. It'll probably take two or three years to get fully operational. He wants to get moving on this as soon as he's fully in charge of the WVB&C."

Jules looked at the three men who were watching him. "Now, you got to keep this quiet, boys—on pain of excruciating death." Jules had the men's undivided attention. They loved thinking they were in the know before others. "I'm going to tell you something no one else knows. He's going to be making the announcement down at the depot one month from this Monday. But don't tell anyone."

Mule Head sipped his coffee. "It's unbelievable how fast this is coming together."

Chaw spoke up, "Well, that's C.P. for you. He gets the job done."

Jules sipped his coffee. "Yeah, I'll be turning my papers in pretty soon so I can be working full time on getting this thing done. I'm going to work until the end of the year and start my retirement in January."

"What does the lovely Renee have to say about this? I thought you were going to retire?" asked Dusty.

"She's one-hundred percent in favor of it. She's as excited about it as I am."

Chaw grinned, "She's damn happy you're going to be out of her hair."

Chapter 11

"Hey, Mom, need some help?" Miles asked as he bounded down the steps behind Champ.

Teri handed off the bags of groceries as she set down her purse on the small foyer table and headed toward the kitchen. "Thanks, Sweetie. I stopped by the grocery store to get some things for dinner and for tomorrow. How was school today?"

"Fine."

"You already finished with your homework?"

"Naw, but it won't take long."

"How was football practice?"

"It was okay. The varsity has a big game tomorrow night, so we just had a light scrimmage and the usual conditioning so all the coaches could work with them."

"I see. So you got home a little early," Teri said—handing him a pack of peanut butter crackers. "Here, hopefully this will tide you over 'til supper," she smiled. She also slipped Champ a treat as he licked his chops at seeing a snack handed to Miles.

"Thanks." Miles crammed a cracker in his mouth and picked up another as Teri put away the groceries. "Say, Mom, the other day, I heard Dad calling some woman a 'witch' when you all were talking. Well, he said another word, but I don't want my mouth washed out with soap," he grinned. She grinned back and shook her head, but the smile vanished when he added, "I think I know who that was."

"What are you talking about?" she asked.

"Well, it may not be her. I don't know. But Tommy's mother had just dropped me off from football practice, and I opened the door to let Champ out. A white car—it was pretty old and dinged up—pulled up the driveway, and a woman was in it. I guess she must have been afraid of Champ, because she didn't get out. She rolled down the window and yelled to ask if you were here. I told her you weren't and asked if she wanted me to tell you she had stopped by.

"I walked close to the car so I could better hear her. Man, she must smoke a lot. I could smell it as I got closer to the car. I'm sure glad you and Dad don't smoke. Anyway, it was weird. She kept looking at me and asking where I went to school. Stuff like that. I told her I had to do homework. She didn't drive off until me and Champ got in the house."

The bag of potatoes slipped from Teri's hands startling the dog. Miles jumped up and picked up the bag as he shooed Champ to the side. He looked at his mother as he handed her the bag. "Are you okay, Mom? What's the matter?"

Teri shook slightly as she laid the bag on the counter.

Gerald had walked up and heard the conversation. "Son, if she ever does come back I don't want you talking to her. Just take Champ inside and lock the doors."

"But, Dad, what's this all about?" He looked between his parents. "What's going on? Who is she?"

Gerald glanced at Teri. "She's your mother's sister, and she's no good. That's all that needs to be said about it."

Miles looked at his mother, "Mom's sister? She's the one who left a long time ago?"

"Yes. She showed up here the other day out of the blue. It's best if we don't get involved with her again. Do as your Dad told you and don't talk to her. Now, I need to fix dinner. Get up there and do your homework. I'll call you when it's ready."

"Okay. Come on Champ." He palmed the rest of the crackers, and boy and dog took off.

"What the hell was she doing back here?" Gerald kept a low roar so Miles did not hear.

Teri turned around to pretend she was sorting through the rest of the groceries, but her mind was reeling. "I don't know." She turned around. "Look, Gerald, I'll handle this. I'll make it perfectly clear that she is not to show back up here."

"What the hell good will that do? She's not supposed to be here now."

"I know. If I threaten to get an attorney, and maybe even a restraining order, that might be enough."

"Look, Teri, she can damn sure cause a lot of trouble." He swore. "I sure as hell don't want her anywhere around Miles."

"I don't either."

Gerald sat down. "Teri, I know the gallery's grand opening is important to you, since you're on the Garden Club committee and are helping out with the advertisement and arrangements, but I don't want to leave Miles alone here Saturday night in case she comes back. You go, and I'll stay here."

"Oh, no, Gerald, I don't want to be there by myself. People know you're able to get around. It won't look right if you're not there. What if I call Tommy's mother and see if she would mind if Miles stays there Saturday night? She won't care. They love for Miles and Champ to come over."

Gerald paused. "Okay, but that's not the answer for the long-term. Something's got to be done and quick." Gerald stood and hobbled away. Teri sat at the table and put her head in her hands. Her stomach knotted from despair. She knew the situation with Vera was going to get worse.

Chapter 12

Cheryl reviewed hundreds of pages about the May 24, 1957, bridge collapse—including official inspector and law enforcement accounts and engineering reports. To make her research complete, she next moved to researching the railroad files on the aftermath and the documents relating to the rebuilding of the bridge. Many of the post-bridge incident files were mundane, but she occasionally came across interesting notes and facts.

The railroad company's home office had hired an engineering company out of Cincinnati that specialized in rebuilding and repairing train bridges. The engineering project manager reported to the railroad section crew foreman who was located in Bekbourg. The railroad crew foreman, who had responsibility for the train's facilities forty miles east and west of Bekbourg, had overseen the entire bridge replacement project. It was apparent from his reports and notes he wanted to get the bridge constructed and operational as soon as possible. He had maintained a log on the project's status and reports from the engineering company. It was one of the foreman's log entries that had grabbed

Cheryl's attention. In a handwritten note, the foreman had recorded:

> *June 13, 1957. Body discovered by railroad crew working to clear debris about 100 yards downstream of Norton Creek Bridge abutment. Crew called sheriff. Sheriff to investigate. No known affiliation with railroad. Crew foreman and train detectives also to investigate, since body found snagged on hand car lodged on shoreline.*

She thumbed through several inches of the railroad's reports to try and piece together what she could learn about the body's discovery. She then went to Kim, Sean's assistant, to see what files might be in the sheriff department's archives. The newspaper's archives were another source of information she intended to review.

Bekbourg sheriff's records contained a copy of the locally-performed autopsy, which estimated the man had been dead four-to-six weeks. If that was correct, the man had died a week or two before the bridge crumbled, which made sense because the body could not have floated past the bridge's debris after its collapse. The medical examiner did not reach a conclusion as to the cause of death but noted the body's condition was consistent with being swept through raging waters and pinned by the hand car—where objects had crashed into the body. The man was estimated to be in his 40's, was five-feet, nine-inches, and weighed approximately one-hundred-seventy pounds. A metal piece on the hand car had snagged the man's belt and prevented the body from floating away. Tree limbs and other debris then had surrounded the mostly-submerged hand car.

The sheriff's report noted no missing persons reports had been filed during the relevant time frame. Most noteworthy of the file's photos was the silver square belt buckle with markings along its edging. If evidence had been collected, it no longer existed. Identification was impossible, and the body had never been claimed. Cheryl copied the autopsy and sheriff's reports.

Cheryl also talked with C.P.'s archivist and learned that the train crew had to clear out all the debris before the engineering company started rebuilding the bridge. That was what they were doing when they discovered the body trapped by the hand car. He was helpful in explaining that a hand car was a small car with a hand pump used in the old days by the track crew to transport tools and travel along the rails to check the track and make repairs. He suspected the rusted-out hand car had gone off the side of the Norton Creek Bridge years before, and since it was too heavy to carry out and of no salvage value, the railroad had left it. It had likely washed downstream and gotten stuck on the shoreline—where it was found during the debris removal for the new bridge.

The *Tribune's* archives had produced a newspaper story on the body being found with an appeal for anyone with information to contact the sheriff's office. The article gave the man's description and that of what remained of his clothing, like boots and the belt buckle. Two weeks later, the newspaper had run a follow-up story asking for the public's help in identifying the man. No other information existed in the *Tribune's* files.

Chapter 13

Colette Lynch had just finished setting out freshly-baked croissants, bacon and fruit when her husband walked into the kitchen. She greeted him with a cup of coffee. "Good morning, Mr. State Representative."

He smiled. "Good morning. Something sure smells good this morning." He tugged her closer, "And you sure look good. Looks like you're going to work out."

She laughed and disengaged. "Sit down and drink your coffee." She kissed his forehead as she put the plate in front of him. "I am, Sweetie, after I get you fed. Playing basketball in high school taught me how to stay in shape. I want to look good standing beside my handsome man."

"You never cease to amaze me with all your plans."

"Why, thank you. Speaking of plans, what have you got planned for today?"

"Dad wants to talk to me and Mick about some client needs, and then I've got a meeting with the Abbotts about a new computer system for their hardware store."

Colette pursed her lips, "I see. Are you going to have time for lunch with anyone about the campaign?"

"Not today," he said as he took a bite. "What about you. What's on your agenda?"

"I was thinking about calling Belinda today—checking in and that sort of thing. I thought maybe I'd see if she and Marty would be interested in coming here. Maybe we could have a dinner and invite possible donors. They would be perfect to attract people around here to a campaign event."

When she had decided to marry him, the one negative she saw was that he wanted to return to Bekbourg and work in his father's company. She was not thrilled with the idea of living in a small town, but she was not deterred. She could already envision a possible means for them to move back to Columbus if life in Bekbourg was not satisfying. During the Peace Corps, Brian had developed a close friendship with Marty Blake, whose father was a famous politician, and she had become friends with his wife, Belinda. Marty and Belinda had connections, and if the right opportunity appeared, she would find a way to coax Brian to leave Bekbourg.

"Mmm," he sighed. "I don't know if that's necessary. If I wasn't already the state representative, I might agree. Besides, I don't have the funds to pay for a dinner like that. You worry too much."

"Well, I just don't think we can take it for granted. After all, you've only been in the position for a few months, and I've started to see brochures from the other side. I saw her meeting with several people during lunch the other day at the GilHaus. I think there is a lot more going on with her campaign than we know. I still don't think it would hurt to invite the Blakes here. Belinda and Marty are *well* connected. If you think a dinner will cost too much, we could have a reception."

Brian attempted a smile as he took a final drink of coffee. "Let's think about it. I've got to run."

They stood, and he pecked a kiss on her lips before he headed to the door.

Colette frowned as she put away the dishes. She wished Brian shared her ambitions to live in a large city and be wealthy. She had grown up in a small town called Newton Falls, Ohio. Her father had worked at a manufacturing plant in nearby Youngstown. Being the oldest of six children, she had come by responsibility early, but it was watching her parents' struggles and anxieties over providing necessities for their family that had made the greatest impression. She was ashamed that much of the family's clothing was secondhand and learned at her mother's side how to mend and iron patches to get extended use of clothing. When friends visited, she hid the shame she endured from their shabby house and its frayed furnishings.

On rare occasions, her parents took the family to Youngstown. Even though plants were closing and the city was in decline, to the young girl, the large city was exciting with all its stores and restaurants. Growing up, she dreamed of escaping small-city life, marrying a big-shot and living in a big city where people had money and lots of ways to spend it. What little time she had to herself, she pretended to be a wealthy socialite who ordered house staff around and hobnobbed with the affluent.

For two years, she had worked her way through a college in Youngstown—until financial aid made it possible for her to transfer to The Ohio State University to complete her degree. She was used to working, so the fact that the financial aid package included a work program was not a deterrent. She was thrilled to be able to move to Columbus.

She was working in one of the campus restaurants when she had met Brian. She liked that he was easy-going—unlike her own hard-charging personality. He had a baby-face, which she found cute. As she got to know him, she learned his father owned a computer and technology business in Bekbourg, Ohio. Brian wore nice clothes and drove a newer model car and talked about family vacations to the beach. Because he had been in the Peace Corps, she thought him a man-of-the world. After his time in the Peace Corps, he had worked in the family business before starting college.

Occasion of Murder

He was older than her by a few years, but she liked the idea of a mature man. When their relationship started to get serious, he took her to Bekbourg to meet his family. His older brother, Mick, was a jokester and the life-of-the party around the family. Brian's parents were welcoming, and when they went out to eat at the GilHaus, the nicest restaurant in Bekbourg, she noticed employees and several of the guests spoke to them. His family was well-known around Bekbourg, and they were financially secure. So, marrying Brian seemed like a good idea.

After they got married, they moved into a small ranch house near his parents. Brian's mother had her group of friends and did not go out of her way to introduce Colette around town, so she started making friends at their church and volunteering. She learned which people were connected and made a point of staying in touch.

Then, when the state representative for their area died suddenly, she saw a chance for Brian to run for his office. She called Belinda and set up a dinner in Columbus. Belinda spoke about the possibility with Marty ahead of time, and by the time the dinner was over, a plan was hatched on how Brian could be appointed interim representative and then run for the office in the upcoming election. Her goal was for Brian to win the upcoming election, and in two years, run for a state senate position. They would then move to Columbus. Once they were in Columbus, she had ambitions for him to run the statehouse, possibly become governor, and who knew—maybe Washington, D.C. was in their future.

Colette had assumed since his father owned a business, Brian was wealthy. Soon after they married, she came to realize that Brian would never get rich on the salary he was paid in the family business. Another rude awakening was discovering that, having served in the Peace Corps, Brian was content with the basics, and expensive material things were of little interest to him. On the other hand, Colette wanted the finer things in life. She enjoyed the attention of being a politician's wife, and she believed appearances were important to him keeping the office.

Colette's spending was the one source of disharmony in their marriage. When he blew a lid after she bought him an expensive pen to celebrate being sworn in as the state representative and threatened to cancel the credit card, she did not curtail her buying—she reduced her spending. Although she despised bargain-hunting, her upbringing had trained her well. She drove to Columbus to shop sales to keep them looking fashionable. She was living for the day when she could spend as she pleased, but for now, she abided his wishes.

Whatever she could do to help push his career along, she intended to do. Voters loved young families, and she knew in the not-too-distant future, they would need to have children. She had practically raised her younger siblings and was not interested in having children, but being parents would look good in future campaigns. She also knew having children was important to Brian. Mick, his older brother, who worked alongside their father in running the business, had recently announced his engagement. He and his fiancé were already talking about having children, and their parents were thrilled.

Colette told Brian she wanted to start trying for a family after the election was over. When he jokingly said, "Hey, Baby, let's chuck this whole campaign thing and start now," her heart skipped a beat. When he saw her pout, he assured her he was kidding, but she was not so sure. One thing was certain—she was not giving up on her dreams. She had to take baby steps as she schemed about the next moves. Let it all seemingly fall in place gradually, she thought. That way, he will find it difficult to balk, especially if his good friend, Marty Blake, was encouraging him.

Chapter 14

For Bekbourg's leaders, Dillie's decision to open the old cigar box factory as an artist haven was a dream-come-true in the remake of the town's reputation as a tourist destination. Dillie had spared no expense for the gallery's grand opening extravaganza. She purchased notices in the *Bekbourg Tribune,* and posters appeared throughout the downtown businesses. Local political leaders and business owners were expected attendees, and regional musicians with national notoriety were part of the entertainment. Bekbourg rolled out the red carpet, and Dillie provided the glitz for the gallery's grand opening.

Frederic had brought in a decorator friend from California to add pizzazz and glamour throughout the cavernous gallery. Live music blared from the far end of the former cigar box factory as servers swept amongst guests offering hors d'oeuvres and flutes of champagne. Every artist booth area had been uniquely festooned to draw attention. For those wanting something other than champagne, multiple bars had been stationed around the perimeter.

A tented pavilion had been set up in a portion of the large side parking lot to give guests a respite from the loud music with continued access to an open bar and food. Valets wore red coats and black pants, and servers donned black coats and pants, white shirts and black bow ties. Two of Sean's deputies, Darrell Logan, and a new hire, Creed Gallagher, managed the traffic control—while Deputy Sydney Johnson patrolled the rest of the area.

It was a crush of people. Anyone who was anybody from Bekbourg was present, and guests from out-of-town were mingling and talking with the local artists. Sean stood off to the side with his father, Jim Neumann, and boyhood friend, Danny Chambers. "I've never seen anything like this in Bekbourg in all my years of living here," Jim said as he took a swig of beer.

Sean grinned, "And that's your entire life."

Jim nodded, "Yeah, except when I was serving this great country of ours in the Marines."

Danny chimed in. "Sally's beauty salon was booked solid with women getting their hair fixed."

"There are some people I don't recognize," said Jim. "Can't hurt to have people coming in to our town and seeing what it's all about. It's good for business."

"That's a good point, Dad."

Just then, C.P. Traylor walked up with a distinguished-looking gentleman. After greeting the three men, he introduced his guest, "This is Grayson Macafee. We've been friends and worked together for years. He's visiting from D.C."

Grayson smiled at Sean, "I understand congratulations are in order. From everything I hear, it sounds like you are on the winning side in that transaction."

The men laughed. "Spoken like a transactional lawyer," C.P. chuckled. C.P. explained that Grayson was the attorney who had overseen the legal and transactional aspects for C.P.'s long-term lease of the WVB&C Railroad Company.

Sean was grinning. "I'd like to think it's a win-win, but I'm afraid you may be on to something."

Following another round of laughter, Jim asked, "Speaking of my daughter-in-law—is she wearing her reporter's hat tonight?"

"Yeah, she's doing double duty—admiring the artwork and also working on the story. She and Milton have plans to get out a late edition so everyone can read about Dillie's grand opening in the morning's paper."

"She's proactive. She found an old newspaper article about the 1957 bridge collapse and decided to write a series and tie it to the anniversary of when the new bridge opened. I've read other articles where she resurrected something from the past with a current event. Readers like that, and I think it's a good way to remind people of Bekbourg's history. Writing about the railroad is a good thing from my standpoint," added C.P.

"Say, I remember that bridge fiasco," said Jim. "That had the whole town torn up."

"Sally and I have enjoyed following her cold-case stories," added Danny. "She's brought closure to some of them."

"Yeah, but the last one got a little too close for comfort," frowned Jim.

C.P. nodded, "Well, at least the story she's working on about the bridge doesn't involve murder."

"Let's hope not," agreed Sean ruefully.

"She does a good job, Sean," C.P. commented as he sipped his scotch.

Sean nodded. "I couldn't agree more."

"You'd better, Sean, since you're married to her," joked Danny.

The men laughed in agreement. Sean ribbed Danny, "You know what that's like. Sally sure has a successful business, and she's a member of the City Council."

Danny beamed with pride. "Yep, I couldn't be more proud. We're both lucky men."

Officers from the milk plant where Jim worked approached and started talking to Jim. Danny leaned over and whispered to Sean, "I noticed you limping. Is your leg bothering you tonight?"

Danny and Sean were boyhood friends and had played football together during high school. Sean had been the star of the team, leading Schriever High to a state championship during his senior year. However, his plans to play quarterback in college were upended by a career ending injury to his throwing shoulder during the championship game's final minutes. After taking a job on the railroad for a couple of years, Sean had joined the Marines and made a career as a criminal investigator in a specialized unit. After twenty years, he had been severely injured in an ambush that had killed his best friend. Being forced to retire from a job he loved, he returned to Bekbourg to heal physically and mentally. Through a turn of events, he became sheriff and married Cheryl, and they had made Bekbourg their home. His healing process was not complete, however. He still had shrapnel in his body, which was more painful at some times than others, and nightmares of the horrendous explosion plagued him, although not as much since Cheryl had come into his life.

"It's fine, Danny. I've learned to live with it. The better days outweigh the others."

Danny nodded. He remembered when Sean had first returned to Bekbourg—how much thinner he was from his high school playing days and how much more distinct his limp had been. To observers, Sean was handsome in a rugged way with thin lips and square jaw. His sandy colored hair now sprinkled with gray was longer, resting on his collar. The pain that had filled his piercing brown eyes when he returned home was gone. Danny smiled to himself, because Sean looked more relaxed than he had ever seen him. He gave Cheryl credit for his friend's turnaround.

"Say, what do you think about the football team this year?"

Sean shook his head. "I don't think they're going to District."

"I don't either. I hear a lot of grumbling from people stopping in at the station. They know I played and want to know what I think."

As Sean and Danny talked about the football team, Grayson looked into the crowd and asked C.P., "I take it you're going to introduce me to the hostess of this stellar affair before the night is over?"

C.P. followed Grayson's line of sight and spied Dillie, breath-taking in her cream flowing pant suit, gold accessories and blond hair bunched on top of her head with curls flowing past her shoulders. Her arms and hands were dancing with expression as she talked to the enthralled couple. Grayson had been a widower since the time his children were young. After the tragedy, he had devoted himself to raising his family and throwing himself into his legal practice, but still, C.P. suspected there had been women over the years.

C.P.'s humor was in check as he enjoyed another drink of fine scotch. "Of course. We can't let the night get away without saying hello to Dillie."

Danny and Sean had fallen silent as they listened to Jim's co-workers discuss the milk company's business. While listening to the conversation around him, Sean observed the crowd.

Standing six-feet-four-inches tall, little escaped his notice. Many he knew from Bekbourg, but a woman caught his attention as she slinked through people. She held her wine glass close to her chest as she tried to peek over and around people. Her dress was tight and short, and her balance was thrown off either from stilettos, too much alcohol, or both. Sean caught glimpses as she meandered among the throng until she came to where Dillie was talking with a couple. Sean watched as the woman squeezed in near Dillie. The couple glanced her way but turned their attention back to Dillie, who was talking. Shortly, the woman appeared to interrupt Dillie as the threesome, in unison, looked toward her. The couple nodded and said something and then stepped away. Dillie said something, and the woman followed.

Sean's attention was diverted as his dad was saying something to him. When he was able to disengage from the conversation, he scanned the tops of people's heads until he finally saw Dillie approaching what looked to be an office near the front of the building with the woman following close behind. Dillie opened the door and then closed it after they entered.

After several minutes had passed, Sean's curiosity was registering on the meter. He debated whether he should walk over. There were glass panels running down both sides of the door, so he would be able to look in. Right before he started to head that way, he saw Frederic, Dillie's assistant, briskly moving toward the door. Frederic peeped in and then rapped his knuckles and opened the door. He said something and then entered.

As Sean watched, he saw what looked to be Frederic escorting the woman out. He waited for Dillie, who emerged. Frederic took her arm and looped it through his and leaned toward her and said something. He patted her hand and grabbed a flute of champagne from a passing server for her and dashed her back into the crowd. Sean looked around for the woman but could not locate her.

Bri returned from the back room where the caterers had set up. She was pleased with the way the night was going. Cheryl was one of Bri's best friends. She laughed as Cheryl handed her a glass of sparkling water. "Here, Bri. You deserve a break. The night is a huge success. Congratulations." She held up her sparkling water for a toast. The women laughed and then took a drink.

"Ah, this tastes so good. Thank you, my friend."

Cheryl smiled, "This is maybe the largest party in Bekbourg's history, and it's wonderful. The food and service are terrific. You must be very pleased."

Bri smiled as she took another sip of the refreshing water. "Thank you. I am *very* happy with the caterers, and I've seen several people from Bekbourg working tonight."

"That was such a good idea, Bri, to ask the caterer to hire locals for tonight."

"Well, I thought the more local people who could work this event, the better for Bekbourg, and Dillie enthusiastically agreed."

Cheryl started to say something when Colette Lynch walked up. "Hello, Ladies. This is my lucky night seeing you both together. Hhooww arrre you?" a practiced smile spread across her face.

Bri first responded, "Fine, Colette. Are you enjoying the party?"

"Ooh, yes. Isn't this amazing? Dillie thinks of everything. I had to sneak a cig, and the smoking area out back looks like a miniature park—ash trays, benches. She even put out pumpkins with cornstalks. Brian keeps trying to get me to stop. I guess I should since we're talking about getting pregnant." Cheryl noticed Colette's eyes scanning the room as she talked. She had met politicians who similarly surveyed their surroundings rather than focusing on the immediate audience.

"I am sooo glad Dillie moved here. Just think of all the famous and important people she knows. She can put our little town on the map." Colette glanced to Cheryl. "How are you doing, Cheryl? I just couldn't believe all that awful business. My goodness, I don't even like to think about it. We had just dined with the Brigadier and Skylar and Brian's parents a few weeks before her death. The Brigadier was considering a large donation to Brian's campaign."

"I'm fine, thank you." Even though she had recovered, the last thing Cheryl wanted to be reminded of, or discuss, was that episode. She pivoted the topic. "The election isn't far off. Brian must be getting ready to gear up for that."

"Oh. He's *already* busy going to meetings to talk to people about his economic plans for this area. People come up to him all the time to talk about what's on their mind. Speaking of the campaign, do you know our dear friends, Marty and Belinda Blake?" she looked expectantly at Bri.

Bri nodded. "I have heard of Marty. Isn't he a state senator from the Columbus area?"

"Yes, and of course, his father was the Lt. Governor and was going to run for governor but decided against it when he got the diagnosis. Fortunately, he is in remission and doing fine. Anyway, Marty and Belinda want to support Brian, and I was hoping you and Max could cater a reception."

"We should be able to."

Before Bri could ask about the details, Colette stiffened, and her eyes widened at someone or something she saw further in the room. She abruptly turned to Bri, "I'm sorry, but it looks like Brian is looking for me. I'll get back to you on the details. Good to see you both." With that, she was off. Cheryl and Bri exchanged looks and changed the topic.

Since the incident that had nearly cost Cheryl her life, Sean had found himself more aware of his stunning bride's whereabouts. He did not need to be protective of her—certainly, she was self-reliant and resourceful—but it was instinctive. Somehow, despite the mass of people, he soon located the five feet, ten inches of beauty with her dark long hair amassed on top of her head, which drew focus to the glow on her face and the shine in her eyes. She was standing with Bri and Colette Lynch. Cheryl had commented over recent months how Colette seemed to be everywhere since her husband, Brian, had been appointed to fill the local representative position. Colette frequently popped into the newspaper wanting coverage of him at this-or-that event, and offering to assist in any publicity they might be willing to provide. Sean had also observed Colette making rounds at the GilHaus during lunch meetings. As if she was the one running for office, she could not resist glad-handing as the hostess attempted to show her to the table.

He watched Colette talking as Bri and Cheryl gave polite attention until Colette disengaged and moved onward. Out of mild curiosity, his eyes followed as she darted toward her husband, who oddly stood alone. When she approached, Sean noticed she said something. Brian flicked his arm to break the contact where her hand had come to rest above his elbow. They briefly talked before a couple walked up. Sean's eyes drifted back to where Cheryl now stood with Sally and Bri. They were obviously enjoying themselves.

The merriment began to break up around eleven o'clock. Most of Sean's family and friends had already left, and Sean was ready to get home and walk Buddy. After taking his wife home, Milton was going to meet Cheryl and her photographer at the newspaper to get out the late night edition. Sean and Cheryl left, but not before they had given their praise to Dillie.

By midnight, the last of the guests had departed. Most of the artists had closed up their booths and gone home. Frederic finally convinced Dillie to leave—saying he would see to the clean-up. The tables and chairs under the large tent were being disassembled, and the caterers and custodial staff were cleaning up when gut-wrenching screaming erupted from behind the factory.

Those outside sprinted to see what had happened. There, they saw a woman bent over—gasping between screams. One of the workers pushed ahead and saw the reason for the woman's hysterics—a body with bloody wounds lay crumpled on the ground behind the hedge.

Sean had walked Buddy and was waiting for Cheryl to return home from the newspaper's office when he got the call. He requested dispatch put out the call to his deputies as he was heading out the door.

Chapter 15

Darrell and Creed had already left when the call came in, so Sean was the first officer to respond. No one was there to direct him, but he caught sight of people huddled in the parking lot where the tent was still standing and headed in their direction. He noticed that most of the tables and chairs had been loaded into a large truck. Lights still shone through the factory's front windows and the grounds were well lit. As he drew closer, he heard one of the men utter, "Here's the sheriff now."

They turned to look at him. He did not recognize members of what he surmised to be the clean-up crew. "I'm Sheriff Neumann. I got a call about someone finding a body." He looked at each of the six men and two women. "Who can tell me something about this?"

A Hispanic man, likely the crew chief, spoke up, "It's around back, Sheriff," he tilted his head in the direction. "The man in charge, Mr. St. Fleur, told us all to hang around. He's back there."

Sean nodded, "Okay. My deputies are on the way. They'll need to talk to each of you about what you know. Don't leave until they give the okay." He looked at each of them to impress the importance of his directive.

The crew chief asked, "Is it okay if we get all this cleared up," he pointed his thumb to where the tent and other fixtures waited to be dissembled and loaded.

"Hold off until we get a better handle on what happened here. I may need forensics to examine that area." The man nodded.

Sean heard him tell the others they "might as well go inside" as his long strides carried him toward the back of the large building.

When he turned the corner, Sean nearly collided with the stylish Frederic wearing a black jacket and designer scarf wrapped around his neck. "Oh, good, you're here." Frederic was uncertain if Sean would remember meeting him at Bri's over cocktails when Dillie had first arrived back in town, so he reintroduced himself. "I am Frederic St. Fleur, Dillie's assistant. The body is over there," he turned and pointed to a dimly-lit area about ten feet away where two EMTs were kneeling. "That's the smoking area."

Sean could see a bench and two wrought-iron chairs on either side of a small, square table. Cigarette receptacles were strategically placed. Pavers covered the entire area, except for a long row where tall hedges had been planted. "The victim is behind those hedges. We planted them in a row to block the view of the back of the factory but left enough room so workers could get back there as necessary to make repairs or access the building."

Sean walked to where the EMTs were, assessed the situation, and returned to where Frederic was standing. "Who found the body?"

"Juana did when she went to empty the cigarette butts and clean out the receptacles. As you can see, the smoking area itself is lit, but the area is dark behind the hedges. She went to clean out the receptacle located at that end and saw something. She took a closer look and saw it was a body and what looked like blood on the woman."

Sean observed Frederic did not seem the least ruffled as he proceeded to tell Sean that some of the workers from the side heard her screaming and ran to see what was happening. When they found Juana, one of the women escorted her inside as another came to find him. "I waited here to ensure no one else disturbed the area." Frederic was efficient as he relayed what then happened. "I felt she was deceased, but of course, I checked for a pulse. There wasn't one. That's when I called 911."

One of the EMTs approached. "Looks like she's been stabbed, but we can't say for sure."

"Thanks. I'll call the state coroner and forensics." Sean made the calls as Frederic waited.

Alex Ogle, the assistant sheriff, came up. Sean briefed him and asked that the deputies interview all the workers—since the state people would look for evidence. After Alex walked off, he turned to Frederic. "Do you know who she is?"

"I do not remember her name, but I briefly met her earlier in the week when she came by to talk with Dillie about a booth for her paintings."

"She was here tonight at the party. What can you tell me about that?"

"She is not one of our artists. I saw her off-and-on throughout the evening. Invitations were sent to select people, but we invited the public at large through public announcements. Anyone could have wandered in."

"Do you know if Dillie knew her?"

"My impression was no."

"What about tonight?" Sean asked. "Do you know if Dillie talked to her tonight?" Sean recognized her as the woman who had gone into Dillie's office.

"Well, yes, she did, but not for very long. I try to anticipate Dillie's preferences and run interference for her. I saw them walking toward Dillie's office, and I was on my way to see if I could be of assistance when one of the guests stopped me to talk.

"By the time I was able to turn my attention, I didn't see Dillie or that woman. I made my way to her office as quickly as I could—given the number of guests I had to navigate. When I opened the office door, Dillie gave no indication she wanted to be alone with the woman, so I took the cue to excuse my interruption and showed the woman out and then escorted Dillie back to her guests."

"Do you know what she and Dillie were talking about?"

"No. Dillie did not tell me, and we never had the opportunity to discuss the woman."

"Do you know if she and Dillie talked after that?"

"I don't believe so. After that incident, I was more attentive and stayed closer in Dillie's orbit."

"When was the last time you saw the woman?"

"I don't remember. I did not keep track of her—except to ensure she didn't get to Dillie again."

"You seem certain it was important to keep her away from Dillie. Why is that?"

"Oh, I do not mean to give that impression. As I mentioned, Dillie was certainly not familiar with her when she stopped by to talk about her paintings. It was the woman herself." Frederic wrinkled his nose. "There was something unpleasant about her, and, in my opinion, her paintings were not the caliber we are looking for."

"When did Dillie leave?"

"After the final guests left, I insisted she allow me to drive her to Bri's B&B."

"Was there anything else that stood out about the woman you think I should know?"

"Mmm. Actually there is. I saw her and a man I did not recognize having what looked to be a tiff. I watched, because I thought I might have to intervene, but they went their separate ways. I will say, he did not look happy. She turned away, so I was unable to read her expression."

"You don't know who he is?"

"No. Preparing for this opening has consumed my full attention since landing in town. I've not been able to meet many people. What I can tell you is that he was about medium height, slender, and had short dark brown hair." The description was a start, thought Sean, although several men fit that description.

"Anything else you can think of?" Frederic shook his head. Sean had been observing the young man, who appeared unfazed despite an apparent murder victim lying nearby. "Have you dealt with other situations like this?" he asked.

Frederic's brows arched. "Pardon?"

"Most people would be at least a little shaken under the circumstances."

Frederic gave no indication of offense. "I can assure you this is my first encounter with a dead body. Hopefully, it's my last. But, I am accustomed to a frenetic pace and like to think I can handle whatever arises."

Frederic told him the security video system had not yet been activated. Sean asked for a list of everyone who worked the event and list of invitees. Clean-up could not resume until the crime technicians completed their work.

"We need to get this all in writing. I'll ask one of my deputies to get with you. They're going to need to talk with everyone who is still here.

Here's my card. If you think of anything else, let me know. I may need to talk to you again."

"Of course."

Chapter 16

Before going to Bri's B&B, Sean tasked Alex with directing the state forensics and coroner's teams upon their arrivals. He thought since Bri and Max had overseen the catering, they might know something about the deceased woman or have seen something that could help in the investigation. He also wanted to talk to Dillie.

When Max answered the door, Sean apologized for waking him at such an early hour. Bri quickly put on coffee, and they settled into the parlor. Because the caterer from Cincinnati was in charge of the clean-up, Max and Bri had left soon after the event formally ended. Neither Max nor Bri had heard anything about the woman being found dead. They explained it had been a long day for both of them, and they had gone to bed as soon as they could after returning. Max and Bri each thought they had possibly seen the woman based on Sean's description, but neither could be sure.

After Sean finished questioning them, Bri went to wake Dillie. Bri served everyone hot coffee and left Sean and Dillie in the parlor.

"I must say, Darling. I'm more accustomed to tall, handsome men like you leaving about this hour of the morning rather than arriving, but either way, the pleasure is all mine. Now, Darling, please tell me what this is all about."

Sean hid his amusement at her flirtatious ways. He knew she had been married several times, and even having been waked at this un-godly hour, she was attractive with her blond hair bouncing about her head. She wore a colorful silk robe and satin house slippers.

"When did you leave the party?"

Dillie's eyebrow arched as she sipped her coffee and returned it to the saucer. "Well, Darling, it was naturally after all the guests had departed. I cannot say exactly. I would have stayed longer, but my dear Frederic insisted he would oversee everything, and so he drove me here." Dillie's eyes sparked. "Has something happened? Is Frederic alright?"

Sean explained about finding the woman. After he explained who she was, Sean asked if she knew the woman.

"You say it appears she was murdered?" Both of Dillie's eyebrows were now arched.

"Yes, that's the way it looks, but we'll know more after the medical examiner completes his examination."

"This is shocking. How could such a thing happen?"

"I understand she came to see you earlier in the week at the gallery. Can you tell me who she is?"

Occasion of Murder

Dillie considered as she took another sip of coffee and then poured them each more. "She must have told me her name, but I don't recall it. She walked into the gallery as I was talking with one of our artists. No one was available to greet her, so she walked around until she found me. She was hoping our gallery would display her work. I didn't stay with her long. Frederic handled the matter. Her paintings were not of a collection we wished displayed."

"Did you or Frederic convey that to her?"

"I leave that to darling Frederic. But I know he told her we had a full complement of artists at this time."

"She didn't give you a business card?"

"No. Maybe Frederic would know her name, but I do not."

"Did you see her tonight?"

"Why yes, I did. She came up to me and said she needed to talk. She was quite adamant, so I suggested we go to my office." Dillie flipped back her hair. Sean could not help noticing her manicured nails and flashy ring. *She must sleep in her jewelry,* he thought as he also spied her diamond stud earrings.

"What was so urgent she needed to talk to you tonight?"

"I frankly did not see the urgency, Darling. She was quite insistent we accept her paintings. I told her Frederic handled those matters for me and she would need to talk to him. I told her I would ask him to get back with her at the beginning of the week. She wanted me to agree, but I could not, nor would I, but I handled her with delicacy. She is an artist and, naturally, proud of her creations."

"That was it?" pressed Sean. "She wanted you to agree to accept her paintings?"

Sean watched as Dillie picked up the china cup by the handle without inserting her fingers through the opening as she sipped. "Well, there was one other thing she mentioned, but I do not know the significance, because Frederic popped in and that was that. That dear is remarkable. He steered her out and then returned me to my guests. So, I do not know the further topic she wished to discuss."

"She didn't tell you anything about it?"

"Let's see." Dillie sipped again. "She said something to the effect that there was something she thought I would find very interesting. Oh, she said she thought my gallery was the perfect place for her art. She said something about giving her a booth without financial strings and said maybe I could help her out. Frankly, Sheriff, I was having a difficult time following her, and, I must admit, I was distracted because I needed to return to my guests. Frederic appeared, and I really cannot tell you anymore. That is all I know."

Chapter 17

Late afternoon, Syd was standing in front of the gallery making certain the area remained clear of curiosity seekers and others who should not be on the property until the all-clear was given by Sean. Sean came walking around from the side lot and stopped to update her. Forensics had completed their investigation at the site. Word had been put out through the local media for anyone who may have seen something or with any pertinent information to call the station. Alex and Arlo had interviewed the people who were still on-site when the body had been discovered.

As Sean was speaking with Syd, he noticed Noel crossing the street and thought, "Wonder what he wants?"

Noel Fischner owned the outfitter's shop across the street from Dillie's gallery. Noel was a newly-elected county commissioner who likely owed his victory to two factors. First, there had been a major backlash against the county commission because of corruption that had been brought to light, so it had proved an opportune time to be running on the Reform party ticket. Name recognition from his family's large construction business founded by his father was another reason many thought Noel had been elected. Noel's father had stepped aside due to failing health, and Noel's brother, Cole, had assumed the reins of the family business. Noel had never been interested in the construction business, but he resented the attention his brother had garnered from their parents and the community, so he had jumped into the commissioner's race and ended up victorious.

Sean and Syd had grown quiet as they observed Noel hurrying toward them. "Afternoon, Sean, I'm glad I saw you. There are a couple of things I want to talk to you about."

Sean and Noel had graduated from high school together, but they were not in the same circle of friends—Sean had hung out with the athletes, and Noel tagged along with the group who considered themselves the popular mix.

"Hi, Noel, this is Officer Johnson." Noel glanced at Syd and briskly shook her hand. "Now is not a good time, though, Noel. Maybe you can stop by the station sometime this week."

"This won't take long, Sean. I know you can spare a county commissioner a few minutes."

Sean had time before he needed to return to the office. *I might as well get this over with.* "What did you want to talk to me about?"

"Well, first thing is why your deputies allowed people to park in my lot last night."

Syd jumped in. "We were told by Mr. St. Fleur you had given permission for cars to park there last night during the party."

Sean arched an eyebrow and looked at Noel. Noel pursed his lips. "Well, yes, I did. I support this new business. It's good for the county to bring people in. Of course, a murder did occur. If Dillie's business is going to bring in that type of riff-raft, I might have to talk to the mayor." Noel was annoying, but Sean chose to overlook his pettiness. "I just think your deputies should have been more careful about who they let park in my lot."

"Was any damage done to your property?"

"No, but someone left an old heap parked there all night. It's still there. Probably got drunk and forgot where they left it, but I want if off my property."

"Have you looked inside or touched the car?"

"No. I don't care what's inside. I just want it off my property."

"Okay, we'll take care of it. Do you have a video camera mounted on your business?"

Noel's eyes widened, "No, why?"

"We're going to need any videos from area businesses to see if they picked up anything that might be helpful in our investigation."

"Well, sorry I can't help there. But now that I have you, there's another thing I've been meaning to talk to you about. I know Dillie is popular around town, and she's doing a good thing by opening this gallery, but even she has to obey the law."

Sean looked hard at Noel. "What do you think she's done?"

"She's driving a golf cart on the roads around town."

"Didn't you notice it has a license plate?"

"Huh?" Noel scowled.

"Yes. It's fully legal. The city council issued an ordinance a few months ago approving low-speed vehicles. They are allowed on the city streets because of the speed limit in town. Her golf cart is fully street legal, Commissioner."

Noel blinked, "No one ran that by the county commission," he complained.

Sean did not see that the county had any jurisdiction over the issue, but he was not going there. "I don't know anything about that, Noel, but I've got to get back to the station. We'll take care of the car in your lot. Don't go near it."

"I won't. Trust me," Noel huffed as he stormed away.

Sean turned toward Syd. "Go check on that car, but don't get too close. Take a picture of the license plate and run it through."

"Will do. By the way, what say does the county have with the city authorizing golf carts on city streets?"

"Beats me, but that's the mayor's battle with Noel, not mine."

"I thought so," Syd smirked to herself as Sean headed back to the precinct.

Syd ran the license plate and identified the car as belonging to Vera Keller from Cleveland, Ohio. Through the state's database, she was able to identify the victim as Vera. Sean called Ronnie Vin, the state forensic expert, to take possession of the car. The Keller named sounded familiar, but not knowing of any Kellers in Bekbourg, he called Kim Conner, the department's assistant.

"Hi, Kim. I'm sorry to call you at home on a Sunday evening, but there is something I was hoping you could help me with."

"Sure thing, Boss."

"We have identified the victim from last night at Dillie's gallery, Vera Keller. Her driver's license shows she lives in Cleveland. Does the name 'Keller' sound familiar? Do you happen to know who she might have been here to see or if she had family around here?"

"Vera Keller. Mmm. I wondered what happened to her. Yes, she grew up here but moved away shortly after her mother died. She's been gone many years. She's Teri Olson's sister."

"Gerald Olson's wife?" asked Sean.

"Yeah, that's right."

"Did you know her?"

"Not really. I know Teri better. She and Gerald go to my church. Teri attends almost every Sunday. Gerald is hit-or-miss. Teri was there this morning. They are part of the younger age group." Kim chuckled, "Not that I consider myself old. Anyway, I see her around town sometimes. I never ask about her sister, and she never mentions her."

"I need to go see them and tell them about Ms. Keller."

Chapter 18

The front porch lights flicked on as Sean approached the porch. A dog barked from within, and then the door opened. He heard Teri shush the dog. When she saw Sean, she leaned on the door for support, her voice catching. "Oh, my God, are Gerald and Miles okay?"

Sean hastened to put her mind at ease. "I'm not here about them. I take it they're not here?"

Her shoulders slacked in relief. "Oh, thank God. When I saw you, I thought something had happened. Gerald went to pick up Miles at a birthday party."

"Mind if I come in? There is something I need to talk to you about."

"Of course, please. I know it's late for most people, but I have coffee in the pot. Would you like some?"

Sean petted Champ and thanked her but declined. Once they were settled, Sean said, "I'm here about Vera Keller. Is she your sister?"

Teri hesitated before answering, "Yes. Why?"

"I'm sorry to be the one to tell you, but she's dead."

Teri's mouth dropped open as she absorbed the news. "What happened?"

Sean told her.

"Oh, my God!" Teri frowned. After a pause, she shook her head, "I heard something this morning at church about something happening at Dillie's party." She again paused. "But, Vera? She was killed?" She seemed in disbelief. "You say she was stabbed. Do you know who did it?"

"Not yet, but I need to ask you some questions." She nodded, and he continued, "What can you tell me about your sister?"

"What do you want to know?"

"I understand she has lived in Cleveland for many years."

Sean had not yet received a list of the contents from her car, but forensics had told him that no luggage was found in the car, and the only clothing was a coat that was lying on the back seat. He wondered if she was staying with her sister.

"Yes. When our mother died, Vera moved to Cleveland to try and distinguish herself as a painter."

"So, was she in town for a visit?"

Teri shook her head. "I frankly don't know what her plans were. When she got back in town, she came by here to see me. That was, I guess, on Monday. She told me she was trying to get Dillie's gallery to pick up her work."

"She wasn't staying here with you?"

"No."

"What was your relationship with her?"

He noticed Teri started to rub her thumb along her finger. "We weren't close if that's what you're asking. When she stopped by, she told me she was running low on money and was hoping to find a place here to sell her paintings, but I'm not sure what she was planning to do."

"When was the last time you talked to her?"

"I saw her briefly at the party last night. We didn't talk long. I was busy with our table for the Garden Club."

Sean paused and watched Teri, who frowned as she looked at her hands. "Before she showed up here the other day, when was the last time you talked to her?"

"It's been fourteen years. The last time was after our mother passed away. Vera went through a hard time. That's when she moved to Cleveland. We lost contact after that. Frankly, I didn't know if she was still in Cleveland."

"Mind telling me why you and she didn't talk?"

Teri looked at Sean and then shrugged, "Sisterly stuff. We weren't close."

"There wasn't any luggage in her car. We found a matchbook in the car from the motel coming into town, but they said she had checked out earlier in the day yesterday. Do you know where she was staying?"

"No. She told me she was staying there."

"Did she have any friends here or other family members she might be staying with or who might know something?"

"There aren't any other family members in Bekbourg or any others to speak of. I don't think she had any friends here. The only friend I ever knew about was Tanya Ellis, but I don't believe they were still friends when she moved from here."

Sean jotted down Tanya's name. "Is she the waitress at Frau's?"

"Yes, that's her."

"I'll need you to identify the body."

"Okay."

He gave her the information. They wrapped up their conversation, and Sean told her about the timing when Vera's body would be released. Teri thanked him but was ambivalent about the return of Vera's remains.

Chapter 19

The state medical examiner, Dennis Douglass, nicknamed "DD," reported to Sean that Vera had been stabbed three times with a long knife—perhaps a kitchen knife. Two stab wounds were to the left chest area, and a third was in the left shoulder area. The fatal wound entered between two ribs and penetrated the heart.

"The victim showed no signs of trying to defend herself. The killer could have caught the victim unaware, but given the level of alcohol in the victim's body, she may have been too impaired to defend herself. The wounds entered from the front and were deep. There was no evidence she was constrained by someone. These were not superficial wounds. The killer had the force to deliver the fatal wound. From the trajectory of the wounds, the killer was right handed and not substantially taller than the victim. She was five-feet, four-inches. I'd say the killer was about four to six inches taller."

"What about blood evidence? Would blood have spattered on the killer?"

"Good question. The victim was wearing a heavy sweater, which absorbed her blood around the wound areas. I believe the knife attack was delivered quickly—that is, the first two stabs.

105

Damage occurred to the deeper internal organs. There possibly could have been blood cast off from the knife as the killer extracted the knife, but the spatter during the attack would have been more localized. The killer was standing in close proximity to the victim to have delivered the blows.

"We didn't find DNA evidence on the deceased's body from an outside source. However, Ronnie found tiny fuzzy balls on the victim's sweater just above her left wrist, which did not match the victim's clothing. I think that could have been pilling from the garment worn by the perpetrator, probably where the killer gripped her arms to drag her. Ronnie said they can't trace the lamb's wool to its source. It's probably from a sweater, although it's not beyond reason that it's from a tweed jacket. She believes it was not a newer sweater, because they didn't find a lot of the tiny wool balls. Ronnie found a wool thread on a hedge. She was running an analysis to see if the wool pilling found on the victim's sweater matches that."

DD also told him Vera weighed ninety-four pounds and suggested someone with reasonable strength could have dragged her body the short distance behind the hedge.

"We believe after she was stabbed, the killer dragged her by her arms to behind the hedge. After she was pulled behind the hedge, that's when the killer delivered the third fatal stab wound."

"I see. When do you think the attack happened?"

"You said most of the guests had cleared out around eleven o'clock, but the body wasn't discovered until about midnight. I'd guess her time of death was about two-to-three hours before midnight." He also told Sean she was a heavy smoker, had been for years, and her physical condition reflected a history of alcohol consumption. No traces were found of recreational drugs or drugs for chronic illness or symptoms. She was wearing a high school class ring, a pair of inexpensive earrings and a sterling silver chain with a pendent of a sizeable green and purple polished fluorite—the type typically sold at art fairs or shops in tourist areas.

Ronnie Vin was as thorough as always in her forensics analysis. At the crime scene itself, minuscule spatters of blood belonging to the victim were discovered on the pavers where she thought the attack had occurred, and blood had pooled where the body was lying. Conjecture was Vera was stabbed and then dragged behind the hedge where it was darker in an effort to conceal her body. Ronnie told Sean there were no discernible footprints on the pavers in front of the hedge or where Vera's body was found.

Through his interview with the cleaning woman, he learned that after she had finished cleaning the cigarette receptacle, she looked around the hedge for trash and saw something lying on the ground. It was dark, so she moved closer and saw the victim and realized something was wrong and started screaming. The tall flood lights on the building itself were off at the time, but Frederic had turned them on before Sean arrived.

The tiny wool balls found on Vera's sweater near her left wrist matched the dark gray wool fiber she had found on a sharp edge of a lower limb on the hedge. "Neither the coat we found in her car— nor the clothing she was wearing—match the wool fibers found on her left wrist or on the hedge. I think it's a reasonable assumption that the wool fibers belong to the killer—since they came from the same garment. If that's the case, I think he or she must have snagged their sweater as they dragged her behind the hedge.

"Near the hedge we found a cigarette butt where the attack occurred and a lighter further away. We suspect the DNA on the butt will match the victim's, because the lipstick color matches that from the tube in her purse. Only the victim's fingerprints were on the lighter. She likely was smoking when the attack happened. A cigarette pack was found in the pocket of her sweater. A key ring was found in the other pocket with a key matching her car and what looks to be a house key."

"What about the car—what did you find there?" asked Sean.

"I was just getting to that. Like I told you when we first took possession, we didn't find any luggage. She wasn't what I would call neat. We're compiling an inventory, but a lot of what we found seems irrelevant to the investigation—thing like wrappers, cough drops, tissue packets. There were receipts from places like fast food restaurants and gas stations—which might help you put together a timeline of her movements, but I don't know if that will help in identifying her killer. That's up to you to decide. Her purse was lying on the front seat of the car." Ronnie's eyes twinkled. "You must be doing a good job, Sean, at least in keeping burglaries down, because someone could have easily taken it overnight while it was parked in the outfitter shop lot—since the car wasn't locked when we impounded it."

Sean hid a grin as he volleyed back, "Well, at least one of our crime statistics is down."

Ronnie's lips curled up. She had assisted Sean on quite a few murder investigations since his return to Bekbourg. "It's nice to have that. Anyway, her purse was filled with all sorts of things, but nothing that appeared out of the ordinary or looked suspicious. It was the same with the glove compartment. Her wallet contained her driver's license and credit cards, but again, nothing that drew my attention. A few dollar bills and some coins were lying at the bottom of the purse. A carton of cigarettes and a half-empty bottle of vodka were on the passenger front seat.

"We believe the coat found in the back seat belonged to her. The size is right, and we saw hair strands matching her hair color and length—all to be confirmed. The coat wasn't wool—that's how I know it's not the source of the wool fibers.

"Canvases of paintings were in the back seat and pushed off to the side in the car's trunk along with painting supplies. The open area in the trunk looked like maybe luggage or a large painting had been there, and the other things had been pushed out of the way to make room."

"Mmm."

"Did the matchbook help at all?" Ronnie asked.

"Yes. I'm glad your team found that on the seat before you took the car. She had been staying at the motel on its cover up the highway but had checked out."

"There *is* one thing that might be of interest. Crumbled beneath the driver's seat was a slip of paper with a name and address scribbled on it. I assume it's a first name—'Brian'—but you can check it out. It's from a notepad from that same motel, and the ink matches ink from pens provided in the motel's guest rooms. We're checking the DNA on the paper, but it's likely from the victim. I'll email you a full report, but I'm going to email a copy of the note with the 'Brian' name and photo of the key we found on the key ring after we get off the phone."

When Sean received the copy of the handwritten note from Ronnie, he looked up the address for "Brian." He was surprised to see the address was for the family business belonging to the local state representative, Brian Lynch. He needed to talk with Brian Lynch. He asked Syd to check out the mysterious key found on Vera's key ring.

Chapter 20

Arlo learned from the motel manager that Vera had paid for a couple of night's stay by credit card, but when she tried to charge another night, the card was rejected. She tried to give the manager a story that there was a misunderstanding with the credit card company, but he had heard all the excuses before and told her she needed to pay with cash or leave. She pleaded, so he gave her until the next day to pay up.

The following evening when the night clerk went to collect, he was surprised to see that she had cash to pay for the night she owed plus one additional night. When those two nights had passed, and she did not have money for the additional night, the manager told her if she did not have payment the next day, which happened to be the day of Dillie's party, she had to leave. He instructed the night clerk to make sure she was out by that evening if she did not pay for the room.

The manager told Arlo he never saw any visitors to her room, but then, he was not there at night and might not have noticed during the day.

Occasion of Murder

Chapter 21

During his early years, Brian Lynch's father had worked as a lineman for the local utility. The family lived in a modest three-bedroom home. His mother had managed the home and volunteered at church and through the PTO. Both boys played knot-hole baseball during their early years and continued playing through high school. Where his older brother, Mick, started at second base both junior and senior years, Brian was a mediocre player and never started.

Brian's father had started a side job out of his home working on computers, and by the time Brian started high school, he had resigned his lineman job and opened his own computer business. Mick majored in programming at The Ohio State University and then joined his father's business.

When Brian graduated from high school, he opted to delay college and worked in his family's business for a few months before deciding to apply with the Peace Corps. He had completed his training and served two years in Cameroon.

After his service was complete, he was not interested in pursuing a college degree, so he returned to Bekbourg and again worked at his dad's company. At his father's urging, he finally enrolled at OSU in their business college. After graduating, he returned to the company business, bringing with him Colette, his new wife.

Sean pulled into the parking lot of Brian Lynch's family computer and technology business and spotted Brian's non-descript black sedan. The receptionist buzzed Brian and announced Sean and then showed him to Brian's office. Photographs were displayed on shelving behind his desk including those of family photos of his parents and Mick, a wedding photo of him and Colette, an assortment of pictures of him with villagers, and his swearing in as a state representative. Sean noted the neatness surrounding him. Two manila folders lay in an inbox, and two wooden figurines stood on the corner of his desk. An expensive pen in a holder seemed at odds with the modest furniture and accessories.

Brian did not have the bluster Sean had observed in other politicians. Brian shook his hand and offered something to drink before they settled into their chairs.

Sean nodded to the photo of Brian, "Looks like you spent time in Africa?"

Brian glanced at the photos. "Yeah, I was in Cameroon working for the Peace Corps."

"Is that where these carvings are from?" asked Sean looking at the wood figures on his desk.

"Yes. Those were carved by a villager from Cameroon. I know you spent time in the Marines. I wasn't really into joining a military branch, but I wanted to do something so I joined and served for two years. Got to see things I wouldn't have otherwise. After I got back, Dad really wanted me to go to college like Mick. Dad never got a degree, so it was important to him. I went to OSU and then ended up back here in the family business."

"Now you're a representative and running for reelection," grinned Sean.

Brian chuckled, "Yep. You know what that's like, too. Can't say I care much for the fundraising, but I like getting to know people and trying to help out where I can."

Sean turned to the reason for his showing up at Brian's office, "I guess you heard about the woman we found dead behind Dillie's gallery. Vera Keller."

"Yeah, I read about that. Shocked something like that happened at Dillie's opening night. Any idea who did it?"

"We're early in the investigation. Did you know her?"

Brian's face tightened. "It was weird, but a couple of days before the party, she came by here. Our receptionist had left for the day, and I heard the front door open. I went to see who it was and found her in the lobby looking for me. I've run into people like her before. They think a representative can cure their woes. She told me she was moving back to

Bekbourg and hoped to sell her paintings. She mentioned she might try Dillie's new place or maybe even set up her own place. She said she had run into difficult times and needed some money to get her past the next few days."

"Why did she come see you?"

Brian shrugged. "Something wasn't right about her, Sean. She wanted me to give her money. Can you believe that? Anyway, I told her about the food pantry at the church—that they might help her. She knew about my family business and thought I had some charity I could spare." He picked up his pen and spun it in a slow circle.

"Did you give her money?"

"Yeah, I gave her a few bucks just to get rid of her. If she came back, I was going to give you a call. I don't mind helping, but I can't have people coming here to Dad's business and begging for money."

Sean thought it odd someone would simply show up at a politician's office expecting a cash handout, but stranger things had happened. "She grew up here. Did you know her from before?"

Brian shrugged. "I can't say one way or the other. If our paths crossed back then, it would have been before I joined the Peace Corps."

"Did you have any communications with her after she was here?"

"Well, I wish I could say I didn't, but she saw me at Dillie's party. She asked about me helping her out again. I told her I couldn't, that she needed to go to a church or charity."

"Did you know she was Teri Olson's sister?"

His eyes widened. "No, I didn't know that."

"You don't know why she was asking you for money?"

Brian shook his head. "It was probably a mistake to give her money the first time. That's probably why she asked me again at the party."

Sean pocketed his note pad. "Nice pen."

Brian chuckled. "Colette got this for me when I was appointed to the house seat. Said it looked better than the coffee mug full of cheap pens I had."

The men stood, and Brian walked him out.

Chapter 22

The investigation yielded snippets into Vera's life during her time in Cleveland. Syd learned Vera had moved around while living in Cleveland. She stayed in her first efficiency apartment for several years but then was forced to move for running behind on rent. She rented single room apartments in old apartment complexes and then in old homes—until being forced to leave in each case for falling behind in rent. Her last residence was a small furnished room in a dilapidated house where she had shared a hall bathroom with others. By the time she moved in there, her possessions merely consisted of clothing items, personal things and art supplies. Her last landlord told Syd Vera left nothing of value to sell for the three months of past due rent.

Syd located a store owner who was most familiar with Vera's time in the Cleveland artist community. He had carried Vera's paintings on consignment during her early years there. He told Syd Vera was never an exceptional artist, but she had a certain artistic flare that appealed to some people. "She was especially good with the use of colors, and her paintings were bold—abstract and dark hues." Vera painted large canvases but also found a niche for her miniatures. Some were stand-alone, and others were miniatures of a grouping. She made enough money in the early years to pay her rent and get by. Vera was difficult to get along with, but her paintings sold, so he continued to carry her work. She appeared at arts and craft shows, and a few local tourist shops carried her paintings.

According to that store owner, "Vera was getting more into the bottle, and word started to get around." A customer of one of the small galleries made a down payment for Vera to paint a large canvas on commission. When it was finished, the customer wanted his deposit returned, because "it looked like she just slapped some paint around." The gallery owner said he asked Vera to see what she could do to make the painting resemble the original sketch, but she refused. The customer was one who returned each year when he was in town visiting family, so the owner returned the deposit out of his own pocket, and—needless to say—dropped Vera's work. She accused another gallery of stiffing her on her consignment percentage. They also dropped her.

The shop owner shook his head. "It's really too bad about Vera. If she'd applied herself, she probably could have made enough to get by. Her problem was her drinking. Maybe there were other problems, too, because she couldn't get along with people. I wish things hadn't turned out as they did."

Syd interviewed an artist acquaintance of Vera's who was convinced that Vera had lost the inspiration behind her abstract works. She told her that Vera then attempted painting impressionism-style scenery from around Cleveland. Some of those paintings sold, but not enough for her to live on. She got to the point where she would borrow money from someone with the promise to repay after she sold the next painting, but as far as the artist knew, Vera never repaid anyone, including herself.

Each time Vera got evicted, she would crash at someone's place until she wore out her welcome—usually fairly soon, and then she'd move on. Toward the end, shops and galleries had pretty much closed their doors to carrying her works. Because money was so tight, she could not afford to participate in art fairs.

At the last place Vera had lived before she decided to return to Bekbourg, Syd talked with an old woman who had lived across the hall. She had once made jewelry to sell at tourist spots, but her eyesight had made it nearly impossible to continue working. The woman was lonely and befriended Vera when she first moved in.

At first, Vera seemed pleasant enough, but then her tale of woes started. She complained that she had been blackballed by the local art community; that her work was better than most, but people failed to see her talent; people chiseled her out of money—those types of grievances. Vera convinced the woman to loan her twenty dollars until she got paid for a painting that was being picked up at the end of the month. "I don't think there was a painting, and I never got my twenty bucks back. After that, if I saw her coming, I'd go in my apartment and act like I wasn't there."

The neighbor knew Vera was in trouble for not paying her rent because she had heard the landlord pounding on Vera's door. He would watch, and when Vera returned, he'd confront her about her overdue rent. She always claimed she would get the money. One of the last times the neighbor saw Vera was when she was returning from the drug store. Vera was coming out of her apartment and followed her into hers. Vera told her she probably would be moving on soon, that she had decided she needed a change of scenery. Vera had heard about a new gallery opening in Bekbourg and thought the new owner would appreciate her paintings. She also told the neighbor she was from Bekbourg and knew people who might help her open her own gallery.

Syd also tracked down a former lover who told her Vera wasn't interested in long-term relationships. He had moved in with her a few months after she moved to Cleveland. "She was into painting and partying. At first it was fun. Not too long after I moved in, I learned she was sleeping around. Two can play that game, I thought. So—no skin off my back. That wasn't why I split. I couldn't take the mood swings. At first, I thought it was because she was on drugs, but she wasn't. She drank, but I don't think that was the reason for her mood swings either. Hell, I drank *and* did some drugs. I knew other people who did, but none of us acted like Vera. Another thing I learned about her was she got weird toward people after a while—kind of a mean streak. She and another woman artist hung out together. I thought they were friends. They both had paintings in one of the tourist galleries. I don't know what happened, but apparently Vera told the owner that the woman was trying to hit on the men customers. The store owner dropped the woman's work. I heard about this later after Vera and I split. I ran into the woman at an art fair and she told me, 'It was like we were friends one day, and the next, she was lying about me to get me kicked out of the store.'"

The former lover told Syd that Vera never confided about her background or talked much about the past. All he knew was she was from somewhere in the southern part of Ohio, both her parents were dead, and she had an older sister.

Vera's four credit cards, none of which had high limits, were maxed out, and she had closed out her bank account, one-hundred-thirty-three dollars, right before leaving for Bekbourg.

The lone key on Vera's key ring along with her car key remained a mystery. A locksmith estimated the key to be at least thirty years old and most likely for a residence—not a commercial establishment. Syd talked to landlords where Vera had stayed in Cleveland, but the key did not match any of those older buildings. Gaps existed between places Vera had rented, so the key could have belonged to a roommate who Vera stayed with, but there was no way to track all those possibilities.

Chapter 23

Arlo knocked on Sean's door frame. "Hey, Chief, got a minute? I found out some more information about what happened at the motel where Vera Keller was staying."

"Sure, Arlo, have a seat."

"Well, I told you what the motel manager told me the first time I was there. There's more to the story. He called me this morning and said he talked to the clerk who was working the night of the party and he had some more information, so I drove up there to talk to the night clerk. They have a video feed that captures what is going on in the parking lot in front of the rooms. The clerk can watch it real-time, but the recording function hasn't worked for several months, so there's no recording.

"Anyway, the night clerk came on duty early that afternoon, because the manager had something he had to do. Before the manager left, he told the night clerk he had already told Vera she had to leave because she wasn't paying, and he wanted the night clerk to make sure she moved out. This was the evening of the party. The night clerk kept tabs on the live-feed to see if she moved her car. He didn't want to have to go talk to her if he didn't have to.

"Around five o'clock, Vera dragged out her suitcase and loaded it in the trunk of the car and then put a smaller duffel-type bag in with it. She slammed the trunk and got in the car and drove off. The night clerk went down and checked the room. There were food wrappings and other trash but no damage to the room. Said it reeked of cigarette smoke. He changed the slide-lock combination so if she returned, she couldn't get back in."

"So, the luggage was in her car earlier in the evening of the party."

"Right. There's something else. About eight-thirty or so, a car pulled into the lot kinda near the office. The person in the car sat there for a few minutes. The clerk said he didn't know what it was about, so he kept watching. A woman got out of the car. She looked around and then came inside. She was looking for Vera. Since Vera was no longer a guest, the clerk decided there was no harm in telling her Vera had checked out. He said the woman seemed uncomfortable—like she didn't want to be there."

"Did he say who the woman was?"

"Yeah. He didn't remember her telling her name, but she told him she was Vera's sister. He didn't remember much about her other than she was about normal size."

Sean cocked an eyebrow. "This was the night of the party?"

Arlo nodded.

"Teri didn't say anything about going to the motel where Vera was staying when I talked to her."

Sean had been leaning back in his chair listening to Arlo. He pulled forward. "She put her luggage somewhere. We need to find out where she went after she checked out of the motel. There weren't any receipts in her car or purse from any motels around here, but check with the motels in the area and see if she checked in somewhere. Also, ask Syd to do another search to see if by chance she used one of her credit cards at a local motel. The credit card companies told Syd they had put a hold on them, but something may have slipped by."

"Will do, Chief."

"Good work, Arlo. Let me know as soon as you find something."

Chapter 24

As the three railroaders watched, Jules went through his ritual of wiping his silverware with a paper napkin, tucking his napkin in at his collar, and then looking over his place setting to ensure things were in order. Dusty was tapping a spoon on the table, Mule Head belched, and Chaw sipped his coffee. "You men ever heard the word, 'persnickety'?" Chaw asked.

Mule Head spun his head toward Chaw. "Is that a word?"

Dusty was looking at Chaw, "Where'd you hear a high-falutin' word like that?"

Chaw had a mischievous grin.

"Hell. He's making that up," snorted Mule Head.

"Naw, it's a word. The old lady read it in a book and didn't know the meaning, so she looked it up in the dictionary. Whatever it means, she said it didn't apply to me."

Jules arched an eyebrow. "I would have to agree with her."

Chaw's grin grew.

Anita brought their breakfast plates.

Dusty's leg was bouncing beneath the table. "I don't get it."

Chaw broke apart his bacon and held up a piece ready to put it in his mouth, "I'll give you a hint—only one of us here can claim that honor."

Dusty and Mule Head's eyes shifted to Jules, who, unlike Chaw, had sliced his bacon using a knife and fork. The men had a good laugh.

Dusty changed the subject. "C.P. ought to be taking control of the WVB&C any day now."

Jules looked at Dusty, "Yes, and I'm glad he won that battle with the OMVX, which wanted to shut our railroad down."

"I thought C.P. couldn't pull it off when it looked like the Feds wouldn't approve it, but then C.P. pulled a rabbit out of his hat and came up with the idea to lease the WVB&C," Chaw said.

"He did that," agreed Jules.

The WVB&C Railroad Company was built from Cincinnati, Ohio, to Wheeling, West Virginia, by the City of Bekbourg in the 1840's to transport goods produced from the area's industries and companies to markets up and down the rail system. The WVB&C ran though the center of Bekbourg and was a flagship for much of the area's growth.

In 1905, in a lucrative arrangement to the city, Bekbourg leased the railroad under a hundred-year-lease to a railroad company which continued train service through the town.

In the 1990's, that train company merged with another large railroad company, forming the

Ohio Maryland Virginia Consolidated Railroad Corporation, the OMVX. The objective of the merger was to capitalize on the strengths and efficiencies between the two rail systems. Where there was overlap in employees and facilities, decisions had to be made about cutting workforces and closing depots and yards.

As time passed, the OMVX moved forward with a decision to shut down the WVB&C by not renewing its lease. C.P. returned to Bekbourg with a plan to keep Bekbourg's train system opened. He was now days away from accomplishing that goal.

"So, I take it you are staying on with the WVB&C and not moving to Cincinnati?" Jules asked.

Dusty nodded, "Yeah. Even if the grandfathered seniority benefits aren't there under the new arrangement, I'm too young to retire, and I didn't want to move to Cincinnati, which is where I'd have to move to keep working with the OMVX."

Mule Head spoke up, "Glad you're still going to be around. Anita might put us back at the smaller table."

The men laughed.

"Hey, Jules, did you know a William Wainright?" asked Dusty.

"Who?"

"William Wainright. I read in the obituaries he died last week. He died in a nursing home in Athens, Ohio."

"Uncle Billy died? I thought he died a long time ago. He must have been near a hundred."

"Who's Uncle Billy?" asked Mule Head.

"He's an old-timer, a conductor, and goes way back. He worked back in the 20's and worked fifty years. He worked with Sean's grandpa and my dad. I remember him. He was quite a character. Back in the days when everybody had a nickname, everybody called him 'Uncle Billy.' I don't know why."

Chaw said, "I remember him when I first started. I worked with him a time or two, but he was an old man then. Seemed like he was always drunk."

"Yes, he did like his whiskey," said Jules. "I heard lots of stories about Uncle Billy, but the strangest one was about the Christmas tree."

"What do you mean, the Christmas tree?" asked Mule Head.

"What it sounds like—Uncle Billy's Christmas tree. One Christmas, his wife laid down the law and told him not to come home on Christmas Eve drunk like he did every year. But, of course, Billy came home that Christmas Eve like he always did—drunker than a monkey. His wife took one look at him and got her suitcase, which she had already packed. Got the kids and presents and left and went to her parents. Billy was too drunk to know what was going on and fell asleep.

"When he woke up the next morning, the house was cold, but the tree was there—the only thing that was left of Christmas. He thought the old lady would come home, but she didn't. He celebrated by getting drunk again. The day after Christmas, he got called out to work and was gone for two days, and when he came home, she still wasn't there, and hadn't been back. In fact, she never came back.

"At first, Billy didn't seem to realize what had happened, but he never took the tree down. He let it sit there in the middle of the living room. It was one of those cedar trees you find in the hills around here. It, of course, dried out, and the needles started to fall off, but he just let it sit there. It stayed there all through the spring. He just ignored it.

"Then, summer came, and he realized she probably wasn't coming back. So, a few days before the Fourth of July, he called everybody he knew to come to his house for free beer and booze on the Fourth. He had a bunch of neighbors and friends show up late that afternoon. When they got there, Billy's Christmas tree was sitting in the middle of the back yard. It was pitiful looking, but it still had ornaments and lights on it. They wondered what it was doing there.

"Billy was about two sheets to the wind and went into the house. Then out he came with a cooler and carried it and a chair to about thirty feet away from the tree. He then brought out his shotgun and a box of shells. He sat down and loaded some shells into the gun. All of a sudden, he took aim and started shooting the ornaments off. Some people took off. Others stayed since he wasn't aiming at them. He'd take a drink of beer and then load the gun and shoot again. By the time he'd worked his way through about six beers, the tree was gone. He picked up his gun and took it into the house and came back outside and sat down and fell asleep."

"Did his old lady ever come home?" asked Mule Head.

"No. Once she heard about the Christmas tree, she filed for divorce and took him to the cleaners."

"Did he have a tree that Christmas?" asked Mule Head.

Jules just looked at him.

Chaw spoke up as Anita brought the check. "I heard that Sean's wife has been asking around about the bridge that fell into Norton Creek. You all know anything about that?"

Everyone shook their head. Dusty looked at Jules, "Has she talked to you?"

"No, but if she does, I will be happy to assist where I can."

"I bet she'll call you since your dad was there," said Dusty.

"That is my assumption, too, but I'll wait until she's ready to talk to me," Jules said as he ironed the dollar bills with his hand to straighten them before Anita retrieved his payment.

Chapter 25

Alex and Syd had been tasked with interviewing people who had worked the party. Some were local, but many were based in Cincinnati where the caterer was headquartered. The wait staff had mostly been hired for the entire evening, although shifts for some of those workers had ended early as the attendees dwindled. Some workers on the clean-up crew started toward the end of the event, but most went on the clock as soon as the party officially ended.

None of the clean-up crew remembered seeing Vera, but various wait staff recalled her. She had made an impression because she was tipsy and never passed up on food offerings as they circulated with serving trays. A couple of workers who smoked remembered seeing her in the smoking area during their quick trips there.

The most significant tip came from the head of the catering service—who had discovered as inventory was taken that one of the large knives was missing. Through photos and details of the missing knife, the coroner confirmed the missing knife might be the murder weapon, but without the knife, there was no way to be sure.

The caterer told them that none of the guests were supposed to have been in the kitchen that night, but a few wandered in and were asked to leave. As they interviewed the kitchen workers, they learned something that raised suspicion. One of the food preparers was complaining that night about "a crazy woman going through the kitchen looking for the smoking area." Unfortunately, he was not available to talk with Syd and Alex, because he had been called away the day after the party for a family emergency, and no one knew how to get in contact with him.

Sean told them they needed to identify everyone who was in the kitchen that night. "We've already started on that," Alex said as he pulled out a folded piece of paper. "We have a list of all the workers. We also showed the kitchen help a picture of Vera. One of the workers there remembered her because she was rude when she was asked to leave."

"Do you think she is the 'crazy' woman the food preparer was talking about?" asked Sean.

"We won't know until we talk to him. Some of the locals, such as Bri, Max, and Dillie, were in the kitchen at times, but they were involved with the party."

Sean was focused on the missing knife and who may have entered the kitchen area. "You may be on to something. Get pictures of people who we know are connected to Vera and were at the party that night, like her sister and brother-in-law, and see if anyone remembers seeing them in the kitchen. Include Brian Lynch on that list."

Syd spoke up. "The state representative?"

"Yes." Sean explained about Vera going to Brian's office asking for money. "I don't see a connection, but let's cover the bases while we're at it. Make it a priority in tracking down the food preparer who saw the 'crazy woman.' Syd, why don't you get started on that? Alex, I'd like you to go with me to talk with the sister, Teri Olson. Arlo learned this morning that she went to the motel where Vera was staying during the party, but Vera had already been kicked out for not paying. We need to know why Teri was there and why she didn't tell me about it when I first talked to her."

Chapter 26

Dillie knew where John Pawley lived. She pulled into the driveway and took in the old wood farm house. The cinder-block well house had been added in the front yard since she had seen it all those years ago. The downspout gutters and weathered rainwater storage tank gave proof to John's rugged existence. Firewood was stacked under a lean-to and on the front porch. A welded wire fence ran along the street and out of sight as it extended toward the back of his property.

"Okay, John," she thought as she opened the door of her new model Italian sports car, "we have some catching up to do."

A monster-sized dog came thundering around the side of the house growling and barking. Dillie stood undeterred as the mastiff roared up to the fence. "Oh, aren't you a handsome one," Dillie cooed in her foreign accent. She opened her gold tote bag as the dog quieted. "Here you go," she said as she threw a large rawhide bone over the fence. The dog took the bone and started wagging its tail as it lay down and started chewing.

About that time, a tall, lean man appeared from around the corner of the house with an M16 strapped on his back and a gun holster around his thin waist. Other than the toboggan covering his head, not a stitch of clothing was apparent—until his socks peeked out from the edge of his leather military-style boots. He slowed as he took in his dog and Dillie. "What the hell have you done to my dog, woman?" he belted in his gravelly voice.

"Is that you, Darling? It's hard to tell behind all that hair?" Dillie said—without giving him time to respond, "What is this regal beast's name? We haven't been properly introduced."

John looked hard at Dillie, his eyes clear and observant. "It's Baby. Now that you've been properly introduced, I don't see that now is a good time to talk, Dillie."

Dillie moved to open the gate. "Of course it is, Darling. Now, John dear, I thought we would visit on those chairs on your porch. I have two delicious coffees in my bag. Dear Max packed them so they would stay hot, so let's get comfortable and catch up. Oh, while your fashion statement is fine with me, if you need something a bit warmer, by all means, while I get our picnic prepared." Dillie thought John's brush with death from pneumonia over the winter would have discouraged him from continuing his perceived health regiment of walking around his place in his "natural" state—but obviously not.

Dillie was walking up the steps in her tight pants, long sweater and gold stilettos by the time John came to his senses. She primly started laying out scones and coffee as he walked past cursing under his breath.

When he returned wearing an old pair of jeans and flannel shirt, Baby was lying beside Dillie's chair. He briefly raised his head to look at John and then plopped his large head back on his paws.

"That damn dog is supposed to be a watchdog. First, the old biddy, and now you, have corrupted him."

"Baby knows I'm harmless. That shows he's a very smart dog."

"Harmless my ass," John growled.

"Now, who is the woman you call the 'old biddy'?" She motioned for John to drink his coffee. "Bon appetite."

"She lives up the road."

"Is she the angel who found you on death's door? Drink some coffee, and the scones are delicious. I prefer not to eat by myself."

"Ah, shit."

Dillie knew hidden behind his gruffness was an intelligent man. John and Dillie had been close friends from the time they were in junior high together. After high school graduation, Dillie had left to attend a university in California, and John had attended a small college for two years and then joined the Marines during the Vietnam War. He became an expert sniper and received two purple hearts during his service. They were pen pals at first, and then their letters became less frequent as life brought on more changes. They had lost contact many years ago.

After his return from the war, John drifted as he worked on a manuscript. He eventually applied to an ivy league, and after graduation, completed his novel about a war vet's attempted adjustment to the life awaiting him after his return from war. Until Sean Neumann discovered that John was a published author, only two other people knew—Dillie and John's agent.

"Why did you not publish your second book?" Dillie asked. "It was certain to be another best seller. Your first book remained on the best seller list for over a year."

"You were living overseas by then, Dillie, so you probably don't know the fallout from my book. While it was on the best seller list, it was quite controversial to many people. The war was not popular, and my introspection was not welcomed by everyone."

"Darling, I am not clear on why that would have precluded you from moving forward with your second book, but in any event, it is not too late. I thought your manuscript for the second book was brilliant. The world should not be denied your gift."

John paused.

Dillie was determined. "Well, Darling. It is time to publish the second novel. It will be an instant success. I am certain the publisher is standing ready."

"Ah, hell, I might as well tell you. The book was ready to go, but I held back. My agent pestered me on and off for years to allow it to be published. I thought he would eventually die, but he didn't. Before I got sick, I gave him the green light. The publisher was chomping at the bit. It is being released next week."

Dillie clapped. "Marvelous! I cannot tell you how thrilled I am to hear this news. You have done well to maintain your anonymity. Are you going to stay anonymous or let the world know what a genius you are?"

He shrugged, "I'm sticking with my pen name, G. Keb. There's no reason for anyone to know." He was ready to change subjects. "So, I picked up a newspaper and saw you have purchased the Schumacher factory. Are you planning to stay?"

"Yes. It's time to settle down, and when I returned for my darling brother's memorial, I decided it was time to come home."

John looked at Dillie as if trying to solve a puzzle. "You really plan to live here?"

She sipped her coffee. "Yes, I do. Of course, I'll continue to travel and spend time at my vineyard in California, but when I came back, I felt I was home. I know this is where I belong."

"What are you planning to do?" asked John.

"I adore artists and the beauty they create. I am having the factory remodeled into a place where artists can create and sell their works. The artists can sell locally of course, but with the internet, they are free to market anywhere. This is a wonderful opportunity to do something I love in a place I love, and I want to spread my love here." She paused as she nibbled on a scone morsel. "John, there is a favor I would like to ask."

Even under his bushy facial hair, Dillie saw his eyebrow arch.

"Now, Darling, please hear me out and do not rush to decide. You have been my closest friend—the only person to whom I ever shared my dreams and despairs. When I heard you had almost died from pneumonia, my heart nearly stopped. I know why you walk around in the nude. You think that makes you physically stronger in order to combat that lung fungus you contracted during the war. I know you enjoy the tranquility here, but maybe it is time to do something different."

"Spit it out, woman."

"You need to publish, John. You must share your talents with the world. I have the perfect place where you can pursue your writing, but it will also relieve my distress. You see, Darling, there is a rather large structure at the back of the factory that used to be a carriage house and an apartment for the night watchman. I need an overseer to the building. Naturally, you would be perfect."

"No way in hell. I have this place to take care of. Besides, Baby likes it here. I cannot live like that. Dillie. I've been here too long."

"Darling, don't be hasty. Come and see what I've done to that beautiful building. I'm also planning to live in the house once the renovations are complete. I will show that to you as well."

"Damn it, Dillie, I knew when I saw you, trouble was brewing."

She reached over and patted his hand as she gathered the picnic items. "Let's set a day." She gave him a day and time. "I will see you at the factory. One more thing, Darling, while your body is much to admire, perhaps you should take more precautions in walking around in your birthday suit in this type of weather. I cannot bear the thought of you contracting pneumonia again." She gave Baby's head a pat and walked down the stairs. Her car roared to life. John was cursing again as he and Baby went inside.

Chapter 27

After Sean and Alex knocked, they heard Champ's nails clicking on the floor as he raced to the front door. Teri was not far behind and was telling him to move back as she opened the door. "Oh. Hi, Sheriff, Alex. Come in."

Sean and Alex took time to give the dog a pat. Teri offered something to drink, but both declined. Champ plopped down next to Teri's chair and laid his head on his paws—looking at Sean with large brown eyes.

"That sure is a friendly dog," Alex commented.

Teri smiled. "He sure is. He's about six-years old. We got him when Miles was eight, and they're nearly inseparable."

"Teri, we need to ask you some more questions about Vera's death," Sean said.

Teri's shoulders stiffened. "Okay." Teri did not want to talk about Vera, or even think about her. God! Even now, there was no escape from the drag she felt from her sister.

"Let's start with you and Gerald attending the party. What time did you get there?"

"Oh, we didn't drive together. I had to be there before it started to set up a table with information about the Garden Club and how we support the arts. I also needed to pack everything up after the party ended. Gerald drove separately. He wanted to get back home in time to watch the second half of the OSU football game."

"Did you cover the table the entire evening?"

She started to rub her thumb over her other hand. "No, other ladies took turns covering the table."

"What did you do the rest of the time?"

Teri pursed her lips a couple of times but remained silent.

"Did you leave the party at any time?"

She slightly slumped forward. "Yes. I drove to the motel where Vera told me she was staying, but she had already checked out."

"Why did you do that? You had seen her at the party."

"I did see her at the party early that night, but after a while, I didn't see her, so I thought she might have left and gone back there. I knew I could get back in time to pack up."

"Why did you go there?" Sean persisted.

She ran her hand through her hair. "I wanted to tell her *again* to leave town. I was going to tell her I would try to see if Dillie or someone local would carry her paintings, but I just wanted her to leave." Her eyes were clear but strained as she looked at Sean. "She was drunk at the party. God, I just hoped she wasn't going to cause a scene there."

Teri stood and walked toward the window and looked out. "She was an embarrassment to me my whole life. God only knows what she was up to." Teri shook her head and whispered to herself, "Poor Dillie."

The faintness of her voice was not enough to keep Sean from hearing, and his interest was piqued. "What's this about Dillie?"

Teri turned slowly. "I'm sorry. I'm just talking to myself."

"You said something about 'poor Dillie.' What did you mean?"

Teri returned to her seat. "Vera was intent on getting Dillie to carry her work. She could be a pest. I felt sorry for Dillie knowing how unpleasant Vera could be."

Sean watched Teri for some indication of her thoughts. When she continued to look at her hands, he said, "You obviously did not want Vera here. Why's that?"

The thought of Vera bringing her venom back to her family and others in Bekbourg who might face Vera's wrath was overpowering to Teri. Her lips firmed, "She was a menace, and it didn't matter who she hurt. In my whole life before she left here I felt like I was walking on egg shells. I never knew when she was going to throw a fit or lie about me to Mom, or embarrass me around my friends.

"Gerald and I married, and I moved out. Finally, for a short period of time, I could relax. I

145

didn't see her often. I'd go see Mom, but a lot of the time, Vera wasn't there. I knew she was probably causing problems for someone in town, but as long as I didn't hear about it, I felt I could block it out.

"Mom's health started to decline, and she needed someone to help her. Vera couldn't be relied on. Gerald and I had been renting, so we decided it was easiest to move back in here. After Mom died, that's when Vera moved to Cleveland, and for fourteen blissful years, she was out of my life." Anger flared in her voice as she continued. "Then, she shows back up here—and in typical Vera fashion, wants money and wants to move back in."

Teri caught herself and looked at Sean. Her voice softened a little. "I told her we didn't have the money to help her and that she couldn't move back in. I said we might lose the house and have to move. Financially, we're hanging by a thread. Also, I didn't want our son around Vera—with the way she acted. He has friends coming in all the time. I couldn't let him go through being embarrassed with his friends like I was when we were growing up. Gerald's not himself after the accident and not being able to get back on a job."

Teri looked at Sean as if pleading for his empathy. "I just couldn't let her back in our lives. Seeing the way she was acting at the party, I made the decision to try and talk to her about leaving. That's why I went there."

"The night clerk told you she had already checked out. Where did you think she had gone?"

"I had no idea. My hope was she had headed back to Cleveland."

"Were there any friends in town she might have stayed with?" Sean asked.

"Like I told you the other day, I can't think of anyone. By the time she left Bekbourg, I don't think she had any friends left. She had a way of alienating everyone around her."

Teri looked down at her hands where she had been rubbing her thumb. "The only person who comes to mind is Tanya Ellis, but they weren't on speaking terms when she left here, so I doubt she would have stayed with her. But, see, that's the thing with Vera, she would push people away, but not think they would be mad at her, so she'd go back and act like nothing ever happened. So, it's possible she reached out to Tanya, but I don't think Tanya would want anything to do with her."

"Is Gerald here?"

"No, he's at physical therapy."

Champ jumped up, and the stub of his tail along with his entire backside was wagging back and forth as he raced to the front door. Sean could hear the dog snorting as he waited for whoever it was to enter. The door swung open, and Miles dropped his things to pat and talk to Champ. He walked into the room, "Hey, Mom." He looked at Sean and Alex. "Is everything okay?"

Both Teri and Gerald were medium height, and Miles looked like he was on the path to follow suit. His hair was dark like Gerald's, and he was a good-looking young man. He had an easy smile and reminded Sean of Gerald's easy-going ways when Sean had gotten to know him after returning to Bekbourg. Sean had not seen Gerald much since his hiking accident.

"The Sheriff and Alex are here to ask some questions about something. There are some brownies left. Go get you a snack."

"Okay. Let's go, Champ."

"Why didn't you tell me you had gone to the motel when I was here the other night?" Sean asked.

Her eyes blinked, "I didn't see the need. She had checked out, and I had not seen her since earlier in the evening at the party."

Sean looked at her with penetrating eyes, and she looked away.

They wrapped up with Teri. As they drove to the station, Alex commented, "Teri had a motive to see her sister dead, and she was at the party. Do you think she did it?"

"We certainly can't rule her out. She doesn't come across as a 'crazy woman,' but then the food preparer might think any guest who came into the kitchen was crazy."

Alex grinned. "Yeah—spoken like someone who feels proprietary over his domain. But we don't know for sure the weapon was the missing kitchen knife."

"That's true, but who brings a knife like the one the coroner described to a party like the grand opening. It seems beyond a coincidence that the knife is missing, and the coroner believes the measurements are close to being a match."

Alex nodded, "So, we really need to talk to the food preparer who saw the 'crazy woman.'"

Sean's lips quirked. "Yeah. When you and Syd track him down, be sure to show him Teri's picture."

"Will do. We don't really have any other suspects, do we?"

"No, but I think we should talk to Gerald to see if he shared similar strong feelings about Vera. Also, let's circle by Frau's and see if Tanya Ellis is working this evening. See if Vera asked her about staying with her."

Tanya was not on duty, and Sean made a note to follow up with her the following day when she was expected back to work.

Chapter 28

Sean wanted to treat Cheryl to a night out, so he reserved a table at the GilHaus toward the back where they would enjoy a semblance of privacy. He had fallen for her the first time she had questioned him about a murder case that had brought her to Bekbourg. He was an unwilling participant in the pull he felt for her, but in the end, love won out, and now she was his wife. Cheryl attacked her work with a passion, but she had plenty of room left for others she loved and cared about. Her energy and positive attitude lifted him and those around her.

A happy glow filled his eyes as he watched her sip the wine. She smiled, "There is nothing more a reporter can ask for than to be invited to dinner by the sheriff whom she can pump for the scoop."

Sean grinned, "Is that right?" and smiled as she nodded. "Well, okay, Ms. Seton, what questions do you have?"

"Let me see. Did you arrest anyone today?"

"No comment," he said with a mischievous glint.

She laughed. "Why am I not surprised with that response? Those were some of the first words you ever spoke to me." He grinned. "I guess that means I won't get any information on Vera's murder. Of course, anything you say is off the record."

They both were smiling as he broke the trance, "Off the record, there's really not anything to say. It's early in the investigation."

She looked skeptical, "Sounds par for the course." Sean laughed—a rarity for him except around Cheryl.

"It's really something how it happened. She shows up in town, and then a few days later, is murdered at Dillie's party. Who would know she would be there?" Cheryl asked as she took another sip. "I spoke with her sister, but she didn't want to comment. Dillie told me she was surprised it had happened and had only briefly met her. Otherwise, we are kind of at a dead end from the newspaper's reporting. No one around here knows much. I've held off going to Cleveland to ask about her, because I'm not sure someone from Cleveland would drive here to kill her."

"Mmm," Sean said as he sipped his beer.

"What I find odd is that she wasn't staying at her sister's house. Vera's gone all those years, and she comes back and is staying in that old motel."

Sean had also pondered that point. Teri had not made a secret that the sisters were estranged, but he did not know why. He understood the antagonism Teri felt for her sister, but he wondered if there was more to the story. What he remembered about Gerald and Teri was not much. Sean was sandwiched in age between the two—Gerald was two years older than Sean, and Teri was three years younger.

Since Gerald did not play football, Sean vaguely knew of him. His father worked for the county fire department and took on side painting jobs for individuals and businesses, and his mother worked part time at the Shopper's Pavilion— Bekbourg's mainstay general store that had morphed into a large box store. Aside from a couple of speeding tickets, Gerald had never run afoul of the law. Sean's dad told him they were hard-working people who went about their daily lives like everyone else.

As for Teri, Sean did not remember her or her family. His parents told him Teri's father frequently traveled on business. His mother remembered when Teri's father had died suddenly, their church rallied around Viola for support. Until she could get through her shock and get the affairs in order, church members took turns mowing the grass, and women spent time visiting and inviting her for brief outings.

He learned Teri's family was not wealthy but they had lived a comfortable lifestyle and a life insurance policy had seen them through the time until Teri's mother had passed away. By then, a large portion of the money had been spent, but there was still the house and five acres. Teri and Gerald bought the house and put the money back into the estate. The five acres had been sold by the estate. Sean also learned that Teri's mother had miscarried twice after Teri was born before Vera arrived.

"Well, I know you will keep on it for your readers. I don't have an official comment, but when I do, I have this favorite newspaper owner who I usually reach out to." They both laughed.

"I have to admire Dillie," Cheryl said. "Most people would be annoyed, or horrified, that a murder had occurred at their grand opening. Naturally, Dillie viewed the death as tragic and was sympathetic to Teri and Gerald. But as far as being concerned about bad publicity for the gallery, she wasn't in the least. She took it like water rolling off a duck's back. Ce qui sera (what will be). I like that philosophy. I need to try to adopt it more often."

Sean's eyes warmed. "I love you just the way you are. Let Dillie be Dillie, and you be you."

Cheryl's smile lit up her face. Sean noticed her attention shift. He looked up to see a foursome being seated. Cheryl's eyes were shining, and he knew where the conversation was heading. "Are C.P.'s friend, Grayson Macafee, and Dillie seeing each other?"

Sean sipped his beer to hide amusement. "I don't know. I don't keep up with things like that."

Cheryl looked like a sentinel as she watched from the corner of her eye. "Well, I know Mary and C.P. have been seeing each other. Bri and I think they may eventually get married, but this is a surprise to see Dillie and Grayson. Doesn't he live in D.C.?"

They were waiting for their food to be delivered, so Sean resorted to taking another drink. "Yeah, I think so. Dillie is friends with Mary and C.P. With Grayson being in town, they probably just asked her to join them. I wouldn't jump to any conclusions."

"I'm not, but the way he is looking at Dillie, there could be something brewing."

Sean did not want to prolong the discussion by asking how he was looking at Dillie. "Wonder where our food is?"

"Wouldn't it be something if Dillie and Grayson got together? I mean, they're both very successful people. I'm sure they have lots in common." Cheryl looked at Sean, "You're not the least bit interested in this."

"Not the tiniest bit. They just met for the first time at the party. He's probably getting ready to head back to D.C."

Cheryl's brow arched, "Well, it didn't take me long to fall for you."

A rare smile appeared. "And, Honey, it sure as hell didn't take long for you to sweep me off my feet. Oh, good. Here comes our food."

As soon as the food was placed, Sean decided it was the perfect opportunity to shift gears from the Dillie/Grayson topic. "What are the next steps on your railroad bridge story?"

Sherrie Rutherford

Chapter 29

Arlo walked into Sean's office carrying a cup of coffee. "Hey, Chief, got a minute?"

"Sure Arlo. What's up?"

"I stopped by Frau's this morning to get my morning java and heard something I thought you should know. It was before the railroaders got there, so Anita had a few minutes to talk. She knew, of course, about Vera being killed, and she remembered her from back in the day. Vera rarely came in Frau's—not really her style—but I guess she left an unpleasant impression.

"Whoever the waitress was who had to serve her felt she had pulled the short straw, because Vera was hard to please and quick to complain. Anyway, a couple of days before the party, she came in. Anita couldn't believe it, because she hadn't seen her in years. Vera sat at a table. Tanya Ellis walked up to take her order and realized it was Vera. You've seen Tanya. Kinda on the heavy side and wears her dark hair pulled back in a ponytail most of the time."

Sean nodded—as he recognized her.

"They kinda got into it. Anita saw them arguing and rushed over and told Tanya it was time

156

for her break and said she would cover the table. Anita said she didn't know what it was about, but Tanya took a break, and Vera left without paying for the coffee Tanya had already poured for her."

"That's interesting," said Sean. "Tanya's name came up yesterday when Alex and I were talking to Teri. Let's go over and talk to her. She should be on duty this morning."

Chapter 30

Since he was supposed to meet Dillie this morning, Pawley decided to stop at Frau's for breakfast—something he had not done in a very long time. Chaw did a double take when he spied Pawley and stood, waved, and yelled across the room, "Hey, John. Over here." John looked around before heading toward the table. "You here for breakfast? Here, have a seat. We've got plenty of room," encouraged Chaw.

"Looks like you men are through," observed John.

Jules spoke up, "We're not in a hurry. It's good to see you. You need a menu?"

"Naw. I know what I want, but I don't know if I belong with this illustrious group of railroaders," John said.

"Sure you do. You're an honorary member," Jules said.

While John was telling Anita his order, Chaw removed his teeth and covered them with a napkin. They had been bothering him lately. He hated thinking about it, but at some point, he'd probably have to go see a dentist.

"Almost didn't recognize you, John, with your clothes on," needled Chaw.

"Good thing he's wearing 'em now," said Mule Head looking around.

"How you boys been doin'?" John asked as he drank some coffee. Even though he was an accomplished author, John had grown up in Bekbourg and found it easy to slip into the speech of those around him.

Chaw stood. "I gotta go take a leak. Don't let 'em pull your leg, John."

"I cannot complain," said Jules. "I'm able to finish out my time with my retirement even though C.P.'s going to buy the railroad."

Dusty spoke up. "I'm still not sure if my seniority is going to count. Even if it doesn't, I'm glad to still be able to work out of Bekbourg. They were going to shut down everything through here."

"Chaw and I ain't affected," said Mule Head. "We're both retired."

"That's good," acknowledged John—as Anita brought John's breakfast, refreshed everyone's coffee, and cleared the table.

"We haven't seen you since you saved Sean," said Dusty.

Chaw rejoined the group and followed up, "That was some doing, John."

"Nothing I care to talk about," John mumbled.

"What brings you into town?" asked Mule Head.

"I got some business."

159

The railroaders talked about the changes that C.P. Traylor planned to make with the train service. C.P. was traveling, talking to investors, customers and potential clients. "It sounds like you men think it's a good thing," John said.

"We do," assured Dusty. About that time, Anita brought everyone's bill and zipped off to pour coffee at another table.

As Chaw started to reach for his wallet, he groaned, "Ah, hell!" Dusty's and Jules' eyes got large. Chaw got up and headed toward the kitchen.

Jules said to John, "She took his teeth." Dusty was solemnly nodding.

"That happen often?" asked John. "Him losing his teeth?" Dusty shrugged.

Jules, pressing the dollar bills flat on the ticket to remove any wrinkles, casually commented, "Occasionally."

Anita collected everyone's money, except Chaw's—since he wasn't at the table. When he returned, Jules said Anita had picked up the tabs. Chaw responded, "I'm paid up. I paid 'em after I dug my teeth out of the trash." Turning to John, he added, "Don't be a stranger. We'd like to see more of you. Join us anytime. We meet here most mornings between shifts."

"For once I agree with Chaw," said Jules. "You are always welcomed at our table."

Dusty added, "Anita's giving us this big table, so there's always room." Mule Head nodded.

As he left, John said, "See you men around."

Occasion of Murder

Chapter 31

John Pawley pulled into the large parking lot adjacent to the Schumacher factory in his old model pickup truck—that had seen better days long ago. He looked at the remarkable building so well preserved. *What in the hell am I doing here? Why did Dillie have to come and disrupt my life? It's because that's who Dillie is.* John could not have been more stunned when he had walked around the corner of his house and saw her standing there. He knew instantly who she was, and they quickly fell back into the ease they had always found together. Now, she was asking him to rejoin the world.

A blue contraption caught his eye as it raced around the lot. She was looking around, spied his truck, and whirled in his direction. For a fleeting moment, John considered leaving, but then it was too late—as Dillie cruised up beside him and motioned for him to get in.

"Come on, Darling. I'll drive you around back to see the beautiful carriage house. Then, I'll be your tour guide for the gallery."

Eyeing the golf cart, he said, "I don't mind walking, Dillie."

"Of course we can't walk. I won't bite, Love!"

"Aw, shit," John mumbled as he climbed aboard. "Where the hell did you get this?"

"I asked Danny Chambers, that wonderful man, to make this for me while I was in California finalizing my affairs. He did a lovely job. Now, Love, do strap on your seatbelt. I would simply hate to throw you out as I make the curve ahead." John grudging complied and was glad he did. Otherwise, he'd be lying on his ass in the parking lot.

After Dillie finished showing John the factory, the apartment in the old coach space, and the mansion, she zipped him back to his truck. "It's a good damn thing the engine in this motorized vehicle can't do more than twenty-five-miles-per-hour. You couldn't afford the speeding tickets."

Dillie's laughter floated like musical notes. "Darling, when you and Baby move into that lovely apartment I have for you, you can get one."

"No damn way on either account, woman."

Dillie grinned. "Now, John darling, it would really help me out if you moved here and oversaw the factory and grounds. Baby would love all the people, and they would love him."

"You've got people who can do those things. I'm just fine where I'm at. Now, I've got to get back and check on Baby. You be careful in this thing, Dillie," he said as he looked at her golf cart and then turned to get into his truck.

She called after him, "I'll pay you and Baby another visit soon. Please do take care of yourself. Ta-ta, Love." John shook his head as Dillie motored away in her golf cart.

Chapter 32

Tanya suggested they sit in a backroom at Frau's where she could smoke while they talked. Sean began by asking her about her relationship with Vera.

Tanya shook her head. "We were friends for a while during high school. Girls grow up. One day, I just decided it was time to move on, and that included moving on from Vera. No biggy."

"What about some words between the two of you here recently when she came back to town?"

Tanya blew out some smoke and tapped her cigarette on the ashtray. "Yeah, well. Like I told you, Vera and I drifted apart after high school. Vera could be a bitch, and I had finally gown tired of it. In high school, I knew Vera had issues. But, hey, she was a Keller! Lived in that big house, so I thought it was cool to be seen with her. Be her friend." She took another drag on the cigarette.

"That meant putting up with her shit. I guess Vera didn't like being rejected, or maybe she thought she could just show back up after all these years and be the bully she always was, but I ain't like I was then. No way was I going to let her get by with her snide remarks. I gave it right back, and things escalated."

"Did you see her after that?"

"Well, I saw her at Dillie's grand opening party. I hired on to help with the catering, so yeah, I saw her there."

"Did you talk to her?"

"She came up to me to get a glass of champagne off my tray. Tried to talk, but I was working."

"What did she want to talk about?" Sean suspected Vera was going to ask to stay with her, but it was hard to know.

"Damn if I know. I didn't give her a chance. I moved on."

"Was that the only time you saw her that evening?"

"I may have seen her around the room, but I didn't talk to her."

"When was the last time you saw her that night?"

"I don't remember. Time was a blur. I had to work the early shift here the next morning, so I had arranged with the caterer to clock out an hour before the party was set to end. He didn't have a problem with that since he thought some guests would be leaving early."

"Do you know if Vera had any other friends here who she might have been in contact with? Someone she could stay with?"

"Huh," she sighed, "not that I know of. I take it she wasn't staying with her sister. I can't say I blame her sister."

"Why do you say that?"

Tanya ground out the cigarette. "Just knowing Vera, I can't imagine anyone wanting to live with her." She glanced at her watch. "I really need to get back. Is there anything else, Sheriff?"

"No. Thanks for your time. If you think of anything, let me know."

After they left, Arlo told Sean, "I'm glad I didn't have to cross paths with Vera. She sounded like a real battle-axe."

"Sure doesn't help in narrowing the scope of suspects," Sean commented.

"Nope. Sure doesn't."

Chapter 33

Kim told Sean that Frederic had called while he was out, so Sean paid a call in person. When Sean walked into the gallery, Frederic was directing some delivery men. He glanced over and waved at Sean, indicating he would be with him shortly.

Sean looked around the mammoth space that contained several artist booths. Most of the artists were not in their booths, but a couple of them were unpacking their works to display. Sean ventured around and talked to one of the artists about his watercolors. He told Sean he was so busy with people coming by his booth the night of the party that he did not remember seeing Vera. She had not stopped by his booth.

A booth containing unique ceramic pieces caught his attention, and he walked up just as the artist was lifting a piece from a cardboard box filled with foam peanuts. She was startled, and Sean lunged to grab the vase before it fell out of her hands.

The woman paled as Sean apologized, "I'm sorry. I didn't mean to surprise you," he said as he handed it back to her, making sure she had a firm grip before releasing it.

167

She turned and gingerly put it on a shelf, but Sean noticed her hands were quivering. There were three more boxes sitting unopened. He offered to help her unpack, but she declined with a polite murmur. He saw "Nell Porter" carved on a wood sign along with the words, "Ceramics by Nell."

"Are you the artist?" he asked.

She had gained some composure. "Yes, I'm Nell."

"These are beautiful. I really like the colors."

"Thank you."

Frederic came rushing up. "You've met our Nell. Aren't her creations astounding?"

"Yes, they are," agreed Sean.

"I'm sorry I was busy with those men when you arrived, but if now is convenient, we can go up front."

"Of course. It was nice meeting you, Nell. My wife owns the *Tribune*. I'll tell her about your works. She's always looking for someone in the community to spotlight."

Nell nodded. As he turned to go, Sean thought about the woman. She carried sadness in her life. He had seen it in a few men he served with in the Marines. He wondered what had caused such grief in her.

"This makes it easier, Sheriff. I can show you the picture." Frederic was waving a hand in the air as they walked to the front. "First, I reviewed the guest list, and Vera Keller was not on the list, but of course, it was an open invitation so everyone was welcome. The second thing you asked me to think about pertained to the guest who had a spat with Vera Keller the night of the party. I did not know the gentleman's name at the time, but I recognized him from a photo in the *Tribune* this morning— quite photogenic."

By this time, they had arrived at Frederic's large work table. He moved sketches and miscellaneous things around until he uncovered the newspaper. "This is the man."

Sean looked to see Brian Lynch's picture with a notice that he was giving an address at the Speaker's Club at the end of the week. "You're sure this is the man?"

"Of course."

"Remind me again what you saw."

"I needed to go to the storage room down that hallway." He pointed to a hall leading back from an "Exit" sign. "There are restrooms through there and a utility room as well as a large storage room. I had both the utility and storage rooms locked the night of the party. I was in the storage room looking for what I needed, and I heard a woman's loud voice as she passed by the door— moving toward the back where the restrooms and emergency exit are. Then, I heard a man's voice, which sounded angry. I found what I was looking for and went into the hall. As I pulled the door closed to lock it, I looked up and saw Vera Keller and this man. I heard him say something like, 'You can forget it,' and she said, 'You don't want this out.' I headed to take the box to the kitchen, but then I circled back to see if they were still there. I did not want anything to happen to ruin the night for Dillie." He stopped as his brows arched. Sean knew where his thoughts had gone—there had been a murder after all. "Naturally, I did not anticipate a murder."

Sean took him back to Brian and Vera. "So, what happened next with them?"

"Right. They were gone by the time I got back."

Sean wondered what Vera and Brian had been arguing about—particularly since Brian had not seemed to know Vera.

"About what time did you see them?"

"Oh, I'd say the party had been going on for nearly two hours, so somewhere around eight o'clock."

"This is helpful." Sean heard the bell chime indicating someone had entered. "I appreciate you following up. If you think of anything else, call me."

Chapter 34

"We have more names of people who entered the kitchen area that night," Syd reported to the officers. She ran down the short list. "It includes Bri's husband, Max; Vera's sister, Teri; Frederic; and one of the artists—Nell Porter. Frederic and Dillie were in and out all night as were Bri and Max who were overseeing the service."

"Since they were involved with the party and the caterer, there is no need to talk with Dillie, Frederic, Max and Bri about why they were in the kitchen, but I'd like for you and Alex to talk with the artist and see what she tells you. I'll talk with Teri about why she would have been in the kitchen."

Syd continued, "I could not find any other motels she tried to charge to her credit card. I also went to others in that price range to see if she had paid cash, but no one had a record of her. Looks like the only motel she stayed in was the dinosaur motel." Syd was the most serious of all his deputies, and the most studious. If Sean needed someone to delve into financial details or detailed records, she was the one he typically called on. Even though she rarely smiled or joked around, she got along with

171

the other deputies—even Arlo, who liked to tease the other deputies.

"Hey Syd," Arlo piped up. "What motel is that?"

Alex smirked, "Arlo, don't tell me you haven't ever noticed that oversized green dinosaur out front?"

"Oh, is that the one, Amigo?"

Alex rolled his eyes, and Syd sat expressionless as she watched the two deputies.

"Wonder what happened to her luggage?" asked Alex. "We know she had some. The night clerk saw her load it."

"It's possible someone stole it from her car," suggested Arlo.

"I don't think that's likely. She left her purse lying on the front seat, and the car wasn't locked. It had her wallet. I think if someone was going to steal anything, it would have been her purse or wallet."

"Good point, Alex, but what if there was something in the luggage they were after?"

"You mean the killer took the luggage?" Syd asked.

Arlo shrugged, "It's possible. Her car wasn't much to look at, but maybe the killer thought there was something in the luggage."

"It's worth exploring," said Sean. "Arlo, why don't you check around at the thrift shops and churches and see if anything suspicious has turned up—like a suitcase or duffle or women's clothing. She was a petite woman."

"Will do, Sheriff."

"Do we have a list of persons of interest?" asked Alex.

"I don't think any of them rise to that level yet," said Sean, "but Vera's sister and brother-in-law are on *a* list—also, Brian Lynch."

Sean had been thinking about Brian and Vera having a heated conversation in the hallway at the gallery. Frederic made it sound like there was more to it than what Brian had told Sean the first time they talked. If all she wanted was more money, why argue? But, Frederic thought he heard Vera trying to pressure Brian about something. It was time to talk to Brian again.

Sean and Alex drove to the computer and technology business. When they arrived, the receptionist told them he was due back from lunch, so they sat in the waiting area.

Shortly, Brian and his wife, Colette, walked in. Sean and Alex stood, and the receptionist told Brian they were there to talk to him. Colette looked confused and turned to Brian, "Why do they want to talk to you?"

"It's nothing, Dear. We'll talk about it at dinner tonight."

She glanced at the officers and turned back to Brian. "Sugar, don't forget we're supposed to be at the Kramer's at 7:00."

"Glad you reminded me. I'll get home a little early so I have time to get ready."

She kissed him on the cheek and bid everyone a farewell—viewing Sean with curiosity.

They went back into his office. "Okay, Sean, what can I do for you?"

"The last time we talked, you told me Vera came up to you at the party and asked for more money, but I understand there was more to the conversation than that." When Brian did not comment, Sean continued. "You need to level with me. Tell me what was going on."

Brian's face grew red. He looked between Sean and Alex. He did not know how Sean would know, but maybe someone had overheard him and Vera arguing. "Okay. She came up and said she needed more money. I didn't want people to overhear. You know how people get the wrong impression and talk. I sure as hell didn't plan on giving her any more money. She seemed drunk to me, and the last thing I wanted was a scene. She was a crackpot. She had this notion that since my father has a successful business, I have money to burn. I told her that wasn't the case, and I couldn't help her anymore."

"Did she say something like she knew you didn't want something to get out?"

Sean watched his reaction. It looked like Brian's chest rose, and color again returned to his face. "If you heard that from someone, maybe they misunderstood what they think they heard."

"You don't know what she could have been talking about?"

Brian shook his head, "That's about all I can say, Sean."

"If there's something you're holding back, Brian, I'll find out. That won't look good on you. You're better off telling me."

"Sorry, Sean, that's about all I can say."

"I think there's something he's not telling us," said Alex on the way to the precinct.

"I agree, and we need to figure out what that is. The motel manager and night clerk didn't remember anyone visiting Vera at the motel, but ask Arlo to circle back with them and see if they remember anything else. Also, have him check around area restaurants and see if anyone remembers seeing her with anyone. One more thing—call the caterer and see if he's heard from the food preparer who talked about a crazy woman coming into the kitchen that night. That could be the key to solving this."

Chapter 35

"Brian, why were the police waiting for you when we got back from lunch?"

"It's really nothing, Colette," he huffed as he walked back the hall to get ready for their dinner plans.

"The police don't just show up over nothing," she pressed.

"They're talking to people who were seen at Dillie's party talking with that woman who was killed—Vera Keller."

"Why would they want to talk to you?"

He blew out a deep breath. "You remember her coming up to me the night of the party and wanting money?"

"Yeah, so they wanted to talk to you about that? How did they know?"

"They didn't say, but I guess someone must have overheard."

"What did you tell them?"

"Look, Colette, don't worry about it. They came by the other day and knew she had stopped by the office. I told them she was down on her luck and wanted a handout."

"That's all they asked about?" Colette was chewing her thumb nail. "Oh, my God, Brian, you know how rumors get started. The last thing we need now is for someone to start a rumor. It could ruin your campaign."

"I wish everything we do wasn't measured by this damn election."

She could see he was getting more agitated, so she stood and walked up behind him as he yanked at knotting his tie. As she rubbed up and down his arms, she tried to calm him, "You're right, Dear. Let's not think about any of this anymore. That dreadful woman is dead. We've got better things to think about.

"I've been talking with Belinda about her and Marty coming down for the fundraiser. Bri and Max are onboard with catering it. You've got that speech later this week with the Speaker's Club. Your opponent doesn't stand a chance, but we don't want to take anything for granted."

Brian pulled away and walked into the closet to get a sports coat. "For God's sake, is that all you can think about—the damn election. I hate all this meet-and-greet shit."

Colette wasn't about to let her dreams of getting out of Bekbourg get dashed. She walked toward him and put her arms around his neck. "Sugar, please don't talk like that. Marty and his dad have all sorts of connections. Once you win this election, the rest will be easier. Think how much fun it will be living in Columbus and raising our children there. Which reminds me," she kissed him, "we need to get started soon on that."

He put his forehead against hers and gently pulled her arms from around his neck and stepped back. "I know. There's just a lot on my mind right now."

"It'll get better," she assured him as they left the bedroom. She grabbed the car keys from the peg and handed them to him. "Have you thought any more about us getting a new car?" She rubbed her hand down his arm. "I think the newly-elected representative should drive around in a new car."

"I don't want another car. Besides, most of the people in the district don't drive around in new cars. I should appear more like them."

"Mmm. I don't know. Voters look up to successful people. And successful people drive new cars."

"Let's just get to the Kramer's."

She smiled. "Always the practical one. Good idea, Sweetie." Colette was not feeling as cheerful as she let on. Brian was moody, which was unlike him. But more alarming was his disparaging talk about running for reelection. That damn woman had brought all this on, but she was out of the picture—thank God. But, sadly, the harm had been done to Brian's attitude about the election. Colette had to stay focused and maneuver them though the land mines and detonate any that got in the way. He had to win.

Chapter 36

Jack Rhodes was one of the people Cheryl thought might know something about the body discovered when the railroad crew was clearing debris in preparation for rebuilding the Norton Creek Bridge. The first words out of Jack's mouth when he heard Cheryl on the phone were, "When are you and that husband of yours coming to visit us here in Venice?"

Cheryl laughed, "It's on our to-do list."

He chuckled, "Okay, as long as it's on some damn list."

Jack had spent his entire working career with the Bekbourg County's sheriff department where he had served as sheriff for many years before retiring to Florida. His institutional knowledge had proven helpful to both Sean and Cheryl's respective past investigations.

They chatted for a few minutes, with Jack wanting to assure his wife and himself that Cheryl had recovered from the life-threatening ordeal at the hands of a murderer. Cheryl finally got around to telling him about her research into the 1957 bridge collapse and the body that had been discovered at the time of the clean-up. "Do you remember anything about this case?"

"I'm afraid I may not be very helpful on this one, Cheryl. My memory is vague about this. I was a rookie. It's like you said. The sheriff was called to the site. The local doctor who moonlighted as the medical examiner came out and took the body away. I don't know any more than what's in the autopsy report about the body."

"I didn't see a lot in the file about an investigation," said Cheryl.

"That sounds about right. The budget was tight, and the sheriff wasn't one to spend on something unless he had to. Based on the autopsy, it wasn't conclusive that foul play was involved so he probably didn't pursue it."

"Mmm."

"I remember that spring, and I sure as hell remember the bridge giving way. It rained like the dickens that spring. The rivers and creeks in the whole region were flooded. There weren't any reports of anyone missing around that time, so the sheriff didn't have a lot to go on."

After Cheryl and Jack concluded their conversation, Cheryl leaned back in her chair to think about what she knew. After a while, she spread out her notes and worked up an outline. She wanted to talk to Milton and get his ideas on what her next steps should be. She was not giving up on finding the identity of the man, and then, hopefully, she could determine how he had ended up in the creek.

When Cheryl graduated from college, she joined a small, but highly respected newspaper in Cleveland, Ohio, that prized itself in investigative reporting. Milton Grant was one of those crusty newspaper reporters. With nearly forty years behind his belt, he knew the ropes and had an expansive network of sources and contacts. He had taken Cheryl under his wing and mentored her about the tools of the trade. They had developed a special father-daughter bond, and when Cheryl relocated to Bekbourg and was offered the opportunity to become the owner of the *Bekbourg Tribune,* Milton retired from *The Cleveland Presenter* and moved to Bekbourg to help Cheryl run her newspaper. Cheryl was happy that, in the process, Milton had found the love of his life, Martha Bolton.

"Hey, Milton, I've run up against a brick wall on finding the identity of the body found in the aftermath of the '57 bridge collapse. Do you have time to talk about it?"

"Sure, Cheryl, move that stack and have a seat." Milton's office was packed with file folders, papers, journal and books, but he knew where everything was amidst the clutter.

She explained her review of all the railroad documents, the *Tribune's* archives, and the sheriff's files. She relayed her conversation with the old sheriff, Jack Rhodes.

When she finished, Milton pulled out a gum wrapper and replaced the gum he was chewing with a fresh stick. A few years back, a heart attack had forced him to substitute gum for cigarettes. He picked up a pencil and slid it above his ear. "Okay, we know the body got in the creek somewhere, and there was no missing person's report. Now, it's possible someone went missing and it wasn't reported. If that's the case, the man could have been from around Bekbourg, but without a missing person's report, we don't have any way of knowing."

"I could write a story about the unidentified man being found and see if anyone comes forward," suggested Cheryl. "It's worked for me before."

Milton scratched his chin and thought for a minute. "You could, but let's explore a couple of options. Hold on a sec." He walked over to a bookcase and rummaged through a stack. "Ah ha." He pulled something out and walked over and spread a map over the papers and files lying on his desk. "I bought this when I moved to Bekbourg. Let's have a look." He and Cheryl stood leaning over the map. "Here's Norton Creek, and here's where the railroad runs," he said pointing. "This is where the bridge was—about here." He studied the map. "We know there were heavy rains all spring, and all these waterways had been flooded," he circled a large area with his finger. "What if the body was washed downstream into Norton Creek from somewhere else?"

Cheryl's eyes sparkled. "Somewhere northeast of Bekbourg, you're saying?"

They both looked closer at the map. "There was farmland all up and down this area," Milton said. "If someone was going to be reported missing, it would be to the sheriff in the county where it happened. The next county up in this area is Tapsaw." He continued to study the map. "See this small town here."

Cheryl nodded, "Saltzburg."

"Yeah. Maybe you should check the sheriff's files in Tapsaw County and see if they have any missing person reports for the time period. I'd also check the police records in Saltzburg and see if they have anything."

Cheryl jerked her head up. "You're brilliant! I knew you would have some ideas."

Milton nodded for her to sit as he sat down. "One more thing comes to mind you might want to check. You've got a copy of the autopsy that was done, but let's face it—the local medical examiner didn't have the equipment or special training that an expert in forensic pathology has. I know a fellow in Cleveland who works in a private practice. Families go to him for second opinions on causes of death. I can give him a call and see if he'd take a look at the autopsy report. I don't know if it'd do any good, but it might."

Cheryl shook her head, "Another brilliant idea. He might find something that is more conclusive as to the cause of death."

"Maybe, or maybe not, but it's worth knowing either way." Cheryl agreed.

That evening, Cheryl told Sean about her conversation with Milton and her plans to visit the Tapsaw County sheriff's department and the police station in Saltzburg. Sean frowned.

"What's wrong?" Cheryl asked. "You don't think that's a good idea?"

"It's not that. I just don't like the idea of you going over to the sheriff's office in Tapsaw."

Cheryl's lips shifted to one side. "I see. But it's not like I'm going to talk about the Pinkstons."

"Hell, I hope they weren't involved."

Cheryl grinned. "You don't really think they were, do you? The Pinkston family lived in Bekbourg at the time. Zeke's the one who moved to Tapsaw as a young man."

Sean was still frowning, "I wouldn't put anything past the Pinkstons then or now, but I've had some dealings with the sheriff there—Elmer Puckett. I don't like the idea of you anywhere near that outfit."

Cheryl's eyes lit with humor. "Honey, I'll be fine. I'm just going to ask to see some missing person reports—ancient history to them."

Cheryl could tell when Sean's emotions were churning because his eyes darkened—like now. She grinned. "If something starts to happen, I'll tell them you're my husband, and that should handle it."

Sean dead panned, "I'll have to come break you out of jail."

Her laughter filled the room. "It'll be fine."

Sean's frown deepened. "I want you to be careful."

Cheryl tilted her head to the side. "Would it make you feel better if I took Milton? He'd probably enjoy himself."

Relief posted on Sean's face, but just slightly. "That's better than you going by yourself."

Cheryl rose and moved over and nudged his arm away and sat on his lap. "I'll take Milton to Tapsaw *and* Saltzburg." His eyes were bright as he watched her lean to gently kiss his lips. Cheryl's humor was bubbling beneath the surface. "We won't speed or run stop signs." She planted another feather-like kiss. "Now, let's think about something else."

As she leaned in to kiss him with a lot more passion, Sean forgot to mumble that his concerns were not allayed.

Chapter 37

"Hey, Boss," Kim greeted Sean when he walked in, "my cousin called me at home last night and told me something I thought you might be interested in about Vera Keller." Sean braced himself, because Kim liked to be thorough with facts. She had been around law enforcement a long time and knew when something seemed relevant—it was just a matter of her winding through the tale.

She sat across from him and leaned forward with her hands in her lap. "We caught up on some things, but then she brought up the murder story in the *Bekbourg Tribune*. My cousin's son is best friends with Miles Olson, Teri and Gerald's son. They are freshman at Schriever High School. When my cousin read that the victim was Vera Keller, she knew Vera was Teri's sister."

Sean leaned back in his chair to listen.

"So, on the night of the party—well, let me back up. Teri called my cousin and asked if Miles could stay with them while she and Gerald attended. She wasn't going, so she was fine with that. She even offered for Miles to spend the night and let them pick him up at church the next morning.

Champ, Miles' boxer, is like part of my cousin's family, so he was staying over, too."

Sean was barely staying focused, but figured something important was coming. Soon—he hoped.

"The boys decided they wanted to play Miles' video game, so she drove them back to his house so he could run in and get the game. Champ and Miles went inside. Here's something else. He told her his dad had recently given him a house key. They never used to lock their door. Anyway, when he unlocked the door, Champ started acting funny and high-tailed it up the stairs and was sniffing at the guest bedroom door. Miles got the video game and yelled for Champ, who wouldn't come down, so he went up and opened the door to show Champ there wasn't anything in there.

"When he opened the door, there were a couple of suitcases there, and he smelled cigarette smoke, which he knows his mother doesn't like. When he and Champ got back in the car, he told my cousin about it. She didn't know what to think and just figured they were having guests and hadn't told Miles. Now she wonders if they belonged to Vera, because she remembered Vera was a smoker."

Sean asked, "Do you know if your cousin mentioned this to Teri or Gerald?"

"I asked her, and she said she hadn't. She wasn't sure if Miles had though."

"Did Miles spend the night?"

"I don't know."

187

"Okay. Thanks, Kim. I need your cousin's name and address."

"Got it right here, Boss," she said as she handed it to him.

Chapter 38

Sean and Alex pulled into the driveway and killed the engine. No lights shone from within, and the October cold spell had withered the ferns, adding bleakness to a lusterless house. Sean wondered *what secrets were tucked behind the house walls. What were Teri and Gerald hiding?* Gray clouds hung heavy, and an unusual chilling dampness prompted Sean to tug his coat closer around his neck and push his hat tighter on his head as he started to approach the house.

He heard a dog wolfing an alert, and before he reached the door, Gerald swung it open. He was unshaven, and weariness wore on his face. The house felt cold, and Sean wondered how Gerald stayed warm in the faded short-sleeve t-shirt. Gerald ordered the dog away from Sean and motioned Sean and Alex inside.

"I guess you're here to talk to Teri about Vera. She's working today. I can have her call you when she gets home."

"Actually, Gerald, we're here to talk to you."

"Oh, Okay. Have a seat in here," he said pointing to the living room off the entry way.

189

Sean asked questions leading up to the inquiry he was particularly interested in covering.

"So, you and Teri drove separately, and you left early to come back here and watch the football game?"

"Yep."

"Did you go out after that?"

"No."

"Where was your son?"

"Spending the night with a friend."

"Did you know Teri went by the motel to see Vera the night of the party?"

"Yeah, she told me. Vera wasn't there. The clerk told her she had checked out."

"Why did she want to talk to her?"

"To ask her to leave town. Look, Sean, we didn't want her here. She was a nutcase. We're going through enough right now. The last thing we needed was for her to come back here."

"Did you know where Vera was going to stay?"

Gerald wiped his face. "I didn't give a shit what she did as long as she left us alone."

"Did she plan to stay here?"

"She wanted to, but Teri told her 'no.'"

"But Vera had other plans?"

"What the hell, Sean? What the hell is this all about?" Gerald said as he stretched out his leg.

"Did Teri know about Vera leaving her suitcases here?" Suspecting Gerald had found the luggage, he asked the probing question.

190

Gerald's face reddened as he stared at Sean. Champ stood and laid his head on Gerald's thigh. Gerald rubbed Champ's head and looked at Sean. "That damn bitch. She must have still had a key to the house. After she was here the first time, we started locking our doors. We were concerned she would come by and walk in. I never thought to get the locks changed. Miles called me. They'd run by here to get something, and Champ must have smelled something. Miles saw the suitcases and asked if we were having company. I came home from the party, opened the door, and flicked on the light. Sure as hell, the room smelled like smoke, and sitting by the bed was a suitcase and duffel bag. I knew right away it had to be hers."

"What did you do?"

"I carried them to the shed out back. I didn't want Teri to know. I had already told Miles not to say anything to his mother."

"What did you plan to do with the luggage?"

"I wasn't going to let her in the house. That's for damn sure."

"Did she come back that evening after you found the luggage?"

"No, she didn't show up here after I got home."

"Weren't you curious about why she didn't show up that night?"

"A little bit, but no one ever knew what in the hell Vera was going to do. For all I knew she was sleeping off a drunk, or maybe sleeping with

191

one. I slept with one eye open to make sure I heard if she pulled up the driveway, which she didn't. When I got home with Miles the next evening, Teri told me you had come by and told her Vera was dead."

"You didn't think she might show up while you were gone to pick up Miles?"

"Well, if she had, Teri wouldn't have let her in the house."

"What were you going to do with the suitcase and duffel?"

"I hadn't even thought about that. Teri never goes out to the shed."

"Why didn't you call me about it?"

He looked guilty. "Well, I never thought to. What would her stuff being here have anything to do with her being killed?"

"You should have called me, Gerald. We need to take the luggage. I'd also like to have a look at the bedroom where you found it."

"Sure, Sean."

"Also, I'd like to see the sweater you wore that night." Sean remembered speaking to Gerald at the party, and he was wearing a dark sweater. He could not remember the color."

"What?" Gerald shook his head. "You think I killed her? This is unbelievable. Even with her dead, she's raising hell in our lives."

"I remember you were wearing a dark-colored sweater at the party. What color was it?"

Gerald shook his head. "It was gray. Teri saw a moth hole in it after I put it on to wear to the party. I guess one got in during the summer. Those damn things like wool. She made a fuss and wanted me to change, but I told her I wasn't changing. No one would notice, and even if they did, I didn't give a shit."

"Where's the sweater?"

"She gathered it up with a few other things and took them to the donation bin. I didn't know she was going to do it. She said she'd buy me a new one for Christmas. Hell, we don't have money to buy clothes."

"Where did she take it?"

"Hell, I don't know, Sean. I don't know why you're so interested in my sweater. I didn't kill her—that much I can tell you."

Sean followed Gerald upstairs and looked around the room. Gerald pointed out where the luggage was sitting. Gerald explained that he didn't touch anything else in the room when he went in to grab the luggage. Assuming what he told Sean was true, it appeared that Vera had dropped the luggage and then left—likely heading to the party.

Vera's luggage was sitting just inside the doors of the unlocked tool shed.

"That seems awfully convenient that Teri gave away Gerald's sweater," said Alex as they drove back to the station.

"Especially since they are going through such a hard time financially," agreed Sean. "But I

193

remember my mother would give away sweaters with moth holes." Sean grinned, "Drove my dad crazy."

"Do you believe him that he didn't tell his wife about finding the suitcases?"

"I can see that, especially since she told him Vera had checked out of the motel. I can see him not wanting to upset her."

"That's another thing, Boss. She had been gone for fourteen years. How did they know she hadn't changed? They wouldn't even let her stay with them for a few nights."

"I've been thinking the same thing, Alex. There is more there than they're telling us. We need to look closer into that situation. They said they had no contact during all the years she was gone, but ask Syd to see if she can find any records of contacts between them. Another thing—it doesn't take long to drive between downtown and their house. Gerald had time to go back to the party after he found the luggage and get back home before Teri did."

Alex turned to face Sean. "You think he found that luggage and blew up and then went there and killed her?"

"We can't rule anything out. I need for you to run the luggage to Ronnie Vin in Columbus for a forensic check. I'm going to ask Arlo to check around and see if anyone saw Gerald after he claims he left the party."

Chapter 39

Varying shades of gray and silver heads leaned over the card table as the four retired school teachers contemplated their bids.

Milly pursed her bright pink lips as she contemplated whether to overbid Lucia or pass. "What to do?" muttered Milly to herself. "You certainly put a fly in the ointment, Dear, with that bid." Milly finally decided she could not bid, so she passed.

Lucia smiled at Milly, who always had her pink lipstick freshly applied. "You're rarely stumped, Milly, so your hand must be unusual."

If Milly was not looking at people's lips, she missed much of what was said. She happened to have been looking at Lucia and replied, "It is most unusual, even for an old math teacher like me."

The four women enjoyed their weekly bridge game. It not only gave them a chance to play a game they loved, but they caught up on the latest news and sometimes relived their time in the teaching profession. After they played the hand, it was time to change partners, so Ann suggested a break to refill coffee cups.

"What tragic news about Vera Keller being killed," Ann said as she poured the coffee.

"It was," agreed Kye. "And it's my understanding she had just returned to town. She had been gone a long time."

"Did any of you have her in class?" asked Ann, who was the only elementary school teacher.

Milly frowned, "I did. She was one of those troubled students. She was capable of doing the work, but I could never get her to apply herself the way I thought she could. Her father had unexpectedly died, and I know the family was going through a hard time. I tried to work with her. She passed, thank goodness, but I was never sure how much she had really learned. I think she memorized just enough to get through the tests."

Ann spoke up. "She was in my class at the elementary school. Her mother was such a nice woman. She volunteered when parents were needed, and I know she worked a lot with Vera on her school work."

Ann looked at the other three women, "I worried about the situation. Vera's mother called me one afternoon. A mother of one of the girls in Vera's class had called her and complained about Vera picking on her. During class, Vera would make faces at her, and at recess she supposedly said things that hurt the girl's feelings. I had not seen any of this, but I moved Vera to the front row where I could keep an eye on her. I was more attentive during recess. Later on, I overheard other teachers talking about Vera picking on children, but I tried to tune it out. I hoped she would grow out of whatever she was going through."

Lucia was a retired Spanish teacher. She spoke up and told them that whatever bullying habits Vera had in elementary school had carried forward into high school. A good friend of hers, the high school art teacher, had confided in her about Vera. Vera had taken art classes for three years. She enjoyed art, but she particularly loved painting.

Another student, Tiffany Porter, was in the same grade and same art classes. Where Vera had good technique, Tiffany was a prodigy—"Once in a lifetime art student," Lucia told the three women. The art teacher tried to treat all the students fair, but Tiffany's exceptional gift could not be overlooked. The teacher displayed Tiffany's paintings around the school during special parent events and reached out to her contacts in Columbus and Cincinnati about Tiffany's talent.

"Tiffany's mother is a well-known artist, isn't she?" asked Ann.

"Yes. Where Tiffany was a painter, her mother Nell's medium is clay," responded Lucia. "It was tragic what happened to Tiffany."

Ann set down her coffee cup. "I vaguely remember something about her death. She committed suicide, didn't she?"

"Yes," said Lucia, "but the art teacher who knew both girls well was really shaken up by what happened. During their senior year, Tiffany confided in the art teacher—saying that Vera and another girl were bullying her. The teacher asked how she could help, but Tiffany was insecure and didn't want the teacher to do or say anything. She was afraid it would make things worse. The teacher felt her hands were tied, but she kept the girls separated during class so Vera did not have an opportunity to do anything.

"Tiffany was a sweet, sensitive child according to the art teacher. She was incredibly gifted, but at the same time, she was socially fragile. Later in the school year, the principal informed her that Tiffany was going to be home schooled and arrangements were made with her mother, Nell, to see that she completed her course work so she would be eligible to graduate. My friend never came out and said it, but I think she thought Vera's bullying may have played a factor in what happened to Tiffany."

"I always thought Vera's mother, Viola, had her hands full," said Kye. "Her husband was gone a lot on business, and when he was in town, he wanted her with him for all the social dinners, golf outings, and things like that. They lived with her mother in that large house, and when her mother's health started failing, she took care of her. That was when Vera and Teri were growing up. Her mother died, and then Viola's husband died suddenly with a heart attack, and she was left to finish raising her daughters."

"And now Teri—what she must be going through," Lucia said as she picked up the cards to deal. "All she has been through with Gerald, and now Vera being killed."

"That's a lot," murmured Ann.

Chapter 40

Kye and Buddy were returning from a stroll when Cheryl came walking up the sidewalk from the opposite direction. Kye dropped Buddy's leash just in time for him to sprint toward Cheryl— wagging his tail in greeting. Kye waited for Cheryl and Buddy to meet at the walk leading to the duplex. Kye owned the duplex, and Cheryl and Sean rented one side from her. Not only was Kye their landlord, but they all had come to think of each other as family. Kye took care of Buddy, their Chocolate Lab, when they were away. "He saw you before I did, but I knew it must be either you or Sean when I heard him whine."

They were laughing as Buddy raced ahead to the porch that ran across the front of the duplex. "It's amazing, but Buddy knows to be careful with you. If it had been me or Sean holding the leash, he would have just lunged ahead. He does that all the time when he sees squirrels."

"I was going to fix some coffee. Do you have time to join me and catch up?" asked Kye.

"I'd love that. I'll join you in just a minute."

Kye poured Cheryl's coffee when she heard the door open. They talked for a few minutes, and Cheryl asked if Kye had won in bridge. Kye smiled, "It was one of those days. I only had opening points twice. Lucia had all the cards today."

"I guess that's one of the fun things about bridge—you never know what to expect."

"So true, Dear. No hand is ever the same. Even Milly was stumped today in bidding, and that is rare." Kye sipped her coffee, "I haven't seen much in the newspaper about Vera's murder."

Cheryl shrugged. "No. I guess when the Sheriff's department has something to report, we'll know."

Kye smiled, "I should hope you'll be one of the first to know."

They both laughed. "We talked about it during our bridge game today. I remember Vera was a problem student, and of course, I knew she was a bully, but I didn't realize the extent her bullying had affected one of the students."

"What do you mean?"

Kye told Cheryl about Tiffany Porter committing suicide, and that a teacher close to Tiffany at the time thought Vera's meanness toward her had been a contributing factor.

"That was terrible, Kye."

"Yes, it was. Tiffany was an only child. Her mother is a very talented artist from Bekbourg. Her name is Nell. She's a recluse, so I was surprised when I heard she had taken a booth for her ceramics in Dillie's gallery."

"I remember seeing her work the night of the party. I took pictures for the newspaper story we ran of the grand opening."

"That's where I read about it. But Vera was not alone. I remember Vera and another girl bullied kids. They were always together. I assume they were friends."

"Who was the other one?"

"Tanya Ellis. I don't know that either had other friends. I always just saw those two together. A student who I was close to during their junior year revealed to me in confidence that Vera and Tanya were bullying her. We discussed possible ways for her to handle it. I offered to talk to the guidance counselor for her, but she didn't want me to. We left it up in the air. I told her she could talk to me about it anytime. She never did, but I think after that, she went out of her way to avoid both girls."

Cheryl arched an eyebrow. "The woman who is a waitress at Frau's? That's who you're talking about?"

Kye nodded.

"Huh. She's waited on me. Not the friendliest person, but she does a decent job. She's kind of rough around the edges, but I never pictured her as a bully."

"Well, people change over time. She may have changed since high school."

"Did you know Vera's family well?"

Kye repeated what she knew about Vera's parents.

"Do you know why Vera left town?" asked Cheryl.

"Here is what I remember. Viola, Vera and Teri's mother, was sick for a while before she died. Teri tried to keep her in the house as long as she could, but the last few months, they had to put her in the hospital, and Teri stayed there almost around the clock.

"After Viola died, I guess it was too much for Vera, because I understand she left town. I heard she had something like a nervous breakdown, and so poor Teri had to go stay with her. She was taking care of Vera at the same time she was pregnant. Anyway, Vera never came back as far as I know until recently. Things finally settled down for Teri, Gerald and Miles, their son. But, bad luck struck again for Teri when her husband had that accident, and now this with Vera. That poor woman can't seem to get a break."

"So, Teri had to stay with Vera while she recovered from the nervous breakdown?"

"Yes. It was several months. I just remember Miles was born about the time she returned home. He may have even been born while she was away. I don't remember."

Chapter 41

During dinner that evening, Cheryl told Sean of her conversation with Kye about Tiffany Porter. "Isn't that terrible that Vera may have had something to do with Tiffany committing suicide? Maybe even Tanya if she was in on the bullying, and it sounds like she may have been."

Sean frowned. "I never heard about that. She was Nell Porter's daughter?"

"That's what Kye said. She said Nell is mostly a recluse. Do you know her?"

"I met her the other day at the gallery when I went by to talk with Frederic." Sean took a bite and considered what Cheryl had told him. "Do you think Tiffany would have told her mother about Vera bullying her?"

Cheryl's eyes darted to meet his. "If they were close, I think she would have. You think Nell could have killed Vera?"

"I don't know, but if Nell blames Vera for her daughter's death, that is a motive." Sean paused. "You said Tanya and Vera were a bullying team against Nell's daughter. What strikes me is, if she blamed them for her daughter's death, Nell had all this time to do something to Tanya but hasn't. Why would she kill Vera now, and why not Tanya?"

"Mmm. My brilliant husband sees all the angles."

Sean's eyebrow arched as he grinned. "I sure see what's sitting right in front of me."

Cheryl giggled, "Yeah?"

"Yeah, and I sure like the view. Maybe I should investigate closer and see if there's anything I'm missing."

They both were laughing as they rose to clear the table.

Sean asked Kim to pull the file on Tiffany's death. The mother, Nell, had been working in her shop and did not know Tiffany had left in the car. When she discovered Tiffany was gone, she assumed she had gone to the store. When she had not returned by the time it started to get dark, she called the police. The file reflected Nell was frantic. It took two days before a deputy decided to drive up to the quarry and found Nell's car. Records showed she drove her mother's car to the quarry one afternoon and jumped off the side. According to the report, there was no evidence of foul play. There was no alcohol or drugs found in her system.

Tiffany did not have any close friends. The police interviewed personnel at the school. Notes in the file from those conversations said she was a loner and aloof. Her grades were mediocre except in art class, where she was considered gifted.

Chapter 42

The house was not visible from the road. The cruiser wound along on the bumpy gravel driveway until they saw an older model SUV. Dense trees and a ground cluttered with decaying leaves boxed in the small brick house. As he and Syd walked to the small porch, Sean noticed how quiet the area was. It was a stillness not to be equated with tranquility, though, he thought. Sunlight, unable to penetrate the denseness of the tree canopy, solidified the melancholy of the surroundings.

Syd rapped on a drab fiberglass door. They waited, forcing her to knock twice more. They were almost ready to leave when Nell opened the door enough to peer through the space beneath the night chain. When she saw it was them, she closed the door to remove the chain and opened the door.

"Ms. Porter. We met at Dillie's gallery the other day. I'm Sheriff Neumann. This is Deputy Syd Johnson. We'd like to talk to you. Can we come in?"

"Okay." The room was sparse except for an old, lumpy sofa, two faded chairs, and a small oak table at the end of the sofa. No books, magazines or television. No pictures or throw pillows. Not even

Nell's ceramics were visible. "Please sit wherever you like."

"Thank you." Nell's apron had wet spots. "I'm sorry if we interrupted you working."

She looked at her apron. "It's okay. I was spinning a bowl and had to finish. What can I do for you?"

"We're investigating the death of Vera Keller."

When she did not respond, Sean asked, "Ms. Porter, did you know Vera?"

Her eyes hardened. "No."

"Your daughter, Tiffany, was in school with Vera?"

"Yes, but I never met her then."

"I understand that Tiffany was bullied." Nell's brown eyes darkened as she looked at Sean.

Syd intervened and gentled her voice, "Vera was abusive to your daughter, wasn't she, Ms. Porter?"

Nell shifted her attention to Syd. After a while, she spoke, "Yes, she was. That girl was evil. She tormented my poor Tiffany beyond what she could handle. Tiffany was a gentle soul." Her eyes softened as she talked about her daughter, but the chill was noticeable when she thought about Vera. "That evil girl couldn't leave her alone. She couldn't stop making fun of her clothes or her shyness. She couldn't stop saying cruel things to her when other kids were around. She couldn't stop until she drove my Tiffany to kill herself."

"Did Tiffany tell you Vera did this?" Syd was tender as she spoke.

"Yes. At first another girl was cruel to my daughter, but Vera Keller was the worst abuser."

"Why do you say that?"

"She told *vicious* lies about my Tiffany. She said she was sleeping with a boy. Tiffany couldn't take the embarrassment. She quit going to school. Even though she was cut off from the abuse at school, she couldn't shake what she knew kids had been doing—talking about her and laughing at her."

"Was it Tanya Ellis who also bullied Tiffany?" Nell nodded. "How do you know Tanya wasn't involved in the rumors?"

Nell had connected with Syd's empathy. "Tiffany didn't say her name when she talked about the rumors. She only talked about Vera Keller."

"Did you know Vera was back in town?" Nell nodded. "Did you talk to her?"

"She came to the gallery to talk to Dillie, and Dillie introduced us, but there was no reason. As soon as I heard her name, I knew who she was."

"Do you know if she recognized you?"

"She didn't act like she recognized me. Someone like that probably doesn't even remember my Tiffany and what she put her through."

"Did you see her after that day when Dillie introduced you?"

"I saw her at the party, but I was busy at my booth. The less I saw her, the better."

"Did she come up to your booth?"

"No."

"I understand you went into the kitchen area that night. Do you remember that?" Sean asked.

"Yes. I was so busy that I hadn't eaten since that morning. I asked the man in the booth next to mine to cover for me. I went to the kitchen to get something to eat—away from all the customers. I wasn't comfortable eating in front of people."

As he and Syd stood to leave, Sean turned and said, "Ms. Porter, I'm sorry about what happened to Tiffany. I'm sorry for your loss."

She looked into Sean's eyes—as if she was searching his soul. "You're a good person, Sheriff." She looked at Syd, "Your soul is gentle."

As they pulled away, Sean asked Syd what she thought. "I think she could have killed Vera."

"Do you think she did it?"

Syd was quiet as she considered his question. "I don't know. If she killed her, she got revenge for Tiffany's death in her mind and probably feels it was justified. On the other hand, she puts a lot of herself into her artwork—she obviously cares about her pottery."

Sean considered Syd's response, "Don't most murderers feel justified?" he asked in reply.

Syd answered, "Yes, that's probably right. All our persons of interest felt they were justified in their feelings against Vera."

Sean agreed, "Only one felt strong enough to act on it, and we need to find who that was."

Chapter 43

Cheryl and Milton drove to the Tapsaw County sheriff's station and asked to look at the missing person's records for 1957. They explained that they were doing a story about the anniversary of the reopening of the Norton Creek railroad bridge and learned that a body had been discovered during the cleanup but never identified.

At first, the deputy did not understand how Tapsaw County could be involved, but after they explained the possibility of a body washing downstream in the heavy rains that spring, he wrote down their contact information and said he needed to talk to the sheriff and would get back with them.

They made a similar stop in Saltzburg, a city which had its own police department. There, the deputy was more accommodating and told them he would need to locate files for that time period and would call.

She had to follow-up with the deputy in Tapsaw, but he finally came through. The only missing person's report was of a woman who was reported missing by her husband. It later turned out she had left him for another man. The deputy in Saltzburg called and told Cheryl he had pulled the files for 1957, but he did not have time to look through them.

Occasion of Murder

When Cheryl and Milton arrived at the Saltzburg police station, they were shown into a small, windowless room, with a small table and some chairs. Five boxes were on the table. It did not take Cheryl long to find a file in the third box that raised interest. She put it aside, and they finished their review. She asked the clerk if she could copy the file, but the clerk offered to. Cheryl and Milton thanked the clerk and officer in charge, took the copy to a nearby coffee shop, and started reading.

On May 14, 1957, a woman named Deffy Patterson reported her brother, Hap Lewis, missing. He was forty-years old and lived with his wife, Bethanne. His description given in the missing persons file closely resembled the one in the autopsy report.

Cheryl and Milton went to the courthouse to see what they could find out about Hap, his sister Deffy, and his wife, Bethanne. Deffy and her husband were deceased, as was Bethanne. Milton suggested they visit people living in the vicinity where Deffy had lived at the time. Since she had filed the missing person's report, they might remember something.

The area was still rural and sparsely populated with most farm houses over a century old. No one answered the door at the house once occupied by Deffy and her husband. A nearby house looked deserted. The third home they stopped at was owned by a retired couple who had been teachers. They had moved to the area about ten years before and started raising miniature schnauzers. They knew nothing about Deffy or her brother.

The day was growing short, so Cheryl and Milton decided to return home. Because they had not eaten lunch, they stopped in a local diner ahead of the dinner crowd. An older waitress yelled over for them to sit wherever they wanted and that she would "be right over." Varying styles of antique tables and chairs filled the room, and old pictures and antique implements hung on the walls. Only two tables had patrons, who glanced at Cheryl and Milton and then turned back to their business.

They sat at a table next to a wall and surveyed the surroundings. "I bet they have good coffee," Milton said as he slid a menu from its holder.

"Mmm. I'm hungrier than I thought," Cheryl said as she picked up her menu.

The waitress approached with a water pitcher and filled their glasses. "How're you folks doin'?" Milton told her they were visiting from Bekbourg, which opened a dialogue. "Been there a couple of times. I have a cousin who lives there. It's a lot like Saltzburg. She's been wantin' me to come down again and visit. Probably should do that before I die." They all three laughed.

"What brings you up here?" she asked when she brought their coffee. Cheryl told her and mentioned Deffy Patterson.

"Well, I'll be. Deffy was my aunt."

Cheryl's eyes widened. "Oh! We'd love to talk to you. Deffy's the one who filed the missing person's report about Hap Lewis, her brother."

"That's right." She looked around. "Let me turn you all's order in, and I'll be right back. Saully won't mind if I talk to you all since it's not busy. I'll still need to tend to my customers, but that won't be hard to do. By the way, my name's Minnie."

Cheryl and Milton could not believe their luck. Minnie hurried off to put in their order. She checked on the other two tables and returned to tell them about Deffy and Hap.

"Like you said, Deffy's brother was Hap. He was a hothead but a hard worker and a good man. His wife, Bethanne, had the prettiest face and long, wavy brown hair. She looked like a china doll and was as sweet as all gets. Deffy didn't mean to be disrespectful, but she always said that the one thing Bethanne didn't have was smarts, so someone could pull the wool over her eyes if they had a mind to.

"Bethanne was about ten years younger than Hap. Hap was in the War, and when he got back, he bought thirty acres north of town and farmed the lower fields. At the upper end of his property was a real nice stand of hardwood. He met Bethanne and decided on the spot he wanted her as his wife. Of course, they courted for a few weeks, and then Hap told Bethanne's father he wanted to marry her—that he would support her and treat her right. So, they got married and lived on his place and were happy by all accounts.

"Thing was, there were these two Schuster brothers who were mean as snakes, and they were greedy. I'm tellin' you all this so you have the background. Right now, though, I need to get your food before it gets cold."

Minnie brought their plates and, after checking on the other two tables and cashing out one table, she returned to continue her tale. "Now, where was I? Oh yeah. Bethanne's old man died after she and Hap married—not right away, but it wasn't too many years. Her mother had passed away when she was about twelve, and she didn't have no other kin to speak of. Hap was true to his word in takin' care of her.

"Now, there wasn't no love lost between Hap and the Schuster brothers. Best way to describe them was they were con artists. Well, around the early 50's, a big furniture maker out of North Carolina came 'round here wantin' to purchase lumber. Them Schusters somehow convinced the company they could represent their interest in getting rights to lumber. And they did. They got a lot of people 'round here who had timber to sign over their rights, and the Schusters got a percentage. Dependin' on how smart people were made a difference in how much their percentage was—if you know what I mean. Them Schusters made sure they got the most they could.

"Hap's timber was likely the best 'round here. It was prime virgin forest with different kinds of trees—just what the furniture company was looking for. You know, back then, there wasn't enough trees to satisfy the demand for good furniture. Hap had no interest in selling his timber and wouldn't talk to the company or the Schusters. When they went back up after being warned to stay away, he run them off his property and told them never to step foot on it again unless they wanted their backsides filled with buckshot."

Minnie took a deep breath. "Now, here's where it started gettin' interestin'."

Just then, several people walked in. "Oh, Lordy. I forgot it's Wilma's birthday. I'm sorry, but I got to take care of them. There's a lot more to the story, but I can't talk anymore right now." Minnie invited them to her house a couple of days later. She told them she would try to find the scrapbook containing pictures of Deffy, Hap and Bethanne.

On the drive back, Milton realized he had a conflict. "It's okay, Milton. I can drive up and meet with Minnie."

When Milton exhaled, "Shit," Cheryl grinned, "I promise to take good notes."

He looked over, "Yeah. It's just that I love being part of tracking down the story. I've had fun today."

"Me, too," Cheryl smiled. "It's been a great day."

Chapter 44

"Good morning beautiful." Sean had already been on his morning run and was sitting in their small kitchen sipping coffee with Buddy lying at his feet.

Cheryl smiled, "Nothing like walking into the kitchen and seeing a handsome lawman dressed in uniform."

She walked to him and sat on his lap and kissed him deeply. "Mmm. You taste like coffee," she said as she pulled back.

"Here, let's make sure it's the right flavor before you pour yourself a cup."

She was smiling as he gave her another passionate kiss. Her eyes were glowing when she pulled back to see the glint in his eyes. "Yep, I'm sure that's the coffee I want. I better get up and pour some before we get delayed."

He laughed as she rose. She refreshed his coffee and set out a scone for each of them. "We never have to worry about running out of fresh pastries with Bri's B&B. These are strawberry."

"Look great. So, what does my newspaper owner wife have planned for the day?"

Cheryl glanced at him, but he was reaching for the mug. She hoped she could manage to avoid raising his suspicion. "I've got to run up to Columbus today. There's something I'm working on. If I don't think I'll be back in time for dinner, I'll call and let you know."

He looked at her, "Does this have to do with the railroad story you're working on?"

"No, it's something else. It may turn out to be nothing."

"Have anything to do with your trip with Milton yesterday?"

"No, but we had a productive trip."

"Good. Well, drive safe."

"How's the investigation going into Vera's murder?"

Sean quirked the side of his mouth as he replied, "There's a lot we're sifting through. As you know, these things take time, but we'll get there."

"I know you will," she smiled.

Chapter 45

Sean and Syd were driving back from talking with the manager of the Shopper's Pavilion about a shoplifting problem when Arlo called. "Hey, Sheriff, didn't you tell me that Gerald said once he left the party, he didn't come back?"

"That's what he told me and Alex."

"Well, he may have lied. I talked to a person here in town who valet parked cars the night of the party. I was asking around to see if any of the valets remembered anyone coming in later the night of the party wanting their car parked or acting suspicious. When Gerald first arrived at the shindig, he had the valet park his car. He made a point of telling the valet he had a bad leg and didn't want to park a long way away.

"Then, when Gerald was ready to leave, the same guy pulled his car around. He remembers it clearly, because Gerald told him he wanted to get home and watch the game. Then, about nine or nine-thirty, he saw Gerald walking toward the tent area."

"He was positive of the time and that it was Gerald?" probed Sean.

"Oh, yeah, he was positive on both accounts. He looked at his watch because he was surprised to see him, since Gerald had left to go home and watch the game, and here he was back. His thought was Gerald was missing the game. He knows it was Gerald, because he knew he was the assistant fire chief."

Sean was quiet on the drive to the station. When they arrived, he asked Kim to have Alex and Arlo join him and Syd. Syd could tell her boss had something on his mind. "What's going on?"

"I'm debating whether to bring Gerald in. He lied about not going back to the party, so let's go over what we know about Gerald," Sean said. "Arlo, let's start with you."

"We know he and his wife did not want Vera around. They weren't happy at all about her returning to town."

Syd ask, "Why is that?"

Arlo rubbed his chin. "Chief, you want to address that?"

Sean was leaning back in the chair in the deputies' room. Arlo was standing at the white board, Alex was sitting on the edge of a desk, and Syd was learning back in a chair fumbling with a pencil. "That's a good question. I know what he and Teri told us—that Vera caused tension around the family and that she embarrassed them—but I think there's more. Whatever it is, they haven't told us."

"Okay," said Arlo. "There's a possible motive. Could be as simple as they didn't want her

219

back here, but there could be more." He looked at the officers, and seeing no dissent, he continued, "He was at the party, left, found Vera had left the luggage in the upstairs bedroom, and from what I learned earlier today, he drove back to the party."

Alex joined in, "And, don't forget he lied about not going back to the party, and he didn't tell us about finding the luggage in the house until the sheriff asked him."

"Yes, and the only way we found out about the luggage being there was by Kim's cousin telling her," said Arlo. "I guess the fact he didn't get rid of the luggage proves something."

Alex addressed that. "Maybe, but maybe he didn't kill her so he saw no reason to dispose of it."

"But it's also possible he was afraid of being seen trying to get rid of it, or maybe he hadn't had time to dispose of it. The fact it was in the shed where Miles and Teri likely wouldn't find it shows he was hiding it," Syd pointed out.

"Did forensics find anything of interest in Vera's suitcase and duffel?" asked Arlo.

All eyes turned toward Sean. "Gerald's fingerprints were on the handles. The techs didn't find anything on the zippers to suggest he had opened the luggage. It was only her fingerprints, so he didn't wipe the zippers. There was nothing suggesting who the killer might have been, but there was one thing of interest. At the bottom of the suitcase was a framed photograph of Vera and Teri. The frame looked to be the original—it was old.

Vera was young. They were holding hands and smiling in front of their house. They were wearing dresses. It looked like a spring day."

Silence momentarily filled the room. Alex broke the spell. "There's another important point. Gerald wore a dark gray sweater to the party. He said Teri gave away the sweater, because it had a moth hole. Since she had to work on Monday, she had been gathering up clothes and decided to drop them off on Sunday, the day after the party."

"Were you able to follow up with the charity that collects clothing?"

"Yes. I'm afraid I struck out," Arlo responded. "The weekend was a big drop off time, so they cleared out the clothes on Monday and sent them to the cleaners. From there, the donated items were sent to Athens, Ohio, where the charities say the need is greatest right now. I drove over there and talked to the people in charge. There was no way to find the sweater. It could be anywhere. There was no way to trace it."

"Pretty convenient for Teri and Gerald," said Syd.

"Getting back to the motive," said Alex, "when Gerald found the luggage, he realized Vera had been in their house uninvited and planned to move in. That could have set him off, and he knew Teri would be upset. They're not in a good place with all the stress and financial woes resulting from his injury. He could have just lost it."

Sean nodded. "That makes sense, but we don't have the murder weapon, and there wasn't DNA evidence on Vera to tie Gerald to the scene."

"What about Teri? We've talked a lot about Gerald, but could Teri have murdered Vera, and Gerald is covering for her?" asked Syd.

Sean arched an eyebrow. "Let's run with that for a minute. Teri had the most reason to want Vera to stay away. All the hurt and embarrassment was from her side. Gerald was impacted because Teri was, but she was emotionally vested."

"Agreed," said Alex. "She also returned to the party after learning Vera had checked out of the motel. She was there at the time Vera was killed."

"Maybe Gerald called and told her about the suitcases? He lied about not returning to the party. He could have lied when he said he didn't tell her."

"Good point, Arlo. Check phone records and see if there was any conversation between the two that night."

"Even though Gerald walks with a cane, he looks strong enough to have dragged Vera behind the hedge," said Alex.

"Yes, and Teri had to take care of Gerald in the early days after his accident, which involved helping him move around, so she had the body strength, too," added Sean.

Arlo reminded them, "Teri was also in the kitchen that night at the party."

"We'll ask her about that," said Sean.

"Do we know if she wore a gray sweater," Syd asked.

"Arlo said the motel clerk recalled her wearing a sweater. We need pictures of what our persons of interest wore that night," said Sean. "I know where we might get pictures of people who attended."

Arlo jumped on that. "You think you have a contact, Chief, who could look for those pictures?" Arlo feigned sincerity with wide eyes.

Alex joined it, "Yeah, don't you know the owner of the newspaper? They had a big spread about the party in Sunday morning's edition. I bet they took lots of pictures of the guests." Alex and Arlo exchanged smirks.

"I think the newspaper might be able to help," Sean dead panned. "We need to break this log jam. Arlo, let me know what you find out about the phone records, and then Alex and I will go talk to Gerald. Maybe we can time it so Teri gets home after we've talked to Gerald and ask her some questions. I'd like to see how those two interact. One more thing: any luck with the caterer about locating the food preparer who saw the crazy woman in the kitchen that night?"

"No, but Syd or I call every day."

"We need to see if any of the co-workers know how to get in touch with the food preparer."

"We have, Chief. The guy doesn't have a cell phone, and he wasn't close with the other workers, so they don't know who the sick relative might be."

"Well, stay on that. I have a feeling it may be important."

Chapter 46

Gerald answered the door, and even though Champ was happy to see visitors, Gerald did not share his enthusiasm. "Sean, Alex, you men back again so soon?"

"We've got some more questions, Gerald. Can we come in?"

Gerald raised an eyebrow at Sean's directness. "Sure."

After they sat, Gerald asked, "So what questions do you have?"

"Let's start with why you lied to me, Gerald. I can charge you for that."

Gerald scowled, "When did I lie to you?"

"About not returning to the party after you got home. You didn't stay here like you told us. You went back to the party, Gerald. You arrived in time to have killed Vera."

"Wait just a damn minute," Gerald barked, causing Champ to stir at his feet.

"What happened, Gerald? Did you find the luggage and blew your stack and went back to the party and killed her?"

"I don't know what in hell you're talking about!"

"Don't lie to me again, Gerald, or we'll arrest you right now."

Gerald put his face in his hands. Sean noticed Gerald's hair was beginning to thin on top. He roughly wiped his hands down his face and sat up. "Okay. I found the damn luggage, and I brought it downstairs. My first thought was to throw it on the lawn and let her find it when she came back. I was furious. We had been keeping our doors locked because of her. We didn't want her coming into the house while we were away, and Vera would have." His voice rose, "She did exactly what we knew she would do."

He paused and lowered his voice. "I didn't want Miles to start asking questions, so I loaded it in my car and drove to the party to find Vera. The party was winding down, and I couldn't find her. So, I decided to take it and put it in the shed. If she came back, I was going to give it to her and tell her to stay the hell away. I would have taken it to the motel where she was staying, but Teri had called me on her way back to the party and said Vera had checked out."

Arlo had found the record of Teri calling Gerald. "Did you tell Teri about finding Vera's luggage?"

He hesitated, "Yeah, I did. I wanted her to tell her sister if she saw her she wasn't moving in, and that I would drop off her luggage wherever she wanted me to, but she wasn't coming back here."

"Why all the lying, Gerald?"

"God, I don't know! It looked bad, Sean. Hell, I ain't no police officer, but it looked bad that I had the luggage and then went back to the party. I didn't kill her." Gerald threw himself back in the chair, "Damnit! Vera was off in the head. She poisoned everyone around her. She made Teri's life a living hell. We thought we were rid of her, and she shows up wanting money and to move back in here."

Sean looked at Gerald, "What do you mean you thought you were rid of her?"

Gerald's eyes widened, "Just that she was no longer living in town."

Sean studied Gerald, wondering if there was more to the story. "Is that the only reason?"

"Yeah, she told us she was leaving Bekbourg and not coming back, and we believed her. At least we hoped like hell that was the truth."

Champ jumped up and ran to the door—his backside in full waging motion as he waited for the front door to open. Teri pushed it, walked into the living room, and looked around. She quickly registered the somber mood and turned to Gerald, "Is everything okay?"

He did not look at her. Her face tightened, and she looked at Sean. "What's happened?"

"You might want to sit down, Teri. We have some questions about Vera's death." Teri looked at Gerald, but he was looking straight ahead. "Teri, did you see Vera when you got back to the party the night after you left the motel?"

227

She shook her head, "No, I didn't see her."

"You didn't see her walking around?"

"No, why?"

"Were you in the kitchen that night?"

She thought about the question. "Yeah, one of the ladies working the Garden Club table is diabetic and needed a glass of orange juice, and I didn't want to wait in line at the bar or try to flag down a server. I rushed into the kitchen to get her a glass, because I knew it was important to be quick."

"Tell us about going in there."

She blinked, "Huh, I just went in the door and told the first person I saw I needed a glass of orange juice, quick, for someone who was diabetic. He poured it for me, and I left."

"Why did you call Gerald after you left the motel?"

She looked questioningly at Gerald, but he had not looked at her. "Well, I called to tell him about Vera checking out."

"What did he say?"

She looked at him and then at Sean and Alex. "He told me Vera had been here and left some things in her old bedroom. We didn't know where she was, so he was going to put them in the shed."

"Did you know he went back to the party to look for Vera?"

"What?" she screeched. She jerked her attention to Gerald.

Sean pressed, "He didn't tell you he was going back to the party?"

Sean saw the moment when it dawned on Teri that Gerald was in a precarious situation.

She shot back at Sean, "Gerald did *not* kill my sister! *No way!* There are other people who had reasons to kill her. Have you talked to them?"

Gerald turned toward Teri. "Teri, stop it."

"No, I'm not going to let them blame you." She swiveled to Sean, "Have you talked to Dillie? What about Tanya Ellis?"

"What would they have to do with Vera?" asked Sean.

"Vera wanted money. My aunt, who was best friends with Dillie's mother, was here visiting about the time Dillie's mother passed away. She confided in Mom about a secret involving Dillie's family. Unfortunately, Vera was hiding at the door like she always did, trying to listen in. Back then, she told me what she heard. Vera's not likely to have forgotten. Her thinking wasn't right, Sean. When she got back to town, she was out of money, and when Vera was desperate, you never knew what she might do. She may have had this wild idea to blackmail Dillie."

"We talked to Tanya. We know about her and Vera bullying kids. Is that what you mean?"

"Teri, this isn't right to be doing this."

She ignored her husband. "No, there's a lot more than that."

"Okay, Teri, we need to know what she might have been blackmailing Dillie about and what you know about Tanya."

Chapter 47

Dillie was talking with Frederic when Sean and Alex walked into the gallery. "Ohh lala! Two handsome lawmen! To what do we owe the pleasure?"

Alex blushed, but Sean was used to Dillie. "Hi, Dillie, Frederic." After Frederic shook their hands, Sean told them they would like to speak with Dillie. She invited them into her office, insisting they have coffee. After they were settled, Sean said, "Dillie, we're here on official business. We have some questions about Vera Keller."

Dillie's eyes were alert. "Of course—whatever I can do to help."

"I understand Vera knew something about your family's history she thought might be a family scandal. Vera may have been planning to try and extort money from you to keep the family secret. Did you know she knew?"

Dillie's eyes were wide. "I am confused, Sheriff. Please, to what scandal are you referring?"

"It involves you mother's relationship with a man."

Dillie swept back her hair. "Ahh. I know what you are talking about now. Do you think this is what she wanted to tell me the night of the party but did not have the opportunity?"

"We suspect it is."

Dillie waved her hand in the air. "Such is life. It's something that I do not discuss, but I am certainly not ashamed of it. It is what happened." She shrugged. "She misjudged me if she thought I would have paid to prevent the affair from becoming public."

"I would like to hear the story from you."

"Well, of course. My mother was devoted to my father, and he loved her. He was a business lawyer, and several of his cases took him to large cities, such as Chicago, Detroit, and others. Men found my mother attractive, but of course, she was married to my father. That did not mean she did not find other men attractive. I do not believe she was unfaithful, though, until this one particular man came into her life.

"When Father was out of town for a trial, she had a flat tire on the side of the road one day, and a man pulled up to change the tire." Dillie smiled. "He was the type of man Hollywood producers dream about. The attraction was too much for both of them, and they found time to be together—naturally being discreet. Owen was old enough to notice, so Mother made sure to be extra careful. Her lover was married, but there were no children yet. Their love affair went on for years.

231

But, at some point, my mother became pregnant, and she knew her lover was the father. I was born, but they continued their affair. Mother never told him, and he never asked if he was the father.

"Then, during high school, I started growing close to a boy. At first, we were friends. I noticed my mother discouraged our friendship, which was a surprise to me, because she had never interfered in my life in that way. After Christmas that year, the boy and I were spending more time with each other working on a senior science project. Mother would not allow us to be alone, and I was never allowed to go out with him, even to get something to eat.

"My mother wanted me to apply to universities in California, which I did, but I also applied in Ohio. I had no intention of going away, because I wanted to stay close to him. We were talking about both of us going to OSU.

"Mother started acting very strange, and one night near our graduation, she walked in and found him with his arm around me. She became hysterical and yelled for him to leave. I told her I was leaving with him. I remember the night like it was yesterday." Dillie sighed, "Ce qui sera. (What will be.) Our lives forever changed. I graduated from high school and left for California. Time passed. Life went on. I never came back until my dear brother passed."

"What did your mother say to you that night?"

She again brushed back her hair. "A couple of months before I was born, the wife of Mother's lover gave birth to a baby boy. As you see, he was my half-brother. That was the same boy who I had started to grow close with during my senior year. You know him, of course. John."

"John Pawley," confirmed Sean.

"I had no idea Vera would know the story. I did not think anyone knew, other than Mother, who is deceased, John and me." Dillie shrugged one shoulder. "Not that it matters, of course. Neither John nor I would be impacted if the story was told. Neither of us have any family who would be impacted. It is just part of what life brings. John is my half-brother. We have not talked about it. I would be delighted to tell people of our relations, but John is such a private person. I do not know how he would feel about people knowing. I am proud of him."

"It's not something that we would tell, Dillie," said Sean, "unless for some reason it became important to the case. It is my understanding that your aunt was best friends with Vera's mother, and she told her about the time of your mother's death. Vera overheard the conversation."

"I see. Mother must have told her sister. When Mother told me, she did not discuss the matter except to tell us of our blood ties. I know my mother loved my father, but she must have loved John's father, too. I wish I had taken the opportunity to talk with her, but I left. Mother called me from time-to-time, and we talked, but I had moved on with my life. It was not until Owen passed away I ever thought of returning. I'm glad to be back, and I have no intention of moving away. I have found home."

"What do you think, Chief," asked Alex as they were walking back to the precinct.

"I think the list of persons of interest keeps expanding."

"You really think Dillie had something to do with it?"

"We have to keep an open mind. She had the motive and the opportunity, but like she said, why would she care if the world found out they were half-siblings? From all I know, Dillie has lived her life like an open book. She does not strike me as caring one way or the other whether people know she and John Pawley are half-siblings. But, we can't rule anyone out until we solve the case." One thing Sean was wondering but did not voice to Alex was whether Dillie would have wanted to protect John Pawley from the attention that could have occurred if Vera had made public their half-sibling relationship. But if Dillie did not care about it becoming public, Pawley seemed even less likely to care—unless he thought he was protecting Dillie from embarrassment.

Chapter 48

Sean pulled up the gravel driveway and looked at the old farmhouse. The lean-to in the front yard protected the upcoming winter's firewood from most of the elements. The remnants of the garden where John Pawley grew vegetables lay flat from the early frost a week ago. Sean knew from a previous investigation John had been a sniper during the Vietnam War and had been decorated for his courage. He eventually returned to the house where he had been raised and survived off the grid, relying on hunting, fishing and gardening for his food. Scraggly facial hair and a long graying pony tail prompted locals to refer to him as the Mountain Man from Mader Valley. He placed extreme value on his privacy—rarely venturing into town, and then only to purchase necessities.

Baby, his huge Mastiff, pushed open the screen door and came bounding toward Sean's cruiser in full guard-dog mode. Sean paused, not wanting to open the gate to the growling and slobbering beast. John had a reputation of walking around his property in nothing but boots, guns and a sock hat during cold weather. When he walked out the screen door, at least he was not carrying his guns, thought Sean.

"Baby, enough!" commanded John in his gravelly voice.

Baby stopped barking but did not take his eyes off Sean.

"Come on in, Sheriff. He won't bother you unless I give the word."

"Nice to know, John," Sean wryly muttered as he opened the gate—eyeing the dog. "How you been?"

"Getting along. How about you?"

"Oh, about the same." Sean eased toward the steps to the porch with one eye on John and the other on Baby.

"Come on up and have a seat. Is your wife doing okay?"

Sean sat down and watched as Baby galloped up the porch steps and plopped down beside John's seat. "Yeah, she's doing fine."

"That's good. I read about it. I'm glad you got that bastard. That was a close one."

"It was close, but it worked out in the end. John, there's something I need to ask you about."

"I figured that."

"Did you hear about the woman who was killed at Dillie's new gallery?"

"Yes, I read about it."

"Did you know her?"

Sean saw hair move above John's eye, so he thought he was raising an eyebrow. "I know about ten people around here, and she's not one of them."

"I'll get right to the point."

"Good."

"Her name was Vera Keller. She grew up in Bekbourg but moved to Cleveland about fourteen years ago. She recently showed back up with the intention of living here. You probably read this. Anyway, she was out of money, and unless she got some cash soon, she was going to be homeless. She was looking for fast cash, and maybe even for a long-term cash stream. I suspect one of her plans was to blackmail Dillie."

Both eyebrows moved under all that hair. "Dillie?"

"Yeah. It seems when Vera was young, she overheard Dillie's aunt, who was a close friend with Vera's mother, talking about a family secret. Vera returned to Bekbourg hoping to get Dillie to carry her paintings in the gallery and maybe to extort Dillie to keep the secret quiet."

"Dillie didn't fall for that shit, did she?"

"No. From what Dillie told me, Vera never got a chance to tell her she knew the secret."

"So, what's this got to do with me?"

"I take it you didn't know Vera knew about the secret?"

John's steel eyes looked hard at Sean. "I got three answers, Sean. First, no. Second, if I had, I wouldn't have given a shit. Third, I read about how she was killed. If I had wanted to silence her, her body would never have been found."

"You would not have killed her to protect Dillie from a scandal?"

"I got two responses to that one. First, Dillie wouldn't be scandalized by something like that, and second, I repeat answer number three to your first question."

"Okay, John. You give any more thought to publishing more of your books?"

"Yes. My second novel is due out."

Sean was surprised, "That's great. I thought you weren't going to publish again."

John shrugged, "What the hell. I still don't want anyone to know."

Sean stood to leave. "I'm not telling."

John stood to walk Sean to the gate. "You take care, Sean. You're in a dangerous job."

Sean reached to shake his hand, "It's getting ready to turn cold, John. You might want to wear more clothes."

"Semper Fi, Sheriff."

"Semper Fi, John."

Chapter 49

Despite the nip in the air, Tanya opened the door wearing a tank top and weathered jeans with flip flops. She lived on the second floor of an older apartment building in a small one-bedroom unit. A haze of cigarette smoke added to the dullness of the room. A drab floral upholstered love seat sat up against the wall with a wood-framed landscape print tilting above. Two laminate end tables offered surface space to a lamp, bills, a TV remote and ashtrays. Sean sat in a small oak-framed vinyl-cushioned chair, and Alex turned around a ladder-back kitchen chair to face them.

Tanya lit a cigarette and looked at Sean. "So, back again? If I had to guess, it's probably to do with Vera."

"Yes," Sean nodded. "We have follow-up questions."

"Okay, shoot." She laughed at her joke. "You got that, right?"

Sean ignored the jest. "Do you know Nell Porter?"

Tanya looked hard at Sean. "I don't know her, but I know about her."

"Tell us about her—what you know."

239

Tanya twisted on the sofa. "She's some type of artist. I saw her at the party that night."

"Did you talk to her?"

"No."

"Do you ever talk to her?"

"No. She never comes in Frau's, and I never see her out. Why?"

"Did you know her daughter?"

Tanya took a long drag and slowly exhaled the smoke. "Yeah, she was in my high school class. I don't want to talk about her."

"Why's that?"

"I just don't."

"Let me tell you what I know then. Vera was a bully. One of her victims was Nell's daughter, Tiffany. You and Vera together bullied Tiffany, and from what I understand, made her life very difficult. One afternoon, Tiffany drove her mother's car up to the old quarry and committed suicide. Did Nell Porter ever say anything to you or Vera about that?"

Tanya had grown quiet. The faint humming of a wall clock was all that broke the silence. Tanya finished her cigarette and then crushed it into the ashtray. For the first time since Sean's last question, she looked at him. He expected to see defiance, but instead, her expression was unreadable. He waited to see what she would do, and he waited another long minute before she spoke. "I don't deny I was Vera's sidekick and bullied some kids. Vera would start making fun of a kid, and I'd go along. We'd laugh at kids, whisper within ear-shot so they thought we were talking about them. We made fun of their looks or what they wore."

She lit another cigarette before continuing. "But there was something about Tiffany that set Vera off. Tiffany was pretty, for starters, and a little weird. She didn't have any friends, which made her isolated prey to Vera. But I always thought the main reason Vera had it in for Tiffany was because she was jealous as hell of her painting skills. Vera was always bitching about the art teacher raving about Tiffany's work and how she displayed her paintings in the hallways at school."

When Tanya became quiet, Sean asked her what she meant by Tiffany being "weird." She shrugged. "She was quiet, and she sometimes acted like she was in her own world. But, the teachers gave her special attention. I guess they saw a special talent that us kids didn't understand. Anyway, I guess Vera saw her as a competitor and didn't like it. She wanted me to start spreading a rumor that Tiffany was screwing with crazy Timmy Vealit—a mentally impaired boy who was in our class—even though he was a couple of years older.

"I didn't want any part of doing that to Tiffany, who wouldn't hurt anyone. I guess somewhere beneath my black soul was some conscience left. Vera kept pushing me, but for once, I stood up to her and refused. God, she was pissed.

"Hell, by our senior year, no one wanted to have anything to do with her, so who else was she going to team up with? She finally got off my back.

241

She started writing things on the bathroom walls and dropping notes around school that were supposed to be Tiffany telling Timmy she loved him and where they were going to meet. You get the picture. I don't know if kids believed it or not, but you know how kids like to gossip. Anyway, it was too much for Tiffany, and she quit coming to school. I guess something happened, because then we heard about her jumping into the quarry."

She watched the smoke rise as she exhaled. "I don't know. It shook me up. I went to the funeral. A couple of other kids were there. I didn't know her mother. I'd never seen her, but this woman walked up to me. I remember it like it was yesterday.

"'You killed my Tiffany.' It was scary as hell. Her eyes were wild-looking. No tears—just scary wide and glassy red. I started shaking my head 'no' and told her I had no part in it. She said I was lying, that she knew I had bullied Tiffany with Vera. I told her how sorry I was I had made fun of her, but I said I had nothing to do with the rumors. I told her I should have never followed Vera, but I repeated I had nothing to do with the rumors. I was scared shitless. I was crying, and people were looking. She told me I was going to hell."

Tanya took another long drag—causing the tobacco to glow orange. "I guess I've been in hell since."

"That was the last time you and Nell Porter talked?"

"Yeah. Like I said, I saw her at the party, but I didn't go near her."

"Was Vera at the funeral?"

"Hell, no. Vera never had remorse about nothing."

"Did you tell her what Nell said to you?"

Tanya shook her head. "No."

"What about you and Vera? What happened after that with your friendship?"

"I knew it was too good to think Vera would forget I wouldn't go along with spreading rumors about Tiffany. She found a way to get back."

"What happened?" asked Sean, but he suspected she was getting ready to confirm what Teri had told him and Alex.

"After that encounter with Tiffany's mom, I started to think about what Vera and I had been doing to kids—the pain we had brought them. I started going to church. I guess I thought I could save myself from going to hell. There was this guy from high school who went to church there, and we started dating. We were going to get married that summer after graduation. I got pregnant but didn't tell him, or anyone. I was just going to wait and surprise him on our honeymoon. Vera called him and said she was having a surprise party at her mom's house for us and not to tell me.

"I found out later that Teri was spending the night at the nursing home with her mom, and Gerald was working night shift, so no one was there. Anyway, when he got there, Vera turned on her magic, and you can guess what happened. That bitch was gleeful in telling me the details. I got violently sick and couldn't get out of bed for days. I guess it was too much because I lost the baby.

"I confronted him about it and called off the wedding. He ended up joining the army, and I never heard from him again. I ended up—well, see for yourself," she said waving the cigarette around the room.

"You told me you got off your shift early the night of the party. Where did you go?"

She looked sharply at Sean. "If you think I killed that bitch, you need to have your head examined. She screwed up my life. No way would I murder her and risk spending the rest of my life in jail." Sean did not react to her outburst as he repeated the question.

"I went home. I had to get up freakin' early to work. You ain't friggin' blaming me for her murder. I ain't the only one she done that to. I bet her sister didn't like Vera screwing her husband."

Even though Sean was not expecting this, he kept his features locked. "What do you mean?"

She looked at Sean. "You don't know? Well, maybe Teri doesn't know, or maybe she doesn't want to talk about it. But, yeah, it didn't matter that he was her brother-in-law, she screwed him, too." Tanya crushed out the cigarette. "Look, I'm through talkin'. You all need to leave."

Sean and Alex showed themselves out as Tanya put another cigarette between her lips and stoked the lighter. Sean felt like he was in a ping-pong match, and he was the ball. He was damn tired of the lies and misdirection.

Sherrie Rutherford

Chapter 50

Sean was in a foul mood when he walked into the duplex and pulled a beer from the refrigerator. He thought about going next door to get Buddy, but he sunk into the loveseat's thick cushion and stretched out his long legs. Based on what Tanya had told him and Alex, Gerald had a reason to kill Vera to keep her from telling Teri about their fling—unless she already knew. In which case, she may have killed Vera as revenge.

Sean took another long drink from the bottle. Tanya was now a suspect because it was obvious she blamed Vera for ruining her life—causing her to lose a baby and the breakup with her fiancé. She had been cast into a life of waiting tables at Frau's and manual landscape labor as a side job to make extra money. Then, there was Nell, a grieved mother, who blamed Vera for her daughter's suicide. He couldn't completely rule out Dillie, but she seemed less likely than any of the others to be the murderer. The murder was much too amateurish for John Pawley.

He took another drink. _I don't know how this case can get any more convoluted_, he thought. Just then, her heard steps on the porch, and Cheryl swung open the door. "Hi, Honey. Is Buddy still with Kye?"

"Yeah, I just got home. I was going to go get him in a minute. You look like you've had a good day."

Cheryl's eyes were shining. "I have. I found out something that is very interesting related to Vera Keller."

He arched a brow, "You're looking into Vera for a story?"

"It's something that Kye mentioned the other day. I didn't want to say anything until I researched it, but I'm glad I followed my hunch." Cheryl pushed off her shoes and sank down close to him. "Ready to hear?"

Sean took a long drink and emptied his bottle. "Ready as I'll ever be."

Her smile lit up her face. "Kye told me soon after Vera and Teri's mother died, Vera left town and had a nervous breakdown. Teri had to go stay with her for several months. Kye said she felt bad for Teri because she had to care for Vera so soon after their mother died—despite the fact that she was pregnant. Thing was, Teri was gone the entire time, so no one knew she was pregnant until after the baby was born and she returned home.

"So, I grew suspicious and went to Columbus to look at records—specifically birth certificates." Sean was beginning to get the picture, but he listened to hear her out. "Vera had a baby, but there is no record of Teri having a baby. The

247

certificate showed the baby was a boy, but only a last name, Keller, was listed. The father's name was not provided. Do you think Miles is really Vera's child, and Teri and Gerald are raising him as their own?"

"Did you happen to make copies of the birth certificate?"

"Yes." She opened her bag and produced a folder. "Here is a copy of the birth certificate. Oh, I almost forgot. Here are all the photographs my photographer took at the party."

"Thank you, Sweetie." Sean studied the boy's birth certificate. He stood. "Mind if I take this?"

"No, it's your copy. Where are you going?"

"I'm going back to the department. There are some things I need to do. I'm sorry about dinner."

"Don't worry about that. I'll ask Kye if she wants to go to Frau's. I'll buy you something and put it in the refrigerator."

His eyes sparkled. "I may want dessert."

She giggled, "Oh, dessert is always a delight."

Sean called Alex and asked him to return to the office. Once they were there, they decided on their plan of action.

Occasion of Murder

Chapter 51

With a posted twenty-five-miles-per-hour speed limit, the state highway ran through the heart of Saltzburg's business district—only a five minute cruise if its two traffic lights were green. Minnie's small home was just on the outskirts of downtown and within walking distance of the diner where Cheryl and Milton had first met her.

Minnie greeted her like she was her best friend as she invited her into her home. "I told people you might have finally found Hap," said Minnie, as she poured them both a cup of coffee and served a slice of custard pie. "I can't remember this much excitement around town in a long time. I feel like a celebrity 'cause everyone who comes into Saully's asks me 'bout it." She patted a book lying off to the side. "I found the scrapbook with pictures of Hap, Deffy, and Bethanne."

Minnie dove in where she had left off. "Okay, so if I remember right, I was to the part where Hap told them Schusters nothin' doin' on his timber. Well, according to Deffy, one night Hap stopped in at the bar to meet up with some buddies. The Schusters dropped in and saw Hap. The bigmouth one said something like, 'Bethanne's daddy shouldn't have let her marry him, 'cause he didn't know his butt from a hole in the ground,' talking about the timber. Hap said he was smarter than both Schusters put together, and they should call themselves the 'Schuster Shysters.' The men in the bar started to hoot, and the bigmouth Schuster took after Hap. Hap floored him before he'd laid a punch on him. The other men broke it up, but not before them Schuster boys were made to look real bad by Hap. Just so you know it, the bigmouth one who attacked Hap ended up in prison a few years later for killing a man with a knife in a fight."

They each took a bite of pie with Cheryl commenting on its tastiness. Minnie coveted the praise and offered to let Cheryl take the rest home. After refreshing their coffee, Minnie continued, "One day, Bethanne called Hap's sister, Deffy, and asked if she knew where Hap was. He had not shown up for three days, which was not like Hap. She drove over to their house 'cause Bethanne couldn't drive, and it was pretty isolated where she and Hap lived. Deffy brought her back to their home. Deffy's husband was an invalid, so he couldn't do much, but he wanted Deffy to tell the police he was missing, 'cause everyone who knew Hap thought something had happened. No one thought he would just leave." Minnie shook her head. "No one ever heard hide nor hair from him again.

"After a few weeks, Bethanne wasn't happy staying with Deffy, so Deffy took her back home but called her almost every day and drove to see her once a week and took her places. Well, several months later, it wasn't the bigmouth Schuster but the other one—he showed up at Bethanne's house. He showed her a paper and claimed it was an IOU from Hap to him. He told Bethanne she owed him the money right then, or he was going to the sheriff and have her arrested and their home confiscated. Deffy repeated the story to me lots of times over the years—that's why I know what I'm telling you is right.

"Poor Bethanne, it scared the bejesus out of her. Schuster told her he could solve it real quick and make the problem go away. All she had to do was sign the paper giving him the right to sell the timber off the land to the furniture company. It'd take care of the IOU; the Schusters would get their finders' fee; and she'd get money for the timber. Bethanne wanted to call Deffy and talk to her 'bout it, but he said he needed an answer then, or he had no choice but to go to the sheriff.

"Bethanne signed the paper. She was too ashamed to tell Deffy. When Deffy went up there and saw the logging trucks and learned what had happened, Bethanne told her it was the saddest day of her life to see them cutting all those beautiful trees." Minnie shook her head. "Poor Bethanne, she only got a pittance of what that valuable timber was worth, but she was able to live on it for a few years until she died of pneumonia one winter." Minnie sipped her coffee. "This goes to show what con men they were. Deffy told me there was no way Hap would have ever done business with those two, which meant that IOU they said he owed them was fake."

"Whatever happened to the Schuster men?" asked Cheryl.

"Well, the bigmouth one died in prison. His brother got run out of town. Never heard what ever happened to him." Minnie scooted her plate out of the way. "Here, let me show you some pictures. This was Deffy's, and I got it when she died."

Frayed edges of yellowed pages had slipped beyond the green cover with black lettering. Minnie gingerly turned past the single sheet of paper bearing handwritten script by the book's owner noting dates and people. Black and white photos were clipped in place at corners by small stickered sleeves on the brittle pages. Cheryl saw pictures of Deffy as a young woman and her husband. They had two children—one had died as an infant, and the son was killed in a car crash in his twenties—Minnie explained as they viewed pictures of Deffy's son whose life had been cut short. "Now, somewhere—oh yeah, here's a picture of Hap wearing a uniform." Cheryl surmised the gangly young man with the short dark hair was near twenty.

"Here's another picture of him after he got out of the War." He was leaning against an old Model T Ford. She turned the page. "Here's a picture of him with Deffy. They were at their parents. It was Easter." Minnie carefully turned more pages. "Now, here he is with Deffy and her husband." As Cheryl and Minnie looked at the picture, Cheryl tried to conger up what Hap was like. His eyes were sharp and his look intense. His darkened complexion told of someone who worked outside, and his wiry frame suggested manual labor. Minnie confirmed he had started working in his father's fields around the age of twelve, but not being the oldest son, he did not stand to inherit his father's farm.

Minnie continued to turn the pages and periodically commented on a photo. "Ah, this is what I was looking for. Here is when he and Bethanne got married. He was about thirty, and she was close to twenty." Cheryl looked close at the beautiful young woman with a dimple and long, wavy hair—wearing a floral dress that tapered to her waist and then flared to just below her knees. Standing beside her was Hap dressed in dark pleated pants, white shirt and tie, and a sports coat hanging off his frame. Despite time passing, Hap's intense and somber expression had not wavered from earlier pictures.

Minnie turned some pages before she stopped. "These are the last pictures I have of Hap and Bethanne. It was Deffy's birthday, and the whole family showed up. I took these. Here's Hap." Cheryl looked, and her eyes widened as she looked closer. "This belt looks just like the one in the picture the authorities took of the man's belongings." Cheryl opened her bag and pulled out a file. She put the two pictures side-by-side and looked back and forth between the pictures. When she leaned back, Minnie peered closely.

"Well, well," Minnie sighed. Moisture filled her eyes. "That's him, ain't it?"

Cheryl looked again at the buckle and the belt. "The belt in the sheriff's pictures had been in the water a few weeks, but still, it looks very similar, but the buckle looks identical, and it's got those odd markings along the edge."

"Yeah. He got that belt when he and Bethanne took a trip to New Orleans to see one of his army buddies and his family." Minnie shook her head, "After all these years, we finally know."

Cheryl thought Minnie was right but wanted to caution, "We can't know for sure, Minnie, without more proof or a DNA match."

Minnie laid her hand on Hap's picture. "I hear you, but I don't need no more proof. I know that's him. That explains why he never came home."

Minnie gave Cheryl the picture so she could ask a forensics expert to enlarge the photos and see if they could draw any conclusions.

The next morning, the *Tribune's* receptionist knocked on the conference room door, "I'm sorry to bother you, Cheryl, but there's a woman on the phone who says she needs to talk to you. She didn't want to give me her name."

Cheryl glanced at Milton and then at the receptionist, "Okay, can you put her through on this phone?"

"Sure thing."

Milton watched as Cheryl listened. He saw the spark in her eye and knew something was up. "I see. Yes, I'd like very much to talk to you. I'm working with another reporter, Milton Grant. If it's okay with you, I'd like for him to be there. . . Okay. What works best for you? Do you want us to meet you somewhere? . . . Oh, sure. What time? . . . "We'll see you then. Thank you."

"What's going on?" asked Milton as Cheryl hung up the phone.

"That was a woman who lives in Saltzburg. She heard about us possibly finding out about Hap. She thinks she has some information that can help us. She doesn't want people in Saltzburg to know she's talking to us. She's driving down this afternoon."

Milton shook his head. "Always said news travels fastest by way of grapevines. I'm looking forward to hearing what she has to say."

Chapter 52

Gerald opened the door to find Sean and Alex. "Sorry it took me so long to get to the door. I was upstairs when I heard the doorbell. Come in."

When they walked into the foyer, Sean stopped. "We're here to take you into custody, Gerald."

Gerald's face grew flush. "What the hell?"

"We suspect you in the murder of your sister-in-law, Vera Keller. If you need this jacket," Sean's head tilted to the coat tree, "get it. We're ready to go."

"I don't understand what this is all about, Sean."

"First, Alex is going to read you your rights, Gerald. But I'll give it to you in a condensed version. You have lied to me and obstructed our investigation into Vera's death. We know about you sleeping with Vera."

Gerald's face went slack, and he leaned heavily on his cane.

"Alex, tell him his rights."

Afterwards, Sean said, "The dog will be okay left alone?"

Gerald nodded.

"Let's go, then."

"I need to call Teri."

"You can call her from the station."

After they arrived at the station, Gerald called Teri, and then they put him in a holding cell. Sean was called out on a domestic dispute, and he and Alex left to handle that situation. Later, when they returned, Kim told them that Derrick Compton, a criminal defense attorney, and Teri had come to visit Gerald. Teri left before Derrick, "visibly upset."

Later that afternoon, Derrick came to see Sean. "I need to know if you plan to pursue charges, Sean."

"I've talked to the prosecutor, and unless I learn something between now and tomorrow, yes, I plan to—a murder charge. He's also made false statements and obstructed this investigation. Just so you know, Teri could be charged, too."

"I need to talk to Gerald again."

"Sure. You know your way around here."

Chapter 53

Cheryl met C.P. at Max's bistro. "My archivist told me you were looking into the body found downstream of the bridge after its collapse. There being a body found as part of the clean-up surprised me, but you say you believe there was foul play?"

Cheryl explained everything she had learned about Hap. As it turned out, Cheryl and Milton both felt the woman who had come to visit them was credible. She had heard through the scuttlebutt going around Saltzburg that the mystery of Hap's disappearance in 1957 had been solved. The woman had never come forward because she did not know what to believe about her father's tale, because he, too, was skeptical. Her father had served prison time at the same time the Schuster brother was there. According to what her father told her about his time in prison, Schuster was always bragging about things, trying to make the other inmates steer clear of him. One story he boasted about was killing a man named Lewis to "teach him a lesson" and to get rights to his timber. She told Cheryl her father said Schuster was "one dumb SOB" for all the talking he did. His murder in prison was never solved.

"So, Milton and I think the Schusters beat Hap and threw him in the creek when the waters were high from the spring's flooding—thinking his body would wash away. And, it did. Only it got hung up just downstream of the Norton Creek Bridge. Otherwise, it might have floated all the way to the river and been lost forever. Word of the body being found never made it to Saltzburg, and news about Deffy's missing person's report about Hap didn't make it to Bekbourg."

C.P. chuckled. "That's quite a story. I never imagined you would solve a murder mystery when you asked if you could review the railroad files about the bridge incident."

Cheryl smiled. "I didn't either."

"I understand you're about ready to publish the story about the bridge collapsing."

"Yes. Few people probably know the full story. I think our readers will find it interesting."

"I don't know the full story, so I look forward to reading your account."

Chapter 54

Sean shook hands with Derrick Compton. Standing six-feet, four-inches himself, few men towered over Sean like Derrick. The former professional football offensive tackle-turned lawyer warmly shook Sean's hand. "Sean, you know Morgan Ramirez," he said as he stepped back to allow them to shake hands.

"I don't think we've met, but my wife has told me about her. Hi, Ms. Ramierz."

Sean remembered hearing Cheryl talk about the young attorney who had stood up to Zeke Pinkston when he had attempted to take his granddaughter's property. She only stood to Derrick's chest, but her spunkiness was evident as her shoulder-length hair bounced with the long step she took forward to shake his hand. "It's nice to finally get to meet you, Sheriff Neumann."

Both lawyers had yellow legal pads, but Morgan had a couple of files with her, and Sean could see tabs marked certain pages. Morgan sat upright and had her pen in writing position. Sean knew Derrick's bear-like lumber was deceptive as to the speed of which the huge man was capable. *Many holes in the offensive line had been opened by his bulk and speed, allowing running backs and quarterbacks to sprint down the field.*

After Derrick settled back in his chair, his baritone words floated around the room. "The Olsons don't have a lot of money, so our firm is representing them both. Morgan has been assigned to advise Mrs. Olson. I'm taking the lead with Gerald."

Gerald looked to have aged overnight. His eyes looked weary. He was pale and pinched. Red-rimmed eyes with dark circles underneath were new features for Teri. She looked like she had lost weight, and her hair was limp and dull. Both were subdued.

After the preliminaries, Derrick informed Sean and Alex, "Gerald and Teri want to cooperate." Alex had a note pad—even though the conversation was being taped. Leaning back in his chair, Sean nodded.

Gerald looked at Teri, who was looking down. She wiped her eyes with a tissue.

Gerald took the lead, "I don't know how you found out, but it happened." Teri's shoulders quivered. "Teri was staying a lot at the hospital with her mother. We were living at her mother's house, and Vera lived there, too. It was a hard time for all of us with her mother being so sick. I'm not making excuses. There are none. There had been a house fire that evening, and it had been a hell of a fire. A kid was trapped in the upstairs, and by the time we could get to him, it was too late. The mother was asleep at the time in a downstairs bedroom, and her husband was working night shift. It was around midnight when I got home, and Teri was gone. I went in the kitchen and downed a couple of beers, and Vera came in with this see-through thing on. I was weak. Anyway, after it was over—God, I felt horrible about what I had done to Teri. I did everything in my power to stay clear of Vera. We never spoke about it to each other, and I sure as hell never told Teri."

Teri was silently weeping.

"So, Viola died, and we had the funeral. A short time after that, Teri told me Vera was pregnant. We had been trying to have children, but then Teri learned from the doctor she couldn't. Vera didn't want the baby, but Teri did. So, Teri told me she and Vera had decided they would leave town— tell everyone they needed to get away after Viola's death. When Teri came back with the baby, we'd say it was ours. At the time, I thought it could have been mine. Teri didn't act like Vera had told her, so I thought maybe Teri and I could raise a child that was mine."

Gerald took a drink from the water bottle. Teri looked up. Her eyes looked bloodshot from her tears. She said, "When Vera told me she was pregnant, she told me she didn't want the baby. I did, but I didn't want her to know how badly I wanted it, because Vera might have had an abortion or given it up for adoption just to spite me. That's how she was. So, I told her if she wanted my help, I would help her out, but there were things we had to address. First, I needed to know who the father was and asked if she had told him. At first, she resisted telling me, but I insisted in case there was ever a medical emergency. She told me his name and that he was in the Peace Corps and she had not tried to reach him. She didn't want to talk to his parents or anyone. When I talked to Gerald about it, he was good with that, but he didn't want Vera around. He didn't want anyone to know the baby was adopted, and he said we could get her out of our life once and for all.

"We hired Owen Donaldson to handle all the paperwork. Vera would leave town, and I was to follow shortly—telling people I needed to help her deal with Mom's death. She had the baby in a private hospital, and the adoption was handled by Owen. I gave Vera my entire part of the inheritance, and we purchased the family place at fair market value. We took out a mortgage to do that, and Vera got all that money. The deal was she was to never tell anyone about Miles and to never show up around Bekbourg again. I guess I knew deep-down she wouldn't abide with the agreement, but I hoped she would. She stayed away fourteen years."

"We never wanted Miles to know he was adopted," added Gerald, and Teri nodded.

Gerald continued, "I thought I could be the father, but Teri told me about Lynch. I knew Vera slept around, so I couldn't be sure. Brian Lynch had dark hair, too. So, Miles' dark hair wasn't a giveaway. Over time, I just accepted he was mine, and that was that. Then, Teri went to a church retreat one weekend, and it was just me and Miles. He was playing on the play set out back, and I was cleaning the gutters. He climbed on top of the set and was reaching for the swing chain and fell. He broke his arm, and while we were at the hospital, the nurse gave me a copy of his medical records. I knew mine and Teri's blood types were both O. The sheet showed Miles was A. It didn't matter as far as my feelings for Miles—I love him. He is my son. But, in a way I was relieved because if there were ever any questions, Teri would not find out about me and Vera."

Teri wiped away tears streaming down her cheeks. "There is something else. Brian Lynch showed up at our house two evenings ago. I guess Vera went to see him after she got back in town wanting him to give her money. She told him they had a son together. She didn't tell him who had adopted the baby, but I guess he started thinking about it. He said at first he didn't believe her, but it had been eating at him and wanted to know if he was Miles' father."

Tears were streaming harder down her cheeks, and she was becoming more emotional, so Gerald picked up. "We told him we didn't know what he was talking about—that Miles was our son." Gerald looked down. "It has been so important to us to keep the secret from Miles and everyone. Miles is our son, and that's the way we want the world to look at it."

"What did he do then?" asked Sean.

"He left. We thought we had dodged a bullet on the truth about Miles until you showed up yesterday."

Teri looked up. "I insisted we tell you. Gerald didn't want to. He didn't want people to know Miles wasn't our biological son. I can't bear to think that Gerald might be arrested for killing Vera. I know he didn't kill her. He loves Miles too much to destroy their time together--just like I would never kill her for the same reason. I thought if you knew the full truth, you would see we didn't do it. Possibly Brian Lynch did it, or someone else, but we didn't kill Vera."

Sean looked at Gerald and Teri with hard eyes. His lips were firm. "So, this is part of your water drip. Now it's Lynch. Before it was Dillie and Tanya. Neither one of you has been forthcoming with our investigation. What else are you holding back?"

Derrick stirred, "That's enough, Sheriff."

Sean did not look away from Gerald and Teri. "That's not near enough. They have also lied to me. You think it's funny watching me and my deputies chase our tails while you hoard facts, number one, and lie when it suits you because you don't want family secrets out?"

"That's it. We're shutting this down. My clients are not answering any more questions. Either you charge Gerald or he walks."

Gerald spoke up, "Sean's right. We should have laid it all on the table at the beginning. We know that now. We're sorry, Sean."

Sean continued to look at them as he reclined in his chair. The only noise was Teri's sniffles as she wept.

Sean looked at Derrick. "I would like to ask Teri a question."

Morgan looked up. "It's up to you, Teri."

She nodded and turned toward Sean. "We've tried to locate the sweater Gerald wore the night of the party. It was long gone in the system. I've got pictures of several of the attendees at the party. The photographer took a picture of you setting up the table for your committee. You wore a dark cardigan with a white blouse underneath."

"I wore a sweater that night. I don't remember about the photographer taking my picture."

"What color was the sweater?"

Morgan interrupted. "I need to talk to my client. Can we take a break?"

"Sure. Let Kim know when you're ready," said Sean.

Minutes passed, and Kim buzzed Sean that they were ready. He and Alex walked back in. "I have no objections to you asking her about the sweater, Sheriff," said Morgan.

He looked at Teri. "I believe you wanted to know what color my sweater was. It was gray—kind of dark."

"Later in the evening, another picture was taken when you were taking down the table. You and a group of women were standing around. You weren't wearing the sweater. Why?"

"When I returned from trying to find Vera at the motel, some of the crowd had left, and there was a parking spot close to the front door. I asked the valet if I could park there, and he told me I could. I had gotten warm earlier, and so I thought I'd leave it in the car."

"Where is the sweater?"

"At home."

"Have you washed it or had it cleaned since the night of the party?"

"No."

"Would you be willing to turn it over to us for forensics to analyze it?"

Teri looked at Morgan. "I'm okay with that."

"Okay, I'll ask Alex to accompany you home to get the sweater."

Sean turned back to Derrick. "I'm going to release your client, but that doesn't mean he and possibly Teri won't face charges at a later time."

After they left, Sean decided to follow up with someone who might remember Brian Lynch during his youth.

Chapter 55

To give him time to think about the investigation, Sean walked to the duplex where he saw a golf cart sitting in Kye's driveway. He circled it and noticed a license plate. On the passenger seat was a towel. He needed to talk with Kye but questioned whether he should knock on the door and interrupt her and her guest. Since it was not decked out like an antique T-Bird, he knew the golf cart was not Dillie's. As he debated whether to interrupt, Kye stepped outside, and Buddy frolicked out to greet Sean. "Hi, Sean. What do you think?" Kye asked.

"About what?"

"My new car."

Sean's eyebrows arched, "This is yours?"

"Why, yes. I saw Dillie's. I didn't need anything that fancy, but I thought it would be perfect to get around town. Danny told me I can't drive on a road with a speed limit over thirty-five-miles-an-hour, but none of the streets I usually go on are. He'll store it for me during the winter, but since the next few days are going to be nice, he dropped it off so I can putt around."

Buddy jumped up in the passenger seat. "Buddy, get out of there," Sean instructed. "You'll dirty Kye's golf cart." Buddy was sitting straight with his tongue hanging out.

Kye quickly intervened, "Oh, it's okay, Sean. I put the towel there for Buddy to sit on. He and I have already driven around the downtown. I think some of my bridge club friends may get one. Lucia really liked it."

Sean grinned at the elderly woman's spryness. She had taught him junior-year English. She was demanding but likely one of the best English teachers Schriever High School ever had.

"Okay, well, there's something I need to talk to you about. Is now a good time?"

"Sure, Sean."

Sean helped Kye bring coffee cups to the porch where they kept an eye on Buddy, who remained in the golf cart anticipating another ride.

"What can I try and help you with?"

"I was hoping you could tell me about a couple of students. Did you know Brian Lynch?"

"Oh, sure. He was in my English class. What do you want to know?"

"First. What kind of student was he?"

"I also had his older brother, Mick. Both boys were polite, and neither one of them ever got into any trouble that I know of—certainly not around school. Both boys were likeable. The difference was in their school work. Mick wasn't happy unless he was making all A's. He was sort of an attention hound, but in a likeable way. Brian was less motivated and basically got-along to get-along. I remember having a conference with Brian's parents at his dad's request, because he made a C on first quarter report card. His dad wasn't blaming me, but he wanted to know what Brian needed to do to improve his grades. He made B's the rest of the year. I think he probably could have pulled some A's if he had put in the effort. He never came across as having a lot of ambition—a lot different from his older brother Mick."

"What about girlfriends?"

Kye sipped her coffee as she thought. "I don't remember him dating anyone specific. I remember him talking to girls before class started, but I can't really tell you much more about that."

"Do you know if he ever dated Vera Keller?"

Kye shook her head. "No. They weren't in the same class. He was two years ahead."

"What about after he graduated—do you know if they dated then?"

Kye again shook her head. "No."

"Okay, Cheryl told me what you told her about Tanya Ellis and Vera being friends during high school. I'd like to hear what you know about that."

Kye relayed what she had already told Cheryl.

"Did Tanya have a boyfriend?"

"Mmm. Let me think." She drank some coffee. "Yes, she did, but they didn't start dating until toward the end of their senior year. I would see them walking between classes together, and I remember hearing some of the other teachers talking about them getting engaged before graduation."

"I understand they didn't get married."

"That's right. I don't know anything about that. It's interesting about Tanya. Tanya never struck me as having much confidence. She wore her hair hanging around her face and in her eyes. She never raised her hand in class, and when I called on her, she looked like a deer in the headlights. Her face would turn red, and she had trouble articulating a response.

"By the end of senior year, I could not believe the difference. I guess it was because she was dating the boy, but she started wearing makeup and fixing her hair. She looked quite nice. A few years after she graduated, I saw her at Frau's, and she looks like she does now. I don't remember her like this in high school. She now seems bitter about life, but that's just my impression. She's an efficient waitress—not very personable, but that doesn't faze me."

Chapter 56

Cheryl believed she had solved the mystery of the body found during the bridge cleanup, so she was now ready to turn back to the story of the bridge collapse. During her review of the railroad documents, she had come across the name, Yves Leroux, and figured there was a connection with Jules Leroux. He had been helpful before with questions she had about railroad history, so she reached out to him again.

"My dear, Ms. Seton. Oh, pardon me. I should have asked. Did you change your name now that you are married to our esteemed sheriff?"

Jules was unique for a railroader. He prided himself on a French heritage, and as a consequence, was formal in his mannerisms and talk. Even though they were eating lunch at Frau's, a decades-old diner that sported scarred and scuffed laminate table tops along with plastic chairs, he took time to seat her. His paper napkin was tucked in at his chin, and he precisely arranged his silverware in parallel lines to make any etiquette guru proud. Cheryl laughed, "Actually, Cheryl is just fine, but I opted to keep my maiden name."

He nodded as he sipped his coffee.

"Jules, I appreciate the card you and your wife sent me during my recovery. Someone painted a picture of the *Tribune's* building. Did you or your wife paint the cover?"

Jules smiled with pride, "My lovely Renee has many talents, and painting greeting cards is one of them."

"I hope to meet her sometime. Please tell her I framed the card and have it sitting on my desk."

"She will be most pleased to hear that, and I look forward to you two wonderful ladies meeting soon." Anita brought their lunches, and once they were settled, "Now, Cheryl, please tell me how I may assist you."

Cheryl showed him a copy of the newspaper's headlines from the spring of 1957. "I was hoping you could give me some more information about this."

Jules needed only to glance at the headline. "My dear, you have come to the right person. You see, my papa, Yves Leroux, was the fireman on the passenger train that memorable night."

Cheryl's hand raced back and forth across the notepad as he took her back in time.

Early Spring 1957

The two railroad section men were preparing to start their shift. One asked the other,

273

"Have you seen the schedule of work we're going to do this summer?"

"Yeah. Why is it Bekbourg is always the last place to get things done?"

"Actually, I think that bridge is okay for now. It's probably got a year or two left before we need to do anything."

"I don't agree. Have you looked around it? I've climbed around there—and up under it. At the very least, they need to bring in a crew to clear out all that debris and garbage that's built up under there."

"Naw. They'll do it like they've always done. Let Mother Nature clear it out."

May 20, 1957

Sean's grandfather, Clarence Neumann, joined the other railroaders at Frau's before their shift started. Cecil Davis, an engineer, greeted Clarence, "Have a seat C.N. Frenchy Leroux's giving the weather forecast." Yves Leroux, one of the railroad's fireman, was holding a newspaper.

Clarence sat down as the waitress appeared ready to pour his coffee. "Hell. I don't need a newspaper to tell me the weather. Rain, rain, and more rain."

"That's 'bout what Frenchy is saying," said Cecil as he took a bite of egg.

"We've definitely had a lot of rain," agreed Yves as he put down the paper. "It's rained so much *all these creeks are flooding up and down the railroad."*

"Yeah, I've never seen anything like this. It's the wettest time I've ever seen."

"Good thing they fixed up all those bridges and cleared up all the debris around them," said Clarence as the waitress delivered his "Railroader Special" breakfast.

Frenchy shook his head. "They haven't fixed the bridge around Norton Creek."

"Yeah, but that's a small one," said Cecil. "Hopefully, they're going to do that this summer."

May 24, 1957

About fifteen miles from downtown Bekbourg, fifty acres of prime farmland included the Norton Valley Creek and extended all the way to the railroad tracks. The creek was prone to flooding during heavy rains. The old farmer raised a small herd of beef cattle and fenced in his property to keep his cattle off the railroad tracks. The old farmer's son-in-law and grandson had come over to check on his cattle. As they sloshed toward the farmhouse, the son-in-law groused, "This has been one of the rainiest springs I ever remember. It's so muddy out there, I'll never get my fields plowed, or your grandpa's for that matter."

"At least he doesn't raise as much corn and soybeans as he used to," said the boy. "He just plants enough for feed corn for the cattle."

275

Sherrie Rutherford

They splashed through the sizeable puddles. "Maybe we should move the cattle away from the creek," said the nine-year-old boy—as rain continued to pour down on them.

"No. I moved them there so I could help your grandpa plow this year's crop." They splashed a couple of steps more before the son-in-law added, "One thing I've got to do is fix that fence near the railroad. The rain has made a few sections loose."

The boy's face was soaked from the rain. "Well, if it ever stops raining."

May 24, 1957

Al DeMoss was one of the most-senior engineers on the passenger train that ran from Wheeling, West Virginia, to Cincinnati, Ohio. He had joined the railroad in 1915 and was getting close to retirement. Where Mossy, a nickname bestowed by his fellow railroaders, was short and rotund, his much younger fireman, Frenchy Leroux, was a wiry man.

Mossy leaned down and put a paper in his grip as Frenchy walked up to join him at a table in the Wheeling depot. "Just got our train orders," said Mossy. "Capitol Express is late, but I guess it could be worse with all this rain."

"Do you think we'll be late pulling her into Cincinnati?" Frenchy asked as he settled into the chair.

"We're going to lose some time, no doubt about that, but we can make it up here or there. Train orders, though, are telling us to watch for washouts." He paused as he watched the downpour. *"We might even lose some time here at the depot, because it was reported the radio is out on the lead engine, and they're going to try and fix it. It shouldn't take too long, because they'll just switch out the equipment."*

"Look at this rain. There must be tracks that are so saturated they might be washed out. Wonder if we can get there?"

The crusty old engineer had seen a lot over his time with the railroad. *"We'll get there. We'll just have to make up time where we can."*

They heard the train's whistle blow for the depot and watched as the passenger train pulled in. *"That's old Smoothie for you. That was as good a stop as I've ever seen. It's right on target."*

The Operator walked up to the men, *"Just got word that they can't change out the radio. You're going to have to go without one."*

Mossy was not fazed by the news, *"Well, I've been working about fifty years, and most of the time I didn't have one."*

May 24, 1957

Railroad operators were stationed along the railroad and monitored conditions and coordinated signals for train engineers to watch as they drove *the route. Green lights signaled all-clear; yellow signaled slow-down; and red signals meant stop. Operators in a region reported to a central dispatcher, who monitored train movements and coordinated traffic over a large region. In 1957, most trains did not yet have radios, and the radios that did exist were problematic—especially when it was raining. The passenger trains had radios, but they often were not operational. So, the railroad signals were critical to alerting the engineer and his fireman to circumstances up ahead.*

The Operator working out of the train yard in Bekbourg was on the phone with the dispatcher. "What's going on with that coal train that left this afternoon? Has he reported any trouble?"

"Yeah. He's running behind schedule. This rain's not helping much. His engine was slipping a lot; his sanders were clogged up; and he was having a hard time pulling that heavy train. He's got a full coal load," said the Dispatcher.

"Yeah, he went very slowly by me. That just seems to be what's going on," replied the Operator.

"Well, we'll have to put him in the sideline east of Chillicothe until the Capitol Express goes by."

"You do know the crew's on short time."

The Dispatcher responded, "Yeah, I know. If we have to, we'll outlaw them there and send a crew to take them into Cincinnati, but we can't block the line. That passenger train needs to be able to get through.

Occasion of Murder

May 24, 1957

Sitting around the kitchen table, the boy, his father, and his grandfather were listening to the local radio station. Through the static, they heard the report that a very heavy band of rain was coming through before midnight. The old farmer's son-in-law shook his head, "I guess we're going to have to go down and check on the cattle and bring them to higher ground." When the old farmer wanted to come, too, his son-in-law told him he best stay, and they would take care of the cattle. Father and son had often helped him and knew his farm about as well as they knew their own.

Father and son put on their rain gear and boots, grabbed lanterns, and headed out.

Their slickers were soaked by the time they stepped off the back porch. The ground gave beneath their boots as they trudged through the puddles and mud to the gate opening to the pasture. In the blackness, the lanterns were all that could be seen as the two slowly made their way down the slope. The boy slipped and quickly righted himself to stay near his father. To be heard over the pounding rain, the boy yelled, "I've never heard the creek roaring so loud."

"No, I haven't either. This here is what my pap would call a gully washer."

They walked in silence until the father yelled, "Go down there and find the cattle and start moving them up towards the gate at the upper end," he motioned with his lantern. "I'll get the gate opened and get ready to herd them on through."

Having romped across the fields since he was old enough to walk, the boy knew the pastures well. He was aware the creek came out of its banks with heavy rains. His dad had warned him about flashfloods and not to go near the creek when it was raining hard. As he stomped toward where the cattle liked to congregate at night, he heard the swashing of the rushing water and knew the creek was battering everything in its wake.

He held the lantern out front, but it was hard to see with the water hitting his eyes. He finally drew close to the stand of trees and saw a few cattle sheltering beneath the trees. He stirred them and got them moving away from the creek. After he delivered them to his father near the upper pasture, he turned to find the others.

He slipped several times as he walked down the slope, but he finally came to another area where he thought the cattle might be. He held up the lantern and slowly muddled through the puddles and soaked ground. His light caught a reflection, and as he approached, he found about six or seven more. He finally got those roused enough to start them lumbering out of the grove. He herded them up toward the upper gate. It was hard work—soaking work.

As he approached the gate, he saw the light from his dad's lantern moving around. His dad had located four, but there were more to be found, so the boy headed back toward the creek, which was now deafening as water cascaded through the ravine. The boy located two more cattle, and drove them up to the gate, where he waited on his dad, who brought in another one.

Hoping they had them all, the boy asked, "Is that all of them?"

His dad closed the gate. "That damn Angus! Wouldn't you know he's trying to hide from us?"

"I know all his hiding spots. I'll go down and find him."

"No bull's worth that," his dad griped.

"I'll find him," the boy assured his dad. He did not want to let his dad or his grandpa down.

"Just don't get too close to the creek," his dad warned.

May 24, 1957

"We'll, this isn't too bad. We're only fifteen minutes late," said Frenchy as the passenger train sped through the darkness. The fireman and engineer looked out the front of engine as rain pelted down on the windshield. The engine's front light showed the deluge of sparkling droplets and the track ahead.

"Yeah. Had to slow down in all the usual places, so I don't think we'll make it on time, but I think we can make up about five minutes on that straightway in Tapsaw County and maybe on the part east of Bekbourg." Mossy was watching ahead.

"Never seen rain like this before," Frenchy said.

"Yeah, thank god they repaired most of the bridges," replied Mossy.

"Yeah, this is sure a night to remember— rain like this."

"Yeah, this windshield wiper is not very good. No one was at the depot to fix it. It's not doing a good job." When Frenchy did not respond, Mossy continued, "You have to be extra vigilant. I can't see very good since the windshield wiper is not working very good."

"Yeah, I'll do that, but mine's not much better."

"We got one-hundred-sixty-five passengers depending on us to get them there safely," Mossy uttered to himself.

Jules stopped talking and pulled out his pocket watch. "Later than I realized. Get me to talking about old railroad stories, and I lose track of time. I hope I've not bored you too much."

"Not at all. I'm fascinated."

"Well, I'm afraid I have to cut it short, but perhaps we can meet and finish another time."

Cheryl readily agreed, and they set a time. She had noticed the white face and large black numbers and asked if that was his railroad watch. It was indeed his railroad watch. He explained that the large black numbers on the white background made it easier to see at night. Some railroaders carried a

Ball, and others had a Hamilton. The engineers had to carry their watches with them at all times, and to ensure they were synchronized with the dispatcher. They were required to have them checked on a regular basis by the railroad time keeper.

On her return to the office, Cheryl outlined in her head how she would break Jules' account into a series for the newspaper. She wanted to time it so that the conclusion would run during the week of the anniversary of the dedication of the new bridge forty-seven years ago. Back at her office, Cheryl threw herself into typing.

Chapter 57

"Thanks for coming in, Brian. We had some questions we thought best to cover here. Alex will be joining us."

"Sure—not a problem, Sean."

Alex walked into the station's conference room to join them.

"What's this about, Sean?"

"We think there is more to the story about Vera asking you for money. Why don't you tell us about it?"

Brian looked between the two officers. "Why, what did you hear?"

"I think you know, Brian," Sean said as he eased back in his chair.

Sean could see Brian mentally working through his options. Brian must have concluded the truth was out, so why hide it. He told them that one night soon before he was scheduled to leave for the Peace Corps, he had stopped by Knucklepin's to have a drink. A woman he recognized from high school, but who had graduated after him, came up and asked him to buy her a drink. He knew she was flirting and went along. They both had a lot to drink before they stumbled out the door and ended up in a cheap motel away from town. He told Sean he normally didn't drink that much, but he was leaving for the Peace Corps and knew he wouldn't be back for a couple of years. They had the one-time fling, and he never saw her again until she showed up at the business wanting to talk to him.

"I didn't recognize her when she came by and barely remembered that night."

"Tell us what it was she told you."

He wiped his forehead with his hand. "Hell. She told me she got pregnant that night, and that I was a father, and that if I wanted it kept a secret, she needed money."

"What did she tell you about the child?"

He threw back his head to look at the ceiling. He looked back at Sean, "She said it was a boy. He had dark hair like me. She said he lived with a family here in Bekbourg who had adopted him, but she could easily prove it was mine with a DNA test."

"She didn't tell you who the family was?"

"No."

"You went to the Olsons to ask if Miles was yours."

"That's right. I know them. I've seen them around town with their son. After Vera stopped by, I got to thinking and realized Miles was fourteen and I had left for the Peace Corps about that time. He's got dark hair like me, but he reminded me of

285

Mick when he was about that age. I know it's crazy, but I was curious. I asked Gerald and Teri, and they told me Miles was theirs. Hell, I think Vera made that up to get money. People will do that to politicians."

"Did she ever try and get in touch with you after you left for the Peace Corps?"

"No—not that I know of. My parents would have told me if someone was trying to contact me."

"So, she came to you asking for money and threatened to expose this?"

"Yes."

"Did she ask you for more money after that?"

"Yeah, it was that night at the party. She told me she needed to talk to me, so we went down a hall. She said she needed more money—another threat. I had already decided I didn't give a shit if she told people."

"You didn't care if it got out? You weren't worried it might tank your re-election?" Sean found that hard to believe.

"No, I really didn't care. You may not believe that, Sean, but it's true."

"I do find it hard to believe."

"It's important to Colette, and I can do the job, so why not run. She wants me to run for a state senate position next go around, which means we would probably move to Columbus. I don't really want to live in Columbus, but we're talking about starting a family, and Colette likes it there and says there are lots of opportunities for kids."

"So, let's get back to the party. Vera threatened to make public you were the father of a child you knew nothing about. What did you tell her?"

"I told her what I just told you—that I didn't give a shit what she told people. She said she didn't believe me, because she knew I was running for office. I told her I didn't care if I won. She didn't believe that, but so what? She then tried to say it would embarrass my family if it got out. I told her I had already told my wife, and that my parents would just deal with whatever happened."

"What did she do then?"

"I don't really remember. I was done talking to her, so I just turned to leave. I didn't talk to her after that."

"What did you do then?"

"Well, I remember wandering into the crowd, then up to the bar. I needed a drink. Colette must have seen me with Vera, because she came up and wanted to know what happened. I told her Vera tried to shake me down and that I wasn't going to cave."

"You said you had already told Colette?"

"Yeah. Look, I've been around enough to know about people like Vera. I didn't want Colette to get blindsided. Colette can deal with things, but there is no way I'd want her embarrassed by some crazy accusation—especially if I could have prepared her. Let the chips fall where they may has been my philosophy."

"She was okay with that?"

"Yeah. Why not?"

"Why didn't you tell us when we talked to you before?"

"Maybe I should have, but I didn't believe Vera, and even if she did go public with the information, I didn't care. It all seemed irrelevant to me. Why get a rumor going that I might be a father when I doubted her from the beginning. Hell, it had been fourteen years. She'd had plenty of time to tell me about it. She raises it now when I'm running for re-election. Frankly, I thought she was bluffing."

"What time did you and Colette leave the party?"

"After that shit with Vera, I was ready to leave. I really didn't want to be there longer than I had to. I wanted to go home and watch the football game. So, I got Mick to give me a ride home. He and his fiancé were leaving because he wanted to see the game, too. Colette wasn't all that happy I was leaving, but I told her she could stay—that she was more important to folks than me. I left after about two hours. I got to catch the last part of the game."

"The party was a great opportunity for shaking hands and asking people for their votes. You wanted to leave early?" asked Sean.

"Look, Sean. I'm the odds-on favorite. Colette's got some other events planned. Dillie's party was more important to Colette, so she stayed. She's a better campaigner than me anyway."

"Did you return to the party?"

Brian frowned. "No."

Sean and Alex sat in the conference room after Brian left. "Do you believe Vera never told him that it was Teri and Gerald who adopted his son? Why wouldn't she have?"

"I can think of a couple of reasons. Maybe she thought she had some leverage over him if she didn't tell him. Another possibility is she really didn't want him to know. Maybe Vera cared more for Teri than anyone realized. She knew Teri did not want it known he was adopted. A third reason could be that Miles is not his either."

"Yep. When you say Vera maybe had feelings for Teri, you're referring to the framed picture in the bottom of Vera's suitcase of Vera and Teri when they were young?"

"Why keep it all these years unless she had some feelings for Teri?"

"I guess I'm not sure how much I believe Brian that he didn't care about the story hitting the front page around here right before the election."

"It would cause commotion in his campaign, but he may have been banking on people overlooking it since it happened so long ago. I guess it's possible he really didn't care if he won, but his wife may have been upset."

Alex shrugged, "Yeah, but who likes to lose?"

"He said he left the party early, but he could have come back and killed her," Sean suggested.

"Yes, and he obviously had the strength to drag her behind the hedge. You're not writing off Gerald or Teri as suspects, are you?"

"No—not at all. There is a lot about Gerald's actions that puzzles me," said Sean. "Even Teri's—for that matter."

Alex agreed, "Teri is sure pointing the finger at other people. Why do that—unless she is guilty or thinks Gerald might be guilty?"

"Check in with Arlo and Syd and see what they have found out. Let's plan to discuss the status of the investigation in the morning."

Chapter 58

Sean was leaning back in his chair with his feet on the desk reviewing a report when Cheryl knocked on his door. "Hi, Sweetie. Kim said I could come on back."

"Well, this is my lucky day."

Cheryl laughed as she waltzed in and sat down. Sean noticed she held a piece of paper. "I thought you might want to see this," she said—raising the paper, "so I decided to bring it over."

"What is it?"

As she reached to hand it to him, he pushed his feet off the desk and took it. He read it and then looked at Cheryl. "When did you get this?"

"Patti put it in my inbox yesterday afternoon. I just saw it today. I know you're working on Vera's murder. I have no idea who it's from, and I'm not inclined to investigate it from the paper's standpoint. It sounds sincere, but it could just be a smear job against a candidate by going after his wife."

Sean reread the letter and laid it down and looked at Cheryl, who was grinning. He tried to keep a serious face. "You enjoy dropping these

291

bombshells in my lap. First, it's Vera being Miles' mother and now this."

Cheryl's grin widened. "Now, Sheriff, if I can be of assistance, I sure want to do my part."

Sean's eyes brightened. "You certainly do your part."

Cheryl's laughter brought a grin to his face. "I take my job as the owner of the newspaper very serious, and I hate to disappoint my fans, but I thought you should solve this one."

"You do, huh?"

"Well, now that I've done my civil duty for the day, I better get back and publish a newspaper."

Sean watched her leave his office before turning his attention to the letter.

Dear Ms. Seton,

I like to read the Bekbourg Tribune paper every morning. You are doing a really good job. I like the different series you write. I remember my mother talking about the thing with the bridge, but I don't remember what she told me, so I'm interested to see how it ends. I especially like all the cold cases you have written about.

I read your stories about that woman who was killed at the new art gallery the other night. Vera Keller. My husband would have a conniption fit if he knew I was writing you about this, but there's something I wanted you to know. I was at the party and went to the smoking area to have a cigarette. Two women were arguing. One was that state representative's wife. I know it was her, because I've seen her with her husband and also her pictures in your newspaper. She was really mad and said to the other woman that she better not threaten them or she would be sorry. She knew all about trash like her and how to deal with her. I don't think I'll vote for him with a wife who talks like that. Anyway, I didn't want them to know I was there, so I left.

Sherrie Rutherford

I like how you have solved those cold cases, and I hope you can solve this one. I prayed for you when you were hurt and am really glad you are better. Congratulations on your marriage to the sheriff. My husband likes the job he is doing. He also still talks about him winning the state football championship for the high school.

Good luck on solving this case. I hope this helps.

Very truly yours,

Anonymous

Sean pulled a file from his desk drawer. He thumbed through the photographs Cheryl's photographer had taken at the party until he came to the one of Brian and Colette. "Mmm. This is interesting." She was wearing a gray sweater.

Chapter 59

He did not know Colette Lynch well, but he figured it was time to pay her a visit. He called Alex to join him.

"Sheriff?" Colette's jaw dropped when she opened the door and saw Sean and Alex. "What can I do for you?" she managed.

"We have some questions. May we come in?"

"Certainly."

After they were seated, Sean advised her that they were investigating Vera's murder.

"Well, I don't see how I can help with that, Sheriff."

"Your husband told us Vera Keller had come to him and told him he had a son by her who had been adopted. She was threatening to expose that if he didn't give her money."

Anger sparked in her eyes. "That is an unfortunate part of what goes with my husband trying to do the best he can for the citizens of Bekbourg, and people are trying to blackmail him."

"Have there been other people who have tried to extort money from him?"

She paused, "Well, not yet, but I'm sure it's just the first of many."

295

"When did you learn that Vera was claiming your husband was the father of a child she had?"

"Oh, he told me that very night after she came to his office. He didn't want me to be blindsided if news broke. I'm glad he told me so I could be ready."

"What did he tell you about the possibility of him being the father?"

"He told me he didn't even remember the woman. After she left, he started thinking about the time before he left to join the Peace Corps, and said he vaguely remembered being with her one night, but he had never talked to her until she showed up at his office. Look, Sheriff. I hope you're not going to repeat these lies. She was just trying to shake him down with boldface lies during his campaign."

"I understand you and Vera argued the night of the party in the smoking area."

Colette's eyes widened. "Where did you hear that? Sounds like another attempt to smear my husband's campaign."

"You deny you and Vera argued that night?"

Sean was thinking back to when he had seen Colette walk up to Brian during the party and put her hand on his arm, but he had pulled away. From the best of Sean's calculations, that was after Frederic had seen Brian and Vera arguing.

Colette tossed back her head. "I'm busy trying to get my husband elected. I don't remember every conversation I've had with people. I'm sorry, Sheriff, but I need to finish getting ready. I'm meeting some women with the Garden Club about Brian's plans for Bekbourg after he's re-elected."

"Did you go into the kitchen that night?"

Sean saw the frown flash. "I swear. People must watch me like a hawk. I guess that's one of those things I'll have to get used to being married to an important man like Brian."

"So, you went into the kitchen?"

She paused before responding, "Yes. Look I don't like to complain, but as the night went on, the waiters weren't bringing around the trays like earlier in the evening. I dropped in to see if I could get one of those pastry things. That man in there was so rude. He told me I wasn't supposed to be there. I told him I was the state representative's wife. He said he didn't care and told me I had to leave, but he'd ask a waiter to bring around a tray."

"How long were you in there?"

"It couldn't have been too long. At first I didn't see anyone, so I walked around. Then he came in and saw me."

"That's it? You didn't look for anyone to help you find the pastries you wanted?"

"I don't know why you're asking me all this. I need to get ready."

"One other question: I saw a picture of you and Brian the night of the party. That was a nice sweater you had on."

Colette's unsmiling face relaxed. "Why, thank you."

"Would you mind showing us the sweater?"

"Huh? What for?"

"We're trying to solve a murder. It's possible the person responsible for Ms. Keller's death was wearing a gray sweater. Photographs taken during the party show you wearing a gray sweater. We'd like to take it and have forensics look at it."

Colette's eyes were wide. "You surely don't think I killed that woman."

"We can't rule out anyone, but it would be helpful if you allowed us to take your sweater."

Colette paused, "Unfortunately, I pulled it on our gate out back. I don't have the sweater."

"Where is it?"

"I was in Columbus and dropped it off by the shop where I bought it to see if they could repair it. I'm not sure when I'll be getting it back."

Sean found this interesting, particularly since a wool fiber had been found on the branch that matched the wool fibers on Vera's wrist. "I'll be glad to send a deputy there and pick it up. Once the analysis is complete, we can take it back to the shop. What's the name of the shop?"

"I'm not sure I like that idea, Sheriff?"

Sean's expression was unreadable, "Why's that?"

"Brian is a public figure. What will people think if a police officer goes into the shop and asks to get my sweater? All kinds of rumors might get started. I have to think about his campaign and reputation."

"What if I have a deputy drive you up there and you go into the store and get it? That way, the people in the shop won't know the police are involved."

Colette's patience was running thin. "I am very busy. I'm sorry, but I don't have time to do that right now."

"When do you anticipate getting the sweater back?" asked Sean.

"I don't know. She told me she would call and let me know when it's ready."

"You don't mind us getting the sweater then, do you?"

Colette paused, "Frankly, Sheriff, I don't know why you want to see it. I need to talk to Brian and see what he thinks. I don't have any reason to not give it to you, but we have to be extra careful that rumors not get started."

After they left, Alex said, "We need to push her up on our list of suspects. She had the motive to kill Vera to keep her quiet about Brian. Also, when he was first appointed to his position, the *Tribune* did a story about Brian and Colette, and she wanted people to know she works out on a regular basis. I've seen her around town in workout clothes, so she likely had the strength to pull Vera behind the hedges."

"I saw some cigarette butts with lipstick in the ashtray. I suspect they're hers. She probably was in the smoking area that night," said Sean.

"Does Brian smoke?"

"I didn't see any ashtrays in his office or smell cigarette smoke when we were there. But a nonsmoker could just as easily find the smoking area."

"What do you make of her sweater having a snag in it?" Alex asked.

"We need to learn more about Colette. Ask Syd to check her out."

Chapter 60

Brian was watching TV while Colette cleaned up after dinner. She joined him and sat down beside him. "Honey, there's something I wanted to tell you."

Brian looked up from the TV, "What's that?"

"The sheriff and one of his deputies stopped by today to talk to me?"

Brian's eyes narrowed. "What did they want?"

She was twirling the hem on her shirt. "That awful woman. It's terrible how much trouble a liar can cause."

Brian frowned, "Why did Sean want to talk to you?"

She continued looking at her fingers circling the hem. "Well, you remember when I saw you come out of the hall that night of the party and that woman came out after you?"

"Yeah."

"And I came up to you because you looked like you were upset?"

"Yeah."

"Well, I was fed up with that slut trying to ruin you."

Brian's eyebrow twitched, and his frown deepened. "What did you do, Colette?"

"I saw her a little later—after you left the party. I saw her go out the door, so I followed her to the smoking area. No one else was around, so I told her we weren't falling for her blackmail, and she should leave us alone."

"Sean knew about this?"

"Well, I don't know how, because no one was around."

"What did you tell him?"

"Well, I didn't want to tell him about it, so I told him I couldn't remember."

"You lied to Sean?" his voice rose.

She looked up. "That woman was trying to destroy your election. I couldn't let that happen."

"Damnit! I don't give a damn about this election. That's all you care about, Colette. You had no business saying anything to that woman, and you sure as hell shouldn't have lied to Sean."

She stood as her voice rose, "I just told him I couldn't remember."

"Well, that's a lie, because you just told me about the conversation. Sean is smart. Hell, he knows you lied."

"He didn't act like it," she frowned.

"Well, he wouldn't." Brian wiped his hand across his mouth. "It's more than that. I thought Vera was lying about the baby, but I needed to know for certain. I started thinking that maybe Gerald and Teri's son, Miles, might be the boy who Vera claimed was adopted, so I went to ask them."

"What!" she screeched. "It was all a lie! Can't you see she was trying to ruin your chance of winning? How could you be so gullible, Brian?" A child by another woman did not suit the idyllic world Colette had created.

"Don't you see? I had to know. They told me he was their biological son, but I had to know."

Colette sighed in relief. "See. They denied it. That awful woman is dead. Thank god, it's over."

He laid his head back on the sofa and turned to face her. "That's probably right if what the Olsons told me is true, but if they are lying about Miles being their biological son, it's possible it will come out as this murder investigation keeps going."

"Oh, god, after everything I've done to get you re-elected—and now this!"

"What do you mean—all you've done?"

Her eyebrows shot up. "You're not doing anything, so I have to. I meet with people, plan events, hand out flyers. You do none of that, so someone has to!" Brian got up.

"Where are you going?"

"I'm going for a drive. I need to clear my head. One thing is certain to me. You care a hell of a lot more about this damn campaign that I do."

"What are you saying?" she demanded.

"I need to decide if I want to stay in."

"You *can't* pull out! Our whole future depends on this. You can become a state senator. We can move to Columbus and live. Just think about the life we can have there and our kids will have. You can even be governor one of these days."

Brian sighed—shaking his head, "Your dream. Not mine."

After he left, Colette slung a pillow across the room. "Damnit! He'd better not drop out! I've sacrificed way too much!" she yelled as she stomped toward the bedroom.

Chapter 61

Frederic was scurrying by with a couple of boxes when Sean entered the gallery. "Hello, Sheriff. Did you need to talk with me?" he asked as he pulled to a stop.

"Yes, but finish what you're doing."

"I need to deliver these to one of the artist's booths, and I will be right back."

Sean nodded and looked around the massive gallery floor.

"Now, Sheriff, what can I do for you?" Frederic asked as he walked up.

"I was wondering if you remember seeing Colette Lynch the night of the party."

He waved his hand. "That requires a two-part response. At the time, I did not know who she was. I did not learn her name until she came by after the party asking if she could hold an election night party here for her husband. She had the chutzpah to assume use of the gallery would be free. Of course, we would make it available for a notable cause free of charge, but when I told her there would be a charge for her event, she was quite rude about it. So, to answer your question, I did see her throughout the evening of the party, but I did not know who she was until recently."

"Did you see her in an argument with anyone or see her with the victim?"

"I frankly consider anyone she was talking to a victim, but I assume you are referring to Ms. Keller. And the answer is no, I did not see her talking to Ms. Keller."

"What about seeing her arguing with anyone or hearing about Colette having words with someone?"

Frederic pursed his lips. "No, I did not see or hear of that happening."

"Okay." Sean looked toward the back. "I don't see Nell back there."

"No, she's not been in for a few days. But, that's not unexpected for her. She likes to work at her home studio. We have plenty of her beautiful ceramics in stock, and our clerk here handles the sales. I expect her to be here this weekend when more tourists are in town and customers visit."

"Mind if I look around her booth?"

"Of course not. Let me know if you need anything else."

Sean looked around Nell's booth. The pottery was indeed beautiful. A dainty white vase—which was soothing to the touch—caught Sean's eye. He admired its beauty and thought of Cheryl. When he turned it upside down, he saw Nell's initials and the year the piece was made. He almost missed the tiny shape next to Nell's initials. Upon closer examination, he decided that the minuscule carving was a teardrop. He picked up a bowl, which likewise had a tiny teardrop carved beside her initials. Every piece he inspected was identical in that regard. The tiny teardrop logo also was carved in the wood sign hanging on the front of her booth.

As he returned to the station, Sean thought about what his deputies had pieced together about Nell's life. She had never been married, and Alex had been unable to learn the identity of Tiffany's father. As a single mother, Nell had financially supported her and Tiffany through her ceramics. They had lived a fairly solitary life. She did not volunteer at school events, but each year for the annual PTA's fundraiser, she donated a pottery piece, which brought in a nice sum for the school. He thought about his conversation with Tanya, who had described Nell's hatred toward her and Vera. "Such a hundred-eighty-degree difference from the love she carried for her daughter. Love versus hate," he pondered.

Chapter 62

Syd was pleased with what she had learned about Colette on her visit to Newton Falls, where Colette had grown up. Syd had talked with a neighbor who had lived next door to the family. Colette's father had been a high-paid union representative and worked for a steel mill in Youngstown, Ohio. When Colette was about nine, he lost his job like so many others did when the steel companies began shutting down. Colette's mother worked cleaning houses for others, and he took whatever odd jobs he could to make ends-meet for the family.

Colette was a hard worker around their house and at school. At the beginning of Colette's senior year in high school, her parents decided they couldn't hold on any longer, and they moved to Tennessee where her father got a job in a car plant. Colette did not want to move, so her best friend's parents agreed she could stay with them. She told Syd Colette had received financial aid to go to a small college in Youngstown.

Syd learned that Colette's best friend from high school had moved to Akron, but her parents still lived in Newton Falls. Through Krystal's parents, Syd was able to make contact and arrange to meet with her in Akron. Krystal worked at a doctor's office keeping books and handling appointments.

"Thanks for meeting me here," Krystal said. "I thought we'd get some coffee before I headed home. My husband gets off at five, so he's with the kids. It'd be hard to talk there," Krystal said smiling.

"This is as good as any place. I appreciate you meeting me."

"Well, when you said it had to do with Colette, I was curious. I haven't heard from her since she moved to Columbus to attend OSU. Is she in any trouble?"

"We're checking out a lot of people who may have known a murder victim, and her name came up. It's more routine—just part of the investigation."

"I see," said Krystal as the waitress set down their coffees. "Mind if I ask you something?"

"What's that?"

Krystal smiled, "Did you play basketball?"

Syd's lips turned up. "Yeah, I played at a small college on scholarship. That's how I got my degree."

"Then, you became a police officer?"

"I always wanted to be in law enforcement," replied Syd. "After I graduated college, I attended the state policy academy."

"Good for you. With your height, I thought you played. Forward, I bet."

Syd nodded.

"Thought so—that's how I got to know Colette—how we became friends in high school. We both played basketball. She was a guard, and I was a forward."

"What can you tell me about her?"

"Let's see—where to start. She was smart, and she studied hard to keep her grades up. She wanted the hell out of Newton Falls, and she realized good grades were the ticket. She was athletic and a good guard. Not enough for college, but around there, people noticed her for her quickness and scoring."

"Was she liked? Did she get along with people?" asked Syd.

"That depends on who you ask. I always liked her, but I also saw her for who she was. She had a jealous side. For example, our senior year, there was this girl who was a sophomore. She had two older brothers who were good basketball players, and this girl was a very good guard. Maybe even better than Colette, but since Colette was a senior, the coach was one of those who didn't like to let the younger players play over the seniors.

"Colette was having a bad game and had three fouls, so the coach pulled her and put in the sophomore. Colette didn't show it, because she never liked to show weakness, but she was fuming. Kinda got some of the girls talking about how good the sophomore was. A couple of girls who weren't exactly fans of Colette made a couple of snide remarks about Colette and tried to make the sophomore look extra good during practice. You probably know all about cliques on teams."

Syd nodded.

"Then came the Christmas break, and the coach said she'd be in touch with the practice schedule during our break. Since Colette was the captain, she gave Colette the list of phone numbers and called her with the practice schedule and told her to let the girls know.

"The sophomore didn't show up for the three practices, and when school resumed and we had our first practice, the coach called out the sophomore for not showing up. I remember the girl's face twisted in confusion, and she told the coach she didn't know anything about the practices—no one had called her. The coach didn't say anything after that, because she didn't want to stir something up, but I think she realized Colette hadn't called the girl."

"Nothing like being torpedoed by a team mate," Syd quipped.

"Tell me about it." Krystal found camaraderie with a fellow basketball player and kept talking. "I'll give you another example of what she could be like. One time a girl came up to Colette when we were sitting in the lunch room and accused her of stealing her homework. She was on the honor society and our class president. Colette denied it but joked she needed to watch her stuff more closely instead of strutting around like she was 'God's gift to mankind.' God, that girl was mad. Colette was staying with us at the time—since her parents had already moved to Tennessee. I saw her stuff a trash bag in the garbage can, and when she was in the shower, I went outside and looked in. Colette had torn up the pages, but I could still see it was that girl's homework.

"I liked Colette. She had a good personality, but man, if she saw someone as a threat, she went after them. That's the way she played basketball, too. She drove hard, and if she thought it wouldn't be called a charge, she'd flatten out the girl defending her. I even saw her do it if she had penalties to spare if she didn't like a girl on the opposing team. You might not think so by looking at her, but she was strong and physical. She was highly competitive, and in her book, losing was not an option."

"That goes with the territory with most competitive players," said Syd.

"Yeah, I guess that's right. Colette is a survivor. I don't know how much you know about that F15 tornado that hit Newton Falls back in the 80's, but Colette's quick thinking probably saved her and her two younger siblings. When she was about six, the sirens went off, and she grabbed the baby and rushed her younger sister to the storm cellar. The damage around the town was catastrophic. Her family was lucky, because their house was mostly spared. Colette sat with her younger siblings on the front steps uncertain if it was safe to go inside until her mother could get a ride home from her housecleaning job. She stayed calm and protected her little brother and sister."

"That's really something that a six-year-old could do all that."

Krystal nodded, "Yeah. She's got a steel spine, so I would never underestimate her in getting what she wants."

"So, you haven't talked to her recently?"

Krystal shook her head, "No. I guess I'm not surprised. I was yesterday's news once she moved on to Columbus. She told me before she left she was moving up in the world and nothing was going to stop her."

"I'm surprised she smoked if she was a basketball player."

"She didn't smoke in high school. That happened after she started college. Mom wouldn't let her smoke in the house. I never understood it either, especially since she continued to run and did conditioning at the gym at the college."

Chapter 63

Before everyone arrived for the deputies' meeting, Arlo had listed on the whiteboard the suspects' names across the top with the facts down the side. A grid was formed so they could compare the suspects. All the persons of interest had attended the party and had an opportunity to kill Vera. Tanya and Colette were cigarette smokers, but it would be easy enough for any of them to scope out the smoking area. They knew from interviews with the kitchen staff that Teri, Tanya, and Nell had all been in the kitchen that night. Colette admitted she went in the kitchen. Alex and Syd had not yet been able to talk with the food preparer, who had mentioned to his colleagues about seeing a crazy woman coming into the kitchen.

Several pictures taken by the newspaper photographer showed Gerald, Teri, Brian, Colette, and Nell all had worn gray sweaters. Since she was wait staff, Tanya wore a uniform shirt, so they did not know what she wore beneath it, and it was possible she had changed after getting off duty. Sean had heard from Ronnie Vin the wool from Teri's sweater was not a match for that found on the victim. Despite that finding, Sean refused to dismiss her as a suspect.

The deputies all agreed each of the persons of interest—Gerald, Teri, Nell, Tanya, Colette and Brian—had a motive. "If you're adding up the motives each person had, Gerald wanted to keep secret Miles' adoption, keep Teri from finding out about his fling with Vera, and wanted Vera out of their lives," observed Alex.

"But, even if a suspect only had one motive, their reason for wanting Vera dead could be equally strong."

"Good point, Syd. We know Tanya and Nell's feelings were intense toward Vera. I don't know if you could call it hate, but it's in that zip code," said Alex.

"I think they both hated Vera," replied Syd. "They each believed she had ruined their lives. Nell, because her daughter committed suicide, and Tanya, because she lost a baby, she split with her fiancé, and her life took a nosedive from which she never rebounded."

"Like Gerald, Teri was fearful Vera would disclose the truth about Miles, but Vera had made her life miserable. Maybe she couldn't stand the thought of Vera being back in town causing problems for her and her family."

Arlo spoke up, "Does anyone think Gerald or Teri might have been concerned that Vera might try and get custody of Miles?"

"I had not thought of that, Arlo, but that's a good point," said Alex.

"Add that under motives, Arlo," said Sean.

"Okey dokey," Arlo said as he walked to the whiteboard.

Alex and Syd looked at each other—each arching an eyebrow. "Is that long for 'okay'?" asked Alex.

When Arlo ignored him, Alex asked, "What about Dillie?"

Arlo spun around, "Is she a suspect? I haven't heard anything about her."

Sean replied, "Let's focus on these six for now. Without learning more, I don't consider her a suspect."

"Okey dokey," said Arlo as he turned back toward the whiteboard.

"Is he taking an online course on a new police language we've not heard of?" bantered Syd.

Alex looked at Arlo's back and shook his head.

"So all six of them could have dragged Vera's body behind the hedge," he said as he put check marks for that detail. "Right?" he asked as he turned to face everyone.

"Should that be an 'okey dokey?'" asked Syd.

"Glad to see you're catching on."

She rolled her eyes, and Alex smirked.

"Next fact?" urged Sean.

"I've got a question about Nell," said Arlo. "Why not kill Vera soon after Tiffany's death? And why not kill Tanya as well—since she also bullied Tiffany?"

Syd addressed that one. "It wasn't too long after Tiffany's death when Vera left Bekbourg, so maybe she didn't have the opportunity. Maybe what Tanya said to Nell at the funeral was enough to cause her to believe Vera was the real culprit."

"Also, Tanya apologized. It doesn't sound like Vera ever did. Maybe in Nell's mind that was enough to absolve Tanya," offered Alex.

"Every one of the suspects was at the party," said Syd. "With all the people and music, the party became the perfect occasion of murder."

"True," Alex said as he looked at the chart on the whiteboard. "I don't think any of our suspects could have known Vera would be there, which would mean they decided when they saw her to kill her."

"That's a good insight. Whoever killed her acted more on impulse—an emotion—rather that a planned scheme. There wasn't much time for planning," said Syd. "You'd think we could find a mistake the killer made or some evidence."

"Of course, both Brian and his wife had a motive. The secret about the boy could ruin his re-election bid," reminded Arlo.

Alex added, "Yeah, and I'm not sure how happy Colette would be if it became public that

Brian was a biological father—could complicate things."

"Maybe Brian and Colette were in on it together. Heck, Gerald and Teri could have acted together, and they keep covering for each other."

"We've got a lot of the pieces, but we're missing some information," said Sean. "Alex and Syd, you need to make a trip to Cincinnati. Start asking neighbors of the food preparer if they know family members he may be visiting. Talk to the caterer again and talk with the workers and see if they know. We need to step up our efforts to contact him. I'd like to know what he saw in the kitchen. The coroner said the dimensions of the missing knife could be those of the murder weapon. We need to know who the woman was in the kitchen, because it's possible she may have taken the knife. I'm going to see what I can find out about Tanya. I'd like to know if she has exhibited any violent tendencies that haven't been raised with law enforcement."

Occasion of Murder

Chapter 64

Cheryl was reviewing her notes when Jules sat down at the table at Frau's, "How nice to see you again, Ms. Seton. Let's order our food, and I'll tell you the rest of what happened that legendary stormy night forty-seven-years ago."

May 24, 1957

As the boy sloshed through the dark field, his dad worked to secure the cattle in the barn for the night. The boy hoped Angus was not too close to the creek. He might already be swept away, the boy thought as he wiped the water from his eyes. He wished he could see the creek. It must be huge— based on the thunderous crashing. Even if Angus was moving, he would not be able to hear the cowbell from the creek's roar. "I know you're down here, you stubborn SOB."

The boy looked in a couple of thickets and slogged along the upper edge in case a wall of water came rushing down the creek bed. He came close to where the creek and bridge met. There he glimpsed the white spots of Angus in the shelter of some trees. "There you are," he said as he walked toward the bull. "Let's go, you SOB. You're going to get yourself drowned." He reached the bull and swatted him on the rump. Angus snorted and jerked forward.

Just then, the boy was shaken by a tremendous crack. "What was that?" he blurted aloud.

It sounded like it came from the direction of the railroad bridge. Hindered by sliding and nearly falling, he raced toward the bridge. He got as close as he dared to the edge of the rushing creek and held up the lantern to see as best he could. "Shit! It looks like the bridge's gone!"

He held up the lantern higher and could not believe what he was seeing. The trestles had collapsed, but it looked like the railroad tracks were suspended in mid-air. Confused, he slipped through the fence railing and dashed up the embankment to the tracks to see what was going on. He knew the passenger train, if it was on time, would be coming through soon.

He reached the track and ran toward the bridge. "Shit!" The tracks were intact across the creek but the trestles below were gone. "If the train runs across this, it'll end up in the creek."

The boy took off as fast as he could. As he approached the barn, he was screaming, "Dad! Dad! Dad!"

Occasion of Murder

The boy was out of breath when he reached the door. "Dad!" He tried to talk through deep breathes.

His father came hurrying toward him, "What's wrong, Son?"

"Dad. We got to do something," he staggered between gulps for air. "The bridge! It's gone."

` The father told his son to calm down and tell him. When he finally comprehended, he sprang into action. "Oh, my god! I better report this quick. I want you to run to the track and keep cranking on that railroad phone." The boy knew what he was talking about. "Keep cranking—you hear me? When they answer, tell them the bridge is washed out." The boy nodded. "I'll run to your grandpa's and use his phone. It's more reliable."

The boy raced through the rain and slipped through the fence's railing and grabbed the railroad phone. He started cranking. All he could hear was static and crackling. He did not know the ring code, so the operators up and down the line had no idea what was going on with the continuous ringing. No one answered. The boy was yelling into the phone between the cranks to see if anyone had picked up.

One operator hearing the ringing, muttered, "What the hell is that? There must be a short in the line."

Other operators up and down the line heard the ringing, but not recognizing their ring sequence, ignored it. When it didn't stop, the Operator at LG Cabin east of Bekbourg, finally answered. "Who is this? Hello! Who is this? Hello! Hello!"

He heard a young boy's voice repeatedly screaming, "Bridge is out!"

To be heard over the boy, the Operator shouted, "Slow down! Who are you?"

The boy was gasping. Having finally made contact, he took a deep breath and yelled, "Can you hear me?"

"Yeah, I can hear you."

The boy took another deep breath, "The bridge is out! Right outside Bekbourg. The train's coming, and it's going to crash if you don't stop it."

"How old are you, young man?"

"Nine. We got to hurry."

"What's the name of the creek?"

"Norton Creek."

The Operator was perplexed, because there was no signal that a break had occurred anywhere on the line. "Young man, tell me what this is about."

The boy described having gone out with his dad to herd the cattle away from the creek, hearing the break in the bridge and then climbing up on the track to see the track suspended across the creek. "There's nothing under the track."

"Are you sure?

"I'm positive! The track is just hanging there across the creek. It looks like the ties are *under it, but the rest is gone. If the train hits it, it's going to crash in the creek!"*

"Oh, my god! We've got to stop the train!"

The Operator told the boy to hold on and rang the Dispatcher. He explained the situation to the Dispatcher. "The signal's still green, because the track isn't broken. The engineer has no way of knowing the bridge is out. The signal is green. He won't know to stop."

"Where's the train now?" interrupted the Dispatcher.

"He just went by LG Cabin. It was the last positive block I could stop him at. He's going to go right down there. We don't have any way to reach him. That engine doesn't have a radio."

"Is the boy still on the line?"

"Yeah, I'm here."

"Son, can you go up on the track and flag down the train? He'll be there in the next ten minutes. He's only eight miles away."

"Yeah. I'll do it."

"Have you got a light?"

"Yeah. My dad's lantern."

"You have to get right on the track and wave it in a big arc. Just keep waving it over your head—big arc back and forth. Can you do that?"

"I'll do it."

"Okay, Hurry. Good luck, Son. We'll send someone out right away to check it out."

Sherrie Rutherford

May 24, 1957

"We're coming up on the signal." Mossy said as squinted to look. "It's green. I guess everything is okay. We have a clear signal here."

Frenchy spoke up, "Did that signal flicker? Green to red?"

"I didn't see it. I can't see anything."

"I thought it flickered."

When they got to the signal, it was bright green. Mossy slowed the train a little. "It was probably just a loose joint causing the signal to flicker. I've seen that a lot."

May 24, 1957

The boy ran as hard as he could. When he got to the track, he raced as far away from the bridge as he had time so the train could hopefully come to a stop before the bridge. He staked out a position standing on the tracks, swinging the lantern in a big arc as he had been instructed. "I'm going to stop that train or else." There had been no respite from the pounding rain.

Off in a distance, he saw the headlight beam through the rain and mist. His arm was moving in a full motion from one side of his small body to the other. "I hope it's bright enough for them to see me." The engine grew bigger, and its light grew brighter as the train streaked forward. The banks on either side of him were steep—sloping downward into the raging creek. He had to be careful he did not lose his balance and slide into the rushing water. He was going to stand in the middle of the track until the last second.

He waved the lantern as steadily as he could in as large an arc as possible. "Stop! Please stop!" he thought to himself as he stared down the oncoming train.

May 24, 1957

Both Mossy and Frenchy were straining to see ahead through the pouring rain. Frenchy jerked his head toward the windshield. "What is that up there? Do you see something?"

"No. This damn wiper!" Mossy stuck his head out the side window and felt the rain pellets stinging his face. He widened his eyes, "Oh hell. He's giving us a stop signal."

Frenchy stiffened. "We can't stop in time."

"Yes, we can," declared Mossy as he yanked on the brake handle to put on the air. He applied the brakes for twenty seconds and then put the train in emergency.

Not realizing the train had gone into emergency, the boy kept swinging the lantern.

"We're going to hit him!" yelled Frenchy.

The train was screeching to a stop.

"Damnit! Jump man!" yelled Frenchy, as he and Mossy looked on.

Sherrie Rutherford

Right before the train got to where the boy was standing, he jumped off to the side grabbing for anything to keep him from sliding down the embankment. The train abruptly stopped past where the boy had been standing. It came to rest within a hundred feet of the bridge.

Frenchy got off the train and walked around the side where the boy had jumped. The brakeman and conductor had both gotten off the train. Frenchy was the first to find the boy as he crawled back beside the tracks. The boy was covered in mud, and his slicker was soaked.

"What the hell is going on?" demanded Frenchy.

The boy found himself yelling, "The bridge is out. Well, the tracks are still there, but the bridge is gone." He took a deep breath, "I rang the crank phone, and they told me to stand here and swing the lantern."

By then, the conductor and brakeman had joined them. Frenchy and the brakeman followed the boy to the bridge. The tracks looked normal from above, but when they were able to see beneath the track, they saw the collapsed trestle.

"I've never heard of anything like this happening," shouted Frenchy over the roar of the creek and the beating of the rain.

"We would have all died if the train had gone off in that ravine," yelled the brakeman.

Frenchy looked at the boy. "Young man, you just saved about a-hundred-sixty-five people's lives."

Jules drained his coffee. He saw Cheryl had not put down her pen and smiled. "Let me guess. You have some questions."

Cheryl's eyes were bright with interest, "Yes, I do. I saw the picture in the newspaper of the boy and his father. The town and the railroad must have been extremely grateful for everything they did."

"Oh, they were. Some of the executives came to town to show their appreciation and gave the boy his own railroad pocket watch with his name inscribed."

Jules asked Anita to refresh their coffee, and he answered Cheryl's questions.

Chapter 65

"I sure as hell hope we're able to find out something about the food preparer," said Alex as he passed a slow-moving truck. "The Sheriff seems to think he'll tell us something that will make a difference in our investigation." When Syd did not comment, he continued, "All four of the women we're looking at seem crazy to me, so I'm not sure it's going to narrow the list of suspects."

"Nell's quiet, so I'm not sure that's who he's talking about, but that Colette can get wound up."

"Well, I wouldn't want to see Tanya on the war path either."

"Yeah, but she was in and out all night. I'd be surprised if that's who the food preparer was talking about, but she certainly had the opportunity to swipe a knife. Teri doesn't strike me as someone who loses control, but I guess you can never tell what someone might do," Syd said as she looked out the side window. "Anyway, someone doesn't have to be acting crazy to steal the knife. It could have been any of the four, but maybe someone else, too. We can't be one-hundred percent sure we have a list of everyone who went into the kitchen that night. We don't even know that the missing knife is the murder weapon. The coroner says the dimensions work, but we don't have the weapon."

"The sheriff said he's not ready to drop Teri as a suspect—even though Vera's blood wasn't on her sweater and the fibers don't match those found on Vera's wrist. Also, what if she slipped the knife out of the kitchen and gave it to Gerald?"

"How is it Gerald's sweater disappeared?" reminded Syd.

"That's something else that's screwy about this case," agreed Alex. "My mom always just mended moth holes. I just wonder if Colette will give us her sweater to be tested. She really appeared to me to be making excuses."

"The sheriff won't let that drop with her. He was going by there again this morning to ask her about it."

Alex spotted a sign indicating they were entering Cincinnati. "Well, let's hope we at least find out where we can find the food preparer. Surely, someone in his apartment complex knows how to get in touch with him."

Chapter 66

When Alex and Syd showed up at Sean's office door, he could tell something had happened. "Chief, we may have something. The food preparer got back to his apartment last night and was going to call us after he ran some errands. We happened to run into him when we were talking to his neighbors as he was returning from the grocery store. We took pictures of all six suspects with us, even the men. We thought we'd ask if he saw Brian or Gerald in the kitchen.

"He must watch the food prep area like a watchdog. He remembered finding the politician's wife, Colette, in there and ordering her to leave. He remembered Teri and Nell being there, and, of course, Tanya was one of the workers and was in and out all evening. He did not see either Brian or Gerald in the kitchen. So, any of the women could have taken the knife from the kitchen. But here is what is odd. Remember Nell told us she had not eaten since breakfast and took a break to go into the kitchen and get something to eat?"

Sean nodded his head.

"The food caterer confirmed she was in and was looking around the kitchen when he asked her what she wanted. She told him she was hungry, so he put a plate of food together for her. She left, but she came back later. The second time, he had been in the refrigerator to put away some food he didn't think he needed. When he came back into the food prep area, he saw her. She jumped when he said something to her. He said she was acting strange— like she was confused. But, the reason he called her crazy was because when she came in the second time, she was wearing gloves. 'What crazy person wears gloves to eat?' he asked. When he asked her what she was doing back in there, she told him she was turned around and was looking for the smoking area."

Syd spoke up. "I don't think she smokes. When we went to her place, I didn't smell smoke or see any signs of ashtrays."

"Did he say what kind of gloves?"

"They were dark. He assumed they were winter gloves, but she didn't have on a jacket or coat. Best he could remember, she just had on a normal sweater, but she was wearing gloves."

Sean looked at his two deputies.

Syd said, "Also, she has a booth there. Wouldn't she know where the smoking area is?"

Sean was thinking what this could mean. Syd spoke up, "Sheriff, I think we need to talk to her again."

Sean stood and reached for his hat. "Alex, go to the gallery and see if she's there. If she is, stay with her and radio me. Also, call Arlo and have him find Tanya."

"You think if she killed Vera, she might go after Tanya?"

"Don't know, but let's not take any chances. Let me know if she's at the gallery. Syd and I will head out to her house." Syd was already in motion as Sean followed her out the door.

When they arrived at Nell's house, Alex had already notified them that Nell was not at the gallery. It was Tanya's day off, and Arlo had not yet located her. Nell's SUV was not in the driveway. Sean went to the front door and knocked while Syd circled around back. Something did not feel right. Syd came striding around from the back. "She's not here, Sheriff. I can't see any lights on in the house or the other building."

They stood looking around. "I'll call Arlo."

Arlo told them he had not yet located Tanya.

Syd suddenly looked at Sean, "Let's run up to the quarry."

Sean's eyes hardened. "You think she might be there?"

"I don't know, but I think we need to have a look."

Sean had a sinking feeling. He sped to the abandoned quarry. As they approached the top, they spotted Nell's SUV. "You think Tanya is here, too?" asked Syd.

"I don't know, but head around the side there. Try not to let her see you. I suspect she's up along the edge."

Syd slipped out of the cruiser without making a sound and headed off. Sean started walking slowly up the embankment toward the ledge. He suddenly spotted Nell standing at the edge. He did not see Tanya. He did not know if that was a good thing or not. Nell's back was to him, but she turned to face him as he approached.

"Nell, what are you doing here?" He glanced around to see if anyone else was around.

She did not respond.

"You're too close to the edge, Nell. Walk closer to me. Let's talk." Sean maintained a calm voice even though his mind was racing on ways to save Nell.

"Leave me alone."

"Tell me what's going on. How I can help, Nell?"

Her laugh was strangled, "There's nothing. I've lived in hell since my Tiffany died." Her eyes and voice hardened. *"Since that devil killed her."* Her voice trailed off. "It took years, but I had finally started to live with my pain through my pottery. *Then, SHE shows up at the gallery!"* At one minute, her voice was gritted with hatred, and the next, Sean could barely hear her whisper. Her eyes were red-rimmed and glassy. *"That bitch didn't even realize I was Tiffany's mother!"* Nell stopped talking.

"Take a step toward me, Nell. We can talk this out." Sean appeared relaxed as he eased forward, but she was still outside the range where he could lunge and grab her.

"Don't come any closer, Sheriff. I know what you want to do, but it won't work. I'm sorry to put you through this, but this is the way it's going to end. You see, I can't go back to what I went through after Tiffany died. Seeing *that bitch* took me back there. I thought if I killed her, I'd be at peace." She quieted. Sean had inched closer but was still out of range of reaching her.

"Nell, I can get you help. Step away from the edge. We can work this out. Talk to me."

"Please, Sheriff. Please leave. I just want peace."

"I can't do that, Nell. I want to help you. Please. Let's talk this out. Think of your talent. The beautiful pottery you create."

Nell shook her head and took a step toward the edge. "I'm sorry."

Just as she went to take the last step, Sean lunged, but it wasn't enough to get to Nell in time. His gimpy leg stumbled.

Chapter 67

Sean dropped by to see Gerald and Teri, who had good news to share. One of the county employees had to take an unexpected long-term medical leave, and Gerald was going to fill in. The county was going to work with him on trying to find jobs until the permanent position became available in a year. Teri enjoyed her job at the hospital and was going to continue working there. They had also decided to tell Miles he was adopted, which was difficult, but he appeared to have accepted it. They were working with a family counselor.

He was not ready to meet his real father, but they had been in contact with Brian, who was willing to wait for Miles. The three adults all wanted what was best for Miles and did not want to push him. Teri told Sean they were going to store Vera's car, and when he turned sixteen, ask Danny about fixing it up for Miles to drive. She also told Sean she would store Vera's items including her paintings—should Miles one day want to see them.

As he handed her the framed picture of the two sisters that had been in the bottom of Vera's suitcase, tears welled in her eyes. "I remember Mom had this on her dresser for years. I always

335

wondered what had happened to it. That was Vera's fourth birthday."

Teri and Gerald seemed to be working through things. Sean knew their family had been through a hard time but left feeling things were turning around.

Arlo found Tanya at the Shopper's Pavilion that day, so no harm had come to her.

Brian had won his re-election.

Occasion of Murder

Chapter 68

*1957 Passenger Train
Catastrophe Averted
Conclusion
by Cheryl Seton*

*Last week, the City of
Bekbourg celebrated the
start of a new era for the
WVB&C Railroad Company
as local resident and former
railroad executive, C.P.
Traylor, assumed operation
of our local railroad.*

*This week, our town also
celebrates the 47th anniversary of the dedication of the
bridge over Norton Creek.
For those who have been
following this series, you
know on that spring night
47 years ago, a disaster was
averted when a nine-year-
old boy, against all odds,
raced through the torrential
downpour and put himself
squarely on the track in*

front of the oncoming Capitol Express carrying one-hundred and sixty-five passengers plus twelve crew members. Seeing the train's glaring light bearing down, he swung his lantern trying to warn the train to stop. According to recorded accounts at the time, the boy waited until the last possible instance to jump from the track, hoping the engineer would see his light—dimmed by pouring rain and moisture-filled air.

The railroad's fireman, Yves Leroux, said at the time it was a miracle the boy did not slide down the muddy embankment into the roaring creek below him.

C. P. Traylor said, "Had that boy not been there to warn the train, history would have been rewritten that night for the Capitol Express. The entire train would have plummeted into the ravine with catastrophic results. His bravery saved the lives of every man, woman and child on the passenger train that night."

Many of you have asked who that boy was. The Bekbourg Tribune wrote of his heroics in 1957, and the above picture from our newspaper at the time is of the small boy with then Mayor Tobias Schuhmacher receiving the Bekbourg's Citizen of the Year award. He left Bekbourg for a while during his early adult years to serve our country in the Vietnam War—once again exhibiting bravery for which he was awarded two Purple Hearts.

Many years ago, he then returned to Bekbourg to the same house in which he had grown up to live a quiet life. He declined a request to be interviewed for this story— not wanting to bring any notoriety to himself.

Since 1957, the bridge over Norton Creek has been maintained. It is concrete construction versus the old wood construction, and newer technologies have changed the way railroads operate, according to Mr. Traylor. "Because all trains are monitored by GPS and radio and are in constant contact with the dispatcher, and because the systems are constantly being upgraded as technologies improve, such a near disaster should not occur in today's operations, but we remain vigilant to keep our passengers and crew safe and our cargo moving."

When asked about the Norton Bridge dedication anniversary, Bekbourg City Mayor Bri Sanderson said, "Our City owes a debt of gratitude to the courageous boy, John Pawley, who raced through the dark of night in 1957 in pouring-down rain to save a train and the people on it."

Chapter 69

Sean read the last page and raised his head to ponder John Pawley's newly-released novel. He looked out from their front porch. Buddy sensed a change and raised his head to look into Sean's eyes. Considering the lateness of the year, the day was warm, and Buddy had found a sunny spot on the porch. He saw Sean close the book and rose up to get a head pat. "Hey, boy." Sean rubbed his neck. As Buddy returned to continue his sunning, Sean thought about the novel.

The book was about a boy named Bobby, who grew up in a small town experiencing the ebb and flow of life doing what many boys from a small rural town might do—fishing, hunting, hanging out with friends, playing with his dog. Being an only child, he often found himself alone, and then he turned to books to read about the world beyond. As his time in high school was winding down, he found himself mesmerized by a girl. She was a free spirit who planned to reach out and conquer the world—not let it conquer her. They formed a special friendship, but he knew deep down she would fly free once she graduated high school.

Then, one day, the girl was gone. Bobby could not discern the reason for her departure. Had she died? Had she moved? Had she left with friends? He only knew that her vanishing had opened a hole in his heart for which there was no repair. Going off to war would surely banish her memory he thought, so he joined the military and relished what Vietnam might bring.

And, the horrors and devastation of war overwhelmed all senses except for survival. He killed fellow humans. Of course, he knew they were the enemy, but with each death at the hand of his firearm, his mind receded a little more, and his heart, once torn apart by a lost love, calcified. Purpose began to retreat as he sought to clear the disorientation that clouded his mind.

In a split second, Bobby's life changed. The blast was deafening, and his only question was whether he was being hurled into heaven or hell. Miraculously, he survived and woke in a military hospital somewhere away from the combat zone.

As time went on, Bobby began to heal and returned to the states. At the suggestion of a counselor, he enrolled in college. After graduation, he went to law school, after which, he clerked for a federal judge. He married, had two children, and lived an idyllic life. He ran for Congress and after two terms, became a United States Senator—with time, his influence and power grew. He and his wife had discussed a possible run for the presidency.

The last chapter of the book began, "Bobby, It's time for your dinner."

"Huh?" replied Bobby. Bewildered, Bobby looked around the sparse room with the dingy while walls and window fogged by broken seals. The florescent light bulbs above fortified the institutional character of his surroundings.

"It's dinnertime, Bobby." The orderly moved to help Bobby stand.

"You know I prefer to be called 'Senator,' don't you young man?"

"Yeah, yeah, I know."

Not for the first time did the orderly wonder to himself when, during the past twenty-plus years' stay at the sanatorium, Bobby had started telling people he was a senator.

Sean could draw parallels between the novel's "Bobby" and John Pawley. Both has lost a young love, both had gone to war, and both had returned to a world of isolation. Unlike the fictional Bobby, Pawley had learned to cope, but he kept himself wrapped in a cocoon away from so much of the world. He did not want his identity as a best-selling author to be known. He refused Cheryl's request for an interview about his heroics as a nine-year-old boy when he had saved all those lives on the train. The difference was the author had found a way to live on his own, where his fictional character had not.

Sean smiled to himself as he wondered if Dillie would be successful in drawing John out. He would not take that bet either way.

Cheryl walked out and put her arms around his neck. "Did you finish your book?"

"Yes."

She knew Sean had struggled with Nell. He had relived the event untold times in his mind. The episode brought back memories of him being unable to reach his best friend, Clint Neely, during the ambush in Kuwait. The night tremors had returned, but she had been counting the days since the last one. He took hold of her hand and guided her around to sit on his lap—to feel the comfort of her warmth.

"You doing okay?" she asked once again. This time brought the response she had been hoping for—dialogue beyond "yeah."

"Yeah. I just keep thinking what could have happened if Syd had not thrown herself at Nell. I blame myself for not being able to get there, but thank God, Syd was able to stop her."

Cheryl put her hand to his jaw. "I'm glad, too, but, Honey, you saved her, too. You kept talking to her, and she talked to you. That gave Syd time to get there."

He smiled, "I guess that's one way to look at it."

She smiled, "You know I'm right."

His grin widened. "You are, huh?"

"Uh huh. What will happen to her?"

"Dillie has hired a high-powered attorney, who is focused on getting her the help she needs. I don't know what's going to happen."

Cheryl's eyes sparkled as she looked into the eyes of the man she loved. "You think this could start gossip—me sitting on your lap on our front porch?"

Sean pretended to look around and up and down the street. "I don't see any of those nosey reporters from the local newspaper. We're probably safe from scandal."

Cheryl's laughter rang out as Sean grinned at her happiness.

Acknowledgments

I am grateful to have many people in my life who support my writing and encourage me to continue doing what I love—they help make my books beautiful to me. Above all, Larry has been there throughout this journey, enjoying the fun in seeing the characters come to life and the stories unfold. Larry—Thank you, my love, for your dedication and inspiration and for being there to help me fulfill a dream.

My acknowledgments would not be complete without expressing my sincere appreciation to Gary Steinhilber and Pat Goetz, who are so generous with their time in reading my manuscripts and sharing their expertise and insight—thank you for all you do.

The kind words from family and friends, who share their enjoyment from having read my novels and encourage me to continue writing and keep me motivated and striving to keep-on-keeping on.

Of course, how lucky I was to find Clarissa Thomasson, my wonderful editor, whose profound knowledge has helped me in so many ways, and Patti with Cross Ink, Corp., whose cover designs I marvel at.

Thank you to all the people who read my novels. I hope you enjoy reading them as much as I enjoy writing.

ABOUT THE AUTHOR

Sherrie Rutherford lives on Florida's Gulf Coast and has ties to Ohio, East Tennessee and Houston. She and Larry love traveling, hiking (especially in the Great Smoky Mountains), and playing Bridge. She is a retired attorney. Her passion for Appalachia and railroad history inspired the Bekbourg County Series.

Sherrie's website
http://www.sherrierutherford.com

Follow Sherrie on Facebook
Sherrie Rutherford – "Author